# Darkness Captured

**By Delilah Devlin**

DARKNESS CAPTURED
DARKNESS BURNING
SEDUCED BY DARKNESS
INTO THE DARKNESS

# Darkness Captured

Delilah Devlin

An *Imprint of* HarperCollins*Publishers*

This book is a work of fiction. The characters, incidents, and dialogue are drawn from the author's imagination and are not to be construed as real. Any resemblance to actual events or persons, living or dead, is entirely coincidental.



HarperCollins books may be purchased for educational, business, or sales promotional use. For information please write: Special Markets Department, HarperCollins Publishers, 10 East 53rd Street, New York, NY 10022.

FIRST AVON PAPERBACK EDITION PUBLISHED 2010.

*Designed by Diahann Sturge*

Library of Congress Cataloging-in-Publication Data
Devlin, Delilah.
Darkness captured / by Delilah Devlin.
p. cm.
ISBN 978-0-06-149823-7 (pbk.)
1. Vampires—Fiction. I. Title.
PS3604.E88645D38 2010
813'.6—dc22 2010015011

10 11 12 13 14 OV/RRD 10 9 8 7 6 5 4 3 2 1

*For my sister, Elle James aka Myla Jackson,*
*who has shared this journey*
*with me every step of the way.*

# Darkness Captured

# CHAPTER

# I

Moonlight filtered through the dense canopy of the oaks surrounding the estate, offering a camouflage of light and shadow to break up the silhouettes of the silent predators creeping through the darkness.

Already in position, Guntram Brandt had a few moments to reassess his plans, reconnoiter the landscape—and time to think about the South-Central clan's dilemma. Not *his* clan, however, for his loyalty lay with only one person, bought and paid for long ago, reinforced through blood and sacrifice, and cemented by a stifling yearning that threatened to overpower his stoic resolve.

Fear was a luxury Guntram couldn't afford. Not now. Not while the stakes for the battle he was set to wage loomed so high.

Still, fear's bitter taste burned his tongue and the back of his throat. Because he'd rarely allowed himself to indulge in the powerful emotion, he swallowed it down, letting it bathe his stomach in scalding acid. Almost as curious as the taste, his body felt as if it were gripped in a vise, held immobile for long, precious seconds while his frozen mind completed endless, pointless loops of indecision. He had only moments to linger in the chill, allowing the hairs on the back of his neck to prickle and lift.

Fear was rare for him, something that gave him pause and dulled his razor-sharp focus. Not something he should indulge, especially now that he needed all of his senses, even the intuitive ones he often ridiculed because they weren't visceral, weren't concrete. He didn't like acting on instinct or gut. He acted on threats he could see, hear, feel, and *smell*. Scent being the most important and dominant power for his kind.

The faint rustling sounds around him stilled, pulling him back. He breathed deeply through his nose, inhaling the air, calming his racing heart and setting his face into a grim mask—at last suppressing the anxiety that had built steadily over the past few hours while he'd waited for word.

Impatient with the other emotions roiling inside him—fury laced with bloodlust—he forced himself to grow as still inside as the woods around him.

Disquiet, as dense and cloying as the humid night, pressed around him. The thick, dank atmosphere, with earthy undertones made more pungent by the dew that had softened his footsteps, held scents longer than the crisp, dry mountain air of his own home. Good for surveillance, but just another reminder of how far outside their own territory they'd roamed. And for what? To give aid to the enemy?

Guntram curled his fists at his sides. He and the warriors he led despised them all. So, a daywalker was rumored to exist in New Orleans, and a malicious demon targeted the cloistered coven they surrounded. Let them both feast. What did it matter to their kind?

He hated being here, hated sneaking around like a thief, but he'd promised to watch from a distance and not interfere. His contingent was meant only as a weapon of last resort should anything happen to their emissary. A weapon he was very near to unleashing because they hadn't seen or heard from her in too long.

While his men quietly surrounded the pristine estate with its thick carpet of freshly mowed grass, beds of roses, and creeping honeysuckle, he didn't miss the significance of the tall brick and iron gated walls, high-state security system, and vigilant soldiers. Appearances mattered to the bitch who ruled Ardeal, but the beautiful, civilized estate was only a façade. She prized power most of all. Strength gloved in gentility. He hoped their emissary hadn't been gulled by the opulence of the old Victorian mansion into believing anything else.

The fact he couldn't simply rush the compound to find her rankled.

He was a simple man with a straightforward agenda—his true nature as unlike the manipulative, parasitic creatures he stalked now as a dog is unlike rats. He'd earned his name, Guntram—*War Raven*—for his skill in battle centuries ago. He'd rather test muscle and steel against them than wits. He'd rather fight like a wolf.

The plan they'd laid out when the invitation came had been just as simple. Enter a hunt for both of the foul creatures in return for a relaxation of relations between their nations. Now he wondered if the clan had entered a trap.

The ancient one who ruled the vampires in the compound was a wily, secretive foe. Inanna had held the reins through cruel and unscrupulous acts, waging a war of attrition against his kind since they'd all arrived in this hemisphere. In recent decades, the friction that burned between them had cooled. The wolves had grown complacent, trusting the treaties carving up the territory into a patchwork of alliances that served their mutual needs to consolidate power and prosper.

Guntram had sensed the change in the air. Had quietly warned of the dangers of trusting their enemy. But the opportunity to gain access to seaports to further their own enterprises had been too attractive to ignore.

Still, the clan listened enough to ignore the stipulation that only one could enter their territory. A small, skilled, and experienced team infiltrated the region surrounding the meeting place in the bucolic countryside north of New Orleans, surreptitiously gathering on-the-ground intelligence about the strength of their adversaries, looking for weaknesses to exploit should things turn sour.

And they had—as sour as the bile boiling in his belly.

From where he stood just inside the tree line, he could make out the dark figures patrolling the lawn inside the compound. Being the predator he was, he lifted his nose and scented the air, waiting for the wafting breeze to bring him the intelligence he sought.

Undead *Revenants* circled the mansion, their sweet almond odor wrinkling his nose and cramping his stomach with disgust. Vampires. And she was inside their fortress.

Gabriella. *Princess*, he sternly reminded himself. Even if their titles weren't spoken in this New World, the castes that separated them made her forbidden fruit. And because he had to fight his attraction with ruthless diligence, he never let her forget their differing statures.

As her sergeant at arms, an archaic title she'd jokingly conferred long ago, he'd sworn allegiance to her above all others. He'd protected her, watched over her even when she grew restless and slipped away from the pack to wallow with humans.

He didn't judge her. Didn't question why she sought release for her deep passions in dark, sordid corners with men who thought they tamed her when she could so easily slash them to death with teeth and claws. Didn't wonder why she'd never surrendered her mantle as alpha to her own pack when she could have shifted the burden to a stronger mate.

Aside from the wealth that came with leadership, she was beautiful, sexually voracious—and any *were*-creature would happily accept the burden of leadership for the privilege of covering her every night of his existence and breeding fierce cubs to replenish their dwindling numbers.

His body tightened at the thought, remembering the many times he'd stood outside a window or sex-club door, watching over her as she'd succumbed to needs so inexplicable to him he'd sometimes cringed and ached for her. Despite the perverse nature of her desires, he'd been tempted more times than he was comfortable admitting to disguise himself and enter that dark world to deliver the punishment her sexuality craved so that he could stroke her soft skin, inhale the fragrance of her lush desire, and sink deep inside her womanly body.

He breathed deeply, forcing down his arousal with an admonishment. He'd never acted on the impulse because he was a stern master of his own desires. Instead, he'd continued to give Gabriella the only things she wanted—obedience and protection.

A hand landed on his shoulder. "The men are all in place," Udo whispered. "No one's spotted her. The vampire called Nicolas, their head of security, set a fresh shift to guard the grounds. Stefan says he overheard that the visitors are imprisoned in their rooms."

Which didn't speak well of Gabriella's fate if they'd taken their own leadership hostage. "Do we know if it's Inanna, their queen bitch, who's responsible?"

"I'm sorry. That's all we know. What next, Raven? Do we wait for daylight, when they are all sleeping like bats in a cave?"

Guntram shook his head. "Gabriella's scent is dissipating. Something's wrong. We act now."

Udo's teeth flashed white in the darkness. He was as frustrated with their vigilance and as eager for action as Guntram was.

"Capture one of them," Guntram bit out. "We need to know what's happened."

Fear was washed away by a wave of exultant rage. He'd offer them a taste of their own treachery. He'd strike hard and at the very heart of them—just as they'd struck the very heart of him.

* * *

Gabriella landed on her knees in the middle of the Persian carpet. Once again facing the crudely carved stone walls of Alex Broussard's magical bolt-hole. "Alex, you lousy bastard, you can't do this to me—"

Her shout was cut short when the object of her bitter tirade grabbed the hand of the pregnant woman who'd been resting on a deep sofa inside the cavern when they'd flashed inside. He cast Gabriella an apologetic smile and palmed the crystal key to the room. Then they both blinked out in a narrow flash of white light.

"Sonofabitch," she muttered, reaching up to grab the silver-linked choker from her neck that he'd used to subdue her and ripping it off. How could he do this, leave her in his bolt-hole, after everything she'd done to help him in his quest to usurp command of the vampires?

While he'd disappeared for hours, clutching the phoenix-creature he appeared to love against his chest, she'd helped round up the *sabat*, nipping at the council members' heels to herd them toward their rooms, where Nicolas posted guards to keep them in lockdown.

Malcolm, Nicolas's next in command, had led away Inanna's private security force to the barracks for "debriefing" and posted his own men around the compound to keep things quiet while Alex's closest advisors sorted through the chaos that was the aftermath of Inanna's expulsion into hell.

When Alex had at last returned, looking like he'd just had the sweetest sex of his life, Gabriella shook her fur, pulling on her human skin, ready to remind Alex about their agreement when his gaze fled up the staircase, again.

The look on his face, one filled with a mixture of impatience and tenderness, had made her heart sink. When she'd cleared her throat to remind him she was still standing there, another look crossed his face—one that had her backing up a step and stammering.

The collar had been a real kick in the ass. He'd pulled it from his pocket and apologized, all the while grappling her to the ground to loop the damn thing around her neck. "I swear. It's just for now," he'd ground out as she wriggled beneath him. "Just until I get everything sorted out."

If he thought she'd be in any mood to talk to him, to negotiate a transaction to ensure the peace between their nations remained in place—well, he'd have to do a whole lot of begging, preferably on his knees and naked, before she agreed.

The thought of Alex, nude and serving her up a dish of submission, soothed her dented pride for all of a second. Her shoulders slumped, and she released a dejected sigh.

Gabriella never lied. Not even to herself. Alex was lost to her, for good. Once, long ago, she'd hired an assassin to kill him, and she'd grieved for centuries, believing she'd killed him in a fit of jealous rage and lost the only lover who'd ever completely fulfilled her dark, sensual fantasies. The past few days, fighting and loving with him had been a bitter reminder of what she'd missed most—but he'd only been playing her, using her to get what he needed from her. When his other lover had "died," it took only one glance at the desperation tightening his face and the tears filling his eyes to know she'd never hold his heart.

She shook out her hair and glanced toward the bureau standing against the far wall of the cave. With time to kill, she could at least empty his liquor cabinet.

With a glide, she pushed off the floor and strode to the cabinet, lifting one bottle and another until she found a cognac to her taste. Pouring a beaker full of the warm amber liquor, she glanced at herself in the mirror and lifted her glass to toast her reflection.

Noting the red ring around her neck, she wrinkled her nose. Wasn't the first time she'd accepted a noose. Maybe the Dom in Atlanta would be amenable to a little retraining. Her nipples prickled and extended, spiking at the thought of the nasty things she'd beg him to do. As soon as she settled her business with Alex, she'd give him a call.

Her features tightened and the corners of her lips curved downward. She shut her eyes and downed the contents of her glass. When she opened them again, she stared at the mirror and set down her drink.

How many times had Alex stared into the glass, looking into that dreadful room—the hall where the demons and the dead feasted on each other in hell? Remembering Alex's warning about the mirror, she reached up and gingerly touched only the frame.

The hall shimmered into sight. The same scene replayed—people in glittering, bejeweled costumes sitting at long benches in a medieval-style hall. She shifted to the side to catch a glimpse of the Master's entrance—the handsome creature whose black aura resembled a dragon's. With Alex behind her, she'd watched the Master stride into the room, felt a tingle of awareness for his masculine beauty, and shuddered for the power he wielded over the orgiastic bloodletting that had followed. She wouldn't deny the fact that the man fascinated her.

The hellhounds once again stood like sentries at either side of the plank door. She waited for a long while, watched the couple nearest the mirror savage each other on the floor, but still he didn't appear.

Just when she'd decided to drop her hand, a figure stepped in front of the glass.

Her eyes widened as she found herself staring directly into the Master's golden eyes. The narrow, slitted pupils slowly expanded, engulfing the irises entirely in black.

Gabriella told herself he couldn't see her. Perhaps he looked at his own reflection in a matching mirror. Gathering calm around her, she stared back, noting the thick black hair that fell to the tops of his broad shoulders, the neatly trimmed beard and moustache that framed his chin and mouth, drawing her gaze to his lips—full for a man, sensual, and beginning to smile.

A chill gnawed at her spine, causing her to quake.

As though she stared into a cobra's mesmerizing stare, she couldn't break with his gaze as he slowly raised his hand and pressed it to the glass, his long fingers splayed.

Gabriella felt as though she stood outside herself, watching as she reached up, spreading her own fingers to match his, and pressed her hand against the glass.

The glass began to warm, and then dissolved between them. Their fingers met. Before she could jerk her hand away, his fingers slipped to her wrist and tightened there. Triumph glittered in his dark eyes, and he reached up with his free hand to grasp the edge of the mirror and pull. It stretched downward, the bureau in front of her melting away, and he jerked her forward—into the blood-soaked hall.

Gabriella stumbled, falling, her knees slamming into stone

tiles. When she shook back her hair, she noted the faces of the demons and the dead swinging toward her and the silence that closed around her. Her heart hammering against her chest, she drew back her arm, trying to free herself from his grip. Falling to her bottom, she scooted on the floor, pushing herself backward with her heels, but her back met a hard wall. Stunned, she looked behind her and saw that the mirror on this side was small and high up on the wall. The portal had closed and she was trapped. *What have I done?*

Low growls penetrated her terror. The hellhounds closed in on either side of her captor, and then the murmurs began, a slithering, raspy noise that grew into a roar as the creatures inside the room left their seats and surrounded them.

She bent her knees to hug them against her torso, and tucked her arm over her breasts, trying to hide herself from dozens of ravenous gazes.

Her glance swung back to the demon that still held her in his grasp, rising slowly to meet his frightening eyes. His lips twisted. His arm swung out, forcing her to unfold her legs and raising her onto her knees, exposing her body fully.

Her breaths shortened, rasping loudly as panic gripped her as tightly as he did. Would they fall on her, make a meal of her body? Or would they rape her? God, no, she'd sooner be eaten. The shame of her defeat, of her helplessness against greater strength and numbers, would live forever.

The beast holding her shot a glance over his shoulder, and the crowd backed up.

Would he take her first, and then give her over to the others? His lust was palpable, pounding, ticking at the side of one of his black eyes. His nostrils flared, and his head waved as though sucking in more of her scent. A bulge formed at the front of the black breeches he wore, thickening along the inside of one massive thigh.

She couldn't help staring at it, knowing her eyes widened with fear. His sex was long and thick, more than an average woman could take. But she wasn't average. At six feet, her body was proportionately large and powerful, her hips wide, her woman's channel deep and able to stretch to fit the circumference and length of a very large man.

Unbidden, her body reacted, spilling fluid to dampen her labia. She sucked in a deep breath, closed her eyes and tried to will away her attraction. How could she be growing aroused?

Was he causing it? Did he have that kind of power over a woman's desire? Her nipples tightened, beading hard, and again she tried to shield them from his gaze, but he already knew.

She saw it in the fierce light glittering in his eyes.

Another tug of his hand and she was rising, teetering on weakened limbs. He ducked and pulled her over his shoulder.

As the world tilted, she flailed against him, clawing at his back through his clothing, but he turned on his heels and drove through the crowd. And because she was afraid, she didn't lift her face to meet their gazes. She tucked her head against his back and closed her eyes. Wherever he was going—out of the room, or simply to one of the emptied tables to lower her and take her—she didn't want to know.

Her only thoughts were of Alex and whether he'd care enough to search for her when he discovered she was gone—and of Guntram, her protector, whose loyalty she never questioned. Alex might mount a rescue due to the complications her disappearance would cause with both their nations' uneasy alliance, but Guntram would follow her for reasons all his own.

Reasons she'd never had the courage to explore because she thought she might already know, and the last thing she'd ever wanted was the love of a wolf.

# CHAPTER 2

Alexander Broussard stood beneath the eaves on the wide veranda, listening to the sounds of the night—the humming of insects, the croaking frogs, and the faint rustle of leaves whispering in the slight breeze.

The *weres* were good, highly disciplined. They'd made little discernible noise as they approached the compound's gates.

They'd also bathed away their wolf-smell and likely smeared their bodies with dirt to mask their human skin's aroma. If they'd only been cloaking their scent to defy detection by vampires, it would have worked. But Alex was something else. *Something more.*

He'd read the wolf-sign—the imprint of their subtly

masked scent, and seen the lupine grace of their movements as they slunk through the woods. While their eyes weren't bright, reflective discs, his heightened sense of sight could just make out sets of paler shades of gray ovals, peering from behind the trees beyond the far fence. For not only was he the only male Born vampire in existence, he'd trained all his life with a mage, learning other kindred tactics and hunting *weres* for practice. Apparently, waiting for this day.

He'd already had a busy night. He'd usurped power from the ancient Inanna, taken her crown, and imprisoned her council. He'd soothed away Mikaela's fears after she'd been reborn in flames, loving her until she slept the deep sleep of the innocent. His heart still ached for the child they'd lost when the demon he'd sent to hell along with Inanna had murdered his sweet phoenix.

And the battle wasn't over yet. Wolves encircled the estate, looking for their princess. He'd have gladly handed Gabriella over to them with apologies for the delay, but there was a little problem.

"How long have they been here?" Nicolas Montfaucon, his captain of the guard said, pretending nonchalance and keeping his back to the perimeter fence.

"For over an hour."

"You didn't think I'd need to know?" Nicolas asked, a hint of annoyance tightening his voice.

"What would you have done?"

"Put more guards near the walls."

Alex smiled. "And they'd have known we were aware they watch us. That we prepare for a battle. And they'd wonder if we had a reason. For now, I don't want them to know that anything out of the ordinary has occurred."

"Has Simon figured out a way to retrieve her?"

Alex stiffened, fighting the urge to act. Now was the time to leave matters in more expert hands. "Once she touched the glass, she activated the portal. We're lucky nothing tried to enter."

"But we've lost her." Nicolas's lips twisted in disdain. "Didn't like her much, anyway. She's a bit too proud."

"And your Chessa isn't?"

Mention of the woman they both cared for, and who carried another of Alex's offspring, had Nicolas's expression lightening. "Point taken."

"Gabriella may be a wolf, but at heart she's still a woman. And she has to be terrified."

Nicolas nodded, his chest lifting with a deep sigh. "If Simon can't reactivate the portal, or if she's moved away from it, what will we do?"

"We'll have to tell her men she's been misplaced." Although his tone was wry, a fresh wave of guilt poured over him. Gabriella had trusted him.

"That should go over well. Is there nothing we can do to bring her back?"

"If anyone can, it'll be Simon."

"I hate depending on fucking mages," Nicolas spat, his words made almost comical by the French flavoring his inflections. "You'd think if he's relived this time over and over he could manage to give us a little warning about what's supposed to happen next. What good is it knowing the future if you can't use that knowledge?"

Not something Alex hadn't asked the mage himself a thousand times. "Simon has his reasons. He lets us know what we have to know *when* we need the knowledge."

Nicolas locked his gaze with Alex's, his expression growing

pinched. "Alex, tell me the truth. Wouldn't you have preferred knowing ahead of time that your Mikaela was a phoenix, rather than watching her body go up in flames and thinking she was lost forever when the Devourer murdered her?"

Alex's body tensed again, remembering his horror.

But all had ended well. Now, she was safely tucked away in their bed, warming the covers nicely. His preoccupation with her, his need to soothe her when she was remade without memories, was what had forced him to place Gabriella in his vault in the first place. Gabriella's jealousy had been palpable. How was he supposed to know the woman would not be able to resist the one furnishing he'd warned her not to touch the first time he'd brought her to his little cavern?

He sighed, fighting the hollow pit in his gut that churned at the thought of what she must be enduring at this very moment. All his life, he'd gazed into the mirror, seeking a gauge of the activities of the demons inside the distant room, steeping himself in the knowledge that his battle wasn't just about surviving and triumphing over the accident of his birth. His battle ultimately would be with the demon-spawn in that other dimension. Each time he'd peered into the glass and watched their violence increase as they'd become more crowded and desperate, he'd known in his heart that someday they'd find a way to pour into this realm.

He'd never thought he might be the one to provide them the means. The *weres* would never be willing to sacrifice their princess for the good of all. They'd blame him—and expect a similar sacrifice—unless he could find a way to retrieve her, and quickly. And once she was back, he'd worry about Gabriella's state of mind, her anger and hurt with him. Either way, his battle with the wolves had just begun.

"Malcolm hasn't checked in."

Nicolas's tone was level, relaxed. But Alex knew he worried over his second in command. If the *weres* had gotten hold of him . . . "Where was he the last place you saw him?"

"I sent him outside the gates on reconnaissance. To see whether the council members had any security roaming around that they'd failed to mention."

"The wolves aren't savages. They aren't the primitive animals vampires would like to believe."

"But they think like a pack. If they get hold of him, they might rip him to shreds."

"Or they might use him as a hostage."

"He's not as important as Gabriella," Nicolas said softly. "They'll know that. If they don't see him as leverage, they may use him to serve as an example."

Alex nodded slowly, his dread deepening. A clanging sounded from the vicinity of the main gate. "Guess they're tired of waiting," he murmured.

"I'll go."

"Take care. They might not be aiming arrows at our hearts just yet, but they won't pass up an opportunity to claim a greater prize. You're a member of the *sabat* now," he said, reminding him of his newly elevated status as the only *Revenant* to ever sit among the Born council.

Nicolas's teeth flashed white in the darkness. "I'll have a care. The last thing I want to be is wolf kibble."

Alex waited, listening as Nicolas called softly to a couple of his men, and then ran with them in a lightning-fast blur toward the gate. In the shadowy night, he could make out their figures against the iron spokes.

Suddenly, something large was pitched over the ten-foot tall wall to land with a heavy thud.

Curses, low and hate filled, were carried on the breeze, and Alex tightened as something was hefted onto Nicolas's shoulder and carried back. His carriage was stiff, his steps deliberate, fury emanating from the bristling of his body as he approached.

Even before the almond-copper smell of *Revenant* blood reached him, Alex knew they'd found Malcolm. He wrapped his hands around the railing, gripping it tightly, feeling the muscles in his shoulders and arms ripple. He would have preferred to expend his fury in a physical challenge rather than to mentally strategize over every step forward. He'd been trained as a warrior, and now he had to hand the battle off to others because he was too valuable, his sperm and his powers too precious to risk.

Nicolas eased Malcolm to the ground at the bottom of the steps. Blood gleamed in the moonlight from a dozen savage slashes across his throat and arms. His chest struggled to fill with each breath. His eyes were closed, his face ashen.

Security swarmed them, lifting Malcolm to carry him to the barracks to see to his wounds.

"They've made the first move," Nicolas bit out.

"And we will answer it. I promise you. But we have to do so in a way that will capture their attention and serve as a warning that we won't stand for more violence done against our kind."

"*Dieu!* They mauled him," Nicolas said, his voice roughening with hatred and despair.

"And we lost their princess," Alex replied. "About even, wouldn't you say?"

Nicolas dragged in a deep breath, calm settling over his quivering frame. "So do we just stand here?" he asked, his tone deceptively free of the violent rage still simmering in his dark eyes. "Do we wait for them to leap the walls and attack?"

Alex smiled slowly—*wolfishly.* "We show them what we're made of, Nic. Gather your men. And the women . . . especially the women."

"What are they doing?" Udo whispered harshly. "They know we're here, and that we tortured one of their own. Are they so cowardly that they won't come out to fight us?"

Guntram peered through the spokes of the iron gate as the lights inside the mansion were extinguished one by one. "Tell the men to prepare themselves."

"But I don't see them."

"You won't. Not until it's too late."

As soon as the words were out of his mouth, the breeze rustling the branches overhead built. He turned his gaze toward the canopy above him, and then heard a sound that made his blood run cold.

A faint flapping, like a breeze caught in a bedsheet, sounded from above the trees. "They're above us!" he hissed. He squatted low, pulling his crossbow over his shoulder. He slid a steel-tipped wooden arrow along the track, pulled back the linen cord, and latched it in the spring lock.

The need for camouflage and silence long past, he stood, raising his bow and settling the stock against his shoulder. "Wolves, do not transform!" he shouted.

"But they'll have the advantage," Udo complained.

"They already have it in numbers. Aim for limbs, not hearts!"

As his men tightened in, scanning the trees above them for

large winged shapes and watching the undergrowth for *Revenants* closing in from the ground, Guntram said a quick prayer that his words had been heard by the vampires. They'd know his wolves didn't intend murder. Perhaps they'd show the same restraint.

Air brushed against the back of his neck, and he whirled, lowering his weapon and swinging his free arm wide to pluck up the creature swooping down at him from the sky. His arm closed around a bare waist, and he dropped his bow to take the vampire to the ground, crushing her wings beneath her.

Breath left the blonde vampire in a loud gasp. Her blue eyes narrowed fiercely. Fangs slid from her gums, and she whipped her head toward him, opening his neck. She spat. "Wolf's blood!" she cried, disgust drawing her lips away from her white teeth.

She wriggled like a fish against him and a knife sliced at his sides. He brought up a knee and slammed it into her belly, and then reached to nail her hands against the ground, slamming the one brandishing the dagger until she let go.

Then something large and solid slammed into his back, pulling him off the woman. *Revenant* scent surrounded him as fists plowed into his kidneys.

They fought with knives and fisticuffs. Relief poured through him. He and his men weren't going to die tonight. This was just a bloodletting to cow them into surrender. So why not have some fun?

Guntram got his knees under himself and heaved upward, flinging away the vampire on his back, and then whirled to meet the next fist flying toward his chin. He blocked it with his forearm, and rammed a clenched fist into the *Revenant*'s midsection, satisfied with the blunt sound as his knuckles connected with flesh, and even more with the deep grunt as his opponent exhaled sharply.

The *Revenant* kicked out, hooking the back of Guntram's knee and shoving.

Guntram smiled and gripped the man's shoulders, pulling him down with him and rolling until he was on top.

His fist came back.

The woman cleared her throat. "I know you two would love to take a few more digs, but we're wasting time here."

She was right. However much he wanted to beat the *Rev* to a pulp, he wasn't any closer to Gabriella. He lowered his fist, and let the man roll him again. Although not as satisfying as inflicting punishment, he reveled in the adrenaline that continued to spike as the man above him delivered fresh blows. More to his gut, to his chin, to his mouth, opening a gash that bled down his throat.

"Have you nothing more, wolf?" the dark-haired man above him growled.

"Plenty," Guntram gritted out. "But we both know this isn't a battle to the death. You have something we want. We must parlay."

The *Revenant*'s fist drew back again. His lips clamped tight. "You would surrender so quickly? Are you cowards?"

Guntram licked the blood from his lips and narrowed his gaze.

The *Revenant*'s lips twisted with disgust. "*Merde!* Call off your men."

Guntram drew as deep a breath as he could manage with the vampire's knee planted in his chest. "Wolfen! Surrender!"

Bitter growls filled the forest, telegraphing the wolves' resistance and frustration.

He shouldn't have had to repeat the command and vowed silently to remind them each later why he had been given command. He'd make sure the reminder was brutal and left scars. Still, he understood their reluctance.

Bloodlust filled them. Although not in wolfskin, his men were unaccustomed to surrender, resented the implication that they had to lay down their arms and pride to their enemies. They'd get the chance to soothe their bitterness later. "Surrender! Remember why we're here."

The menacing sounds slowly died down around them, replaced by harsh, jagged breaths. Footsteps crunched in the leaves as more of the vampires slipped into the forest around them. Guntram's eyes widened at their numbers. They would have lasted only minutes if they'd tried an all-out attack on the compound.

His gaze took their measure. The women, some with wings unfurled, all bare-chested like mythical harpies, had expressions set in lines every bit as harsh as the undead who served them.

The Frenchman who held him immobile glanced over his shoulder at the blonde. "Natalie, are you all right?"

Already rising, she flared her wings and winced. "Bruised is all, Nic. He's not a lightweight."

The *Revenant* grasped Guntram's shoulders, lifted him, and slammed him against the ground before jumping to his feet.

Watching the male vampire for signs he might reengage, Guntram came slowly to his knees and stood. He wiped the blood trickling down his chin with the back of his hand and forced a feral grin. "This is where I demand that you take me to your leader."

"You're in no position to demand anything," the dark-haired *Revenant* gritted out, the fact he seemed to be the one in charge betraying him as Nicolas, the head of the coven's security. "We have you surrounded. If you make one wrong move, if any one of you transforms, you'll be killed on the spot." To prove his claim he pulled a weapon from the holster strapped along his thigh. "Silver load."

Guntram gave a sharp nod. "You know that we didn't come to do battle."

"Odd, since you left one of our own bloodied at our gates."

Guntram shrugged. "Just our calling card. You will note we didn't send his ashes."

The blonde woman who'd first attacked him stepped up beside the *Revenant*. "Nic," she said softly. "Alex would have this one brought to him."

Nicolas's eyes narrowed on Guntram. "Your men will submit to collars."

Murmurs erupted from his men.

"Only if I have your vow they won't be harmed while wearing them."

Nicolas's brow arched. "You'd trust my word?"

"You're Inanna's mate, the Knight Templar monk. I would trust your word."

Nicolas's firm jaw relaxed and bleakness darkened his eyes.

It seemed strange the mention of the woman who turned him should affect him so. Something had happened here.

"You have my word. If your men come peacefully, they'll be made comfortable in our barracks while you meet with our leader."

Guntram nodded. This was, after all, what he'd come for. And at last, he'd meet the man Gabriella had trusted. The one she'd lusted over. She might be headstrong, but she wasn't a fool.

Udo's gaze met his as a slender silver choker was lowered over his head and cinched. His friend wasn't happy, but his shallow nod said he'd follow his command and make sure the others did as well.

A hand was shoved between Guntram's shoulder blades, forcing him forward. He cut a glance behind him, noted the quiet fury in another *Revenant*'s eyes. Guntram allowed a small smile to curl the corners of his lips. He'd taken great satisfaction in ripping open the one called Malcolm. They were all pissed. It seemed he'd chosen the sacrifice well.

Gabriella pounded the demon's back, her head still tucked close, until she grew weary. Her body shuddered with her strained, quivering gasps and soft sobs. The pummeling was only tiring her, while the monster that carried her didn't flinch once or slow his steady pace. When sunlight warmed her upturned bottom, she turned her head to take a peek.

They'd left the dim hall and entered blazing sunshine. Beneath her was a walkway paved with golden sandstone and framed by crenellated rock. Beyond the notched wall to one side spread a sandy desert, to the other side stretched a fortress so enormous it took away her breath.

This was hell?

The Master of the Demons ducked, and she grabbed for his waist to keep from swinging against the door frame. The stone-walled passage led to a stairwell that circled downward. At a wooden door, he kicked it open and strode inside, bending farther to deposit her in the middle of a nest of satin pillows.

She scrambled backward on a large bed as soon as he released her, wiped away her tears with the backs of her hands, and narrowed her eyes. "I don't know what you think is going to happen," she said, her voice low and fierce, "but I'll fight you."

His strange dark eyes glittered, and he snorted. Then he turned away, and at last, she drew a deep breath, ready to gather her scattered wits and figure out just how bad her situation was.

Only it was hard to believe things were so dire when she was surrounded by an opulence she'd never experienced. Like some sultan's palace, the open airy chamber was furnished for comfort and seduction.

Light spilled into the room from a shaded balcony. White, gauzy curtains stirred softly on a light breeze. The same nearly transparent fabric framed the canopy above the bed, but was bunched and tied off with silken cords around heavy, scrolled bedposts. Veins of precious metals glinted in pale, blush-colored marble on the floor. Columns carved in a deeper skin-toned marble supported the ceiling. Low-backed, sectional sofas, upholstered in brown velvet and peppered with rose, brown, and gold satin pillows, invited one to rest, to sink into their softness. Tall, leafy plants set in deep urns gave the chamber the feeling one was in a lush tropical mansion.

The most remarkable feature was the sunken pool at the center of the room. Three steps surrounded the pool where more plants with long fronds tilted toward the water. The water was clear, with more vegetation floating on the surface—lily pads, white lotus blossoms, and dark vines that trailed along the edges of the pool.

Her captor strode toward the pool and stuck his hand beneath the clear water spilling from a stone pipe before glancing back at her.

Deepening her scowl, she backed up on the bed again, drawing the edge of the coverlet over her naked body, not liking his expression at all.

Dark, sensual promise radiated from a masculine face tightening with resolve.

Turning away, he plucked the ties at the wrists of his black surcoat. Then he reached behind his neck, grabbed a handful of the silk and pulled it over his head.

With his back to her, she could only stare at the black tattoo that covered his skin. Like a modern tribal tattoo, the design portrayed a dragon, its snout pointing toward his neck, furled wings spreading over the backs of his shoulders, and a long sinuous tail trailing beneath his trousers. The body of the black dragon was covered in small scales, each meticulously rendered, yet the wings appeared smooth rather than feathered or scaled.

She remembered blurring her sight the first time she'd seen him in the mirror, and finding the dark aura of a giant dragon surrounding him. She did the same now, but found no such shadow around him. When his trousers loosened, she couldn't look away. They pooled around his soft boots, which he toed off one at a time. He stepped into the water.

When the churning water hid the hewn buttocks, she finally drew a deep breath and glanced away. His allure was a palpable thing, causing her heartbeats to race and her stomach to drop to her toes because she knew she didn't have a hope in hell of resisting him.

Already her mind leapt ahead to thoughts of how his dominance would affect her. The dark promise in his gaze had answered the shameful yearning she suppressed except for those times when she sought the "safety" of a human master.

Her mind was nearly consumed with lustful images when she ought to be considering her escape.

There had to be a way out. She'd have to follow their scents to retrace their steps and find the hall with the mirror. If she made a quick dash for the door, would she have a chance to escape him? He was powerful, but was he quick? And did she really want to escape, or did she want to be captured again and forced to submit?

Without Guntram to watch over her, his presence a reminder of her duty and the honor she ought to protect, could she keep her head in the game, or would she surrender completely to the dark obsession that ruled her?

# CHAPTER 3

For once, Gabriella wished she owned an ounce of Guntram's ability to assess an enemy calmly before selecting the correct tactic. Remorse filled her. She'd often teased her personal guard about his lack of spontaneity, prodded him more than once to see if he would lose his tight-fisted control. She'd sensed long ago his attraction to her, but she'd never crossed that line, never invited him to her bed. To surrender to a male of her kind would spell the end of her independence, however much she'd been tempted to taste his fierce, measured passion.

Instead, her willfulness had landed her in a chamber with a monster. One who didn't care that she watched as he bathed. And one who apparently didn't give a damn whether she tried to escape or attack him.

He'd turned his back on her. Was he so sure of himself because they weren't really alone? Gabriella studied the room again but found no evidence of any modern technology—wall sconces with fat candles would provide light during the night. There was no television, no phone, which meant hidden cameras and bugs were just as unlikely to exist here.

Were there more enchanted mirrors for someone to watch her from? Distressingly, the only mirror she saw in the room was one huge gilt-framed mirror on the ceiling above the bed, but it was too high for her to touch or look behind, so her concerns couldn't be verified.

The deliberate placement of the mirror made her body quiver anew as her mind filled with images of the demon's body rutting into hers while she watched him over his shoulder. A mistake, because now that she knew what his backside looked like, the picture was firmly planted. Her body flushed with languid heat.

The man was made for a woman's pleasure—as handsome as Alex, as powerfully built as Guntram. If she'd met a human like him in one of the clubs she visited, she'd have begged to give him a week's service before being satisfied.

He must know she was curious, and had to know that she was attracted despite her fear. Her arousal wafted in the breeze caressing her skin.

Her gaze turned slowly, reluctantly, to find him again, still with his back to her as he cupped water and spilled it over his shoulders. Broad and powerful shoulders.

He'd subdued her easily and carried her large frame as though she weighed nothing. Physical strength was like an aphrodisiac for her, and he was built like a god—heavy, slabbed muscles rippled along either side of his deeply embedded spine. Arms thick as tree trunks, so like Guntram's, flexed as he splashed water against his chest. As well, she hadn't missed the depth of muscle that wrapped around the long bones of his thighs and calves before he'd stepped into the pool.

She continued to stare now—not because she worried he'd approach her again—but because she wanted him to turn, wanted him to rise from the water and let her look at the part of him that held the promise of being every bit as impressive, *as massive*, as the rest of him.

Her naked skin felt hot, so she shoved away the coverlet to feel the breeze sifting through sheer curtains at the arched windows. Her nipples prickled, tightening into aching points. She'd feared rape in those first few moments when he'd dragged her through the portal. Now, her body prepared to be taken.

At last, the one Alex had called the Master of the Demons turned, aiming a hot, assessing glare her way.

Did he wonder why she hadn't bothered covering herself since she'd been afraid before of inciting lust? As a wolf, she didn't possess a lot of modesty. Running in wolfskin, transforming in the company of her pack, there wasn't anything dozens of men didn't know about her body.

Even her heats were their business. When her body burned with lust to mate, they sniffed around her, fur rising on their backs to warn away the competition as they circled her. She'd reveled in her power to attract them even as she'd scorned their suits. They could sniff and nuzzle her sex, but they couldn't sink their teeth into her neck and hold her—not and hope to live long.

The demon's glance slid over her, pausing on her ripened nipples, gliding down her soft belly to her ample hips and thighs. She wasn't a stick-girl, but she thought he might prefer her frame because he was so large himself.

Perhaps she could use his lust to distract him. Use him long enough to assuage the heat curling around her womb while she sought a way to overcome him and escape.

*There now* . . . she'd shown a modicum of restraint, however self-serving, to come up with a plan. Not that Guntram would have been pleased with the course she'd chosen.

Too bad he wasn't here to watch. She loved it when he watched.

The demon sank beneath the water, then sprang upward, water sluicing down him from the curtain of his dark hair. He shook it back, still staring at her. Funny, how appealing, how youthful the damp clumps of eyelashes framing his golden irises made him appear.

His hand rose, palm up, in an invitation to join him. She should bristle at his arrogance that he thought he could so easily command her.

Yet, instead of lifting her chin in defiance, she damn near preened, her shoulders falling back to raise her breasts in offering.

He curled his fingers, twice, telling her to come now, while his expression hardened.

Her heart thudding hard against her chest, she scooted off the bed because she feared his reprisal and worried that her plan to seduce him would get off to a wobbly start—or so she told herself. But she knew she lied. She wanted him.

So she strolled toward him, rolling her hips, lowering her eyes because his strange slitted pupils unnerved her almost as much as the powerful wave of lust that throbbed inside her pussy.

Gabriella wondered if fucking a demon was any different from fucking a man or a vampire. She knew she was about to find out and hoped she'd survive the act, because the heat in his heavy-lidded gaze was burning her alive.

Guntram's hand remained wrapped around the stock of his crossbow as he entered the room on the ground floor of the mansion. A meeting room, he surmised, from the large ebony table that dominated the space.

At the head of the long table sat a man he recognized, the one he'd battled in an alleyway in New Orleans days ago when he'd gone prowling in wolfskin. He'd thought him unusually skilled for a *Revenant*. The man had managed to choke Guntram with his bare hands until he'd passed out.

Now he didn't feel quite so chagrined at being beaten. This man ruled the coven now. Something he'd learned while the men were led to the barracks. He had to be a Born male, the daywalker they'd been brought to kill.

Gabriella had known exactly what he was all along. This was the man she'd insisted they could trust.

Alexander Broussard sat like a potentate, relaxing against rich leather; Nicolas Montfaucon stood at one shoulder, and another man, older with shoulder-length brown hair and a fathomless stare that seemed as old as time, stood at the other. Knowing vampires' love for magic, Guntram guessed this one was Alex's mage.

Guntram suppressed the urge to slow his steps, to hunch his shoulders and balance his weight on the balls of his feet in case they attacked.

Vampires weren't straightforward creatures. They hid their black souls behind civilized smiles.

"Please, have a seat," Alex said, gesturing toward a chair beside him.

Guntram chose one farther down and took his seat with a show of reluctance.

Alex raked a hand through his brown hair. By his expression, Guntram knew he wasn't going to like what the vampire was working his way up to saying.

"I suppose you know by now, that the *sabat*, our council, is no longer in charge."

Guntram nodded, just suppressing the urge to grunt. Vampires already thought *weres* were primitive creatures, that they belonged to a four-legged subspecies of dog.

Alex's hands curled slowly on the tabletop. "When the smoke cleared, I placed Gabriella in a safe—"

"Placed?" Guntram said softly.

Nicolas, still standing beside Alex's shoulder, folded his arms over his chest, and his lips thinned.

The older man's face betrayed no emotion whatsoever.

Alex nodded. "I *escorted* her to a safe place. Things were happening fast. Although the worst of the danger had passed, I still had vampires loyal to Inanna to deal with. I feared for Gabriella's safety."

He lied. Guntram could tell by the way his eyes blinked at

the last. He couldn't quite hold his gaze. "You imprisoned her for your convenience."

Nicolas's terse expression eased. His lips slid into a cynical smile. "Gabriella is anything but convenient," he murmured.

Alex shot him a cold glare, and then turned back to Guntram. "The place where I left her was perfectly safe, with one caveat that she understood well. But she has somehow . . . disappeared."

Guntram's stomach knotted, icy calm sliding down to douse the anger rising inside him. Now was not the time to punish. "I would see this place," he said, keeping his tone carefully even.

"It's not necessary," Alex murmured.

"It's necessary for me to see how allies who give you aid are kept . . . safe."

The older man touched Alex's shoulder. "Show him."

Alex slowly rose from his seat. Guntram did the same as he approached.

The vampire reached into his pocket, produced a crystal dangling from a keychain, and held it up. "This is the key. When I close my hand around it, we'll enter the room where I left her."

"How do I know you won't do the same to me—leave me?"

"You don't. But since I told my men to allow you your weapons, I'm assuming you'll come armed."

Guntram laid his bow on the table and bent to slide a knife from his boot. "Not wood. Not lethal to your kind. So what other assurances do I have? You have my men in your barracks."

Alex's set expression softened. "You will have to trust that

Gabriella is my friend. I'm just as concerned about her disappearance."

Alex reached out, placed one hand on Guntram's shoulder, and closed his other fist around the crystal.

White light blinded Guntram for a moment. When his vision cleared, he was in another place. A cave. With Persian carpets on the floor, silk tapestries cloaking rock walls, and fine furnishings.

The room reeked of sex. Guntram inhaled. Alex and Gabriella had made love here. So had others. But the scents were fading.

A glance at Alex said the other man knew what he was thinking. His expression remained neutral. He lifted his chin toward the far wall. A bureau laden with decanters of liquor sat below a gilt-framed mirror.

"Touch the frame of the mirror. A lot will be explained."

Guntram stalked toward the mirror, lifted one hand, and pressed his fingertips to the frame. The surface of the glass reflecting his own image shimmered, lightened, and then settled again, offering a view into an orgy of bloodlust and sexual frenzy.

Guntram's chest stilled and his gaze skimmed the room.

"She touched the glass," Alex said softly, urgently, beside him. "Had to, for it to have happened."

"It's a portal, then? Into hell."

"Into the Land of the Dead. Hell, I guess."

"She's not there. Is she already dead?"

"That she isn't anywhere in sight is a hopeful sign."

Guntram swallowed down the deep emotions that tasted like metal in his mouth. "How do we save her?"

"Simon, my mage, has a plan."

Guntram found it nearly impossible to look away from the awful carnage. But he dropped his hand and spun on his heels, his hand coming up to grip Alex's throat and lift him off the floor, the tip of his dagger pressing between the vampire's ribs. "You're responsible," he said between clenched teeth. "Don't think, because you hold my men and we're only a small force, that our kind won't seek vengeance."

Alex lifted his hands. "The last thing I want is trouble with the Wolfen," he said, his voice strained. "You have my word we'll do everything we can to get her back. She's my friend."

"She tried to kill you."

"Long ago, yes. But I know she regretted it. I hold no grudge against her. I didn't intend this."

Guntram lowered the knife and dropped Alex on his feet.

Alex raised the crystal. "Have you seen enough?"

Guntram nodded.

Before his eyes could adjust to the dim light inside the council chamber, something hard slammed into Guntram's side, taking him to the ground. A boot crushed the hand holding the dagger—Alex's. Nicolas had him pinned.

Guntram had the advantage of weight and would have liked nothing better than to take out his rage and frustration on them both, but he lay slack until Nicolas gave his shoulders a shove and climbed off him.

Guntram rose, brushing off his clothing—nothing but an act, because he was already covered with a thin layer of mud. When his gaze met Alex's again, he let him see his fury. "What is this plan you have?"

The older man stepped forward. "What we seek to do may be impossible. While demons have punched through to enter our realm from time to time, no one from this realm has entered the Land of the Dead and returned. Not without negotiating a trade. One soul for the soul you would save."

"I would take her place," Guntram said quickly.

"And then your kind would still have cause to war with us," Alex said, sounding impatient. "I would attempt to enter in secrecy, find her, and slip back. It hasn't been done before. But we were fortunate to obtain a device, something sorcerers use to cross between the realms. We sent Inanna and the demon known as the Devourer to the Land using that device."

"I will take my men."

Alex shook his head. "No, we don't want to leave a large signature. Two of us will go."

Guntram's jaw tightened. "I'll be one of them."

The mage cleared his throat, drawing their gazes. "And I will accompany you."

Alex swung toward the mage. "It should be me," he said heatedly.

Simon shook his head, a small, sad smile easing his expression. "You have work to do here. You're too important to risk."

"Then it should be me," Nicolas said, stepping closer.

"You'd desert Chessa when she's about to give birth?" Again, Simon shook his head. "I've known this was coming. I'm prepared."

"You've done this before. Lived this before?" Alex asked.

Guntram scowled, not following the conversation and wondering if they were speaking in some kind of code.

Simon nodded. "I've lived this before."

"And how does it end?" Alex said, his eyes glittering.

"In death. But I have hopes that this time, I will find a way to prevail."

Alex gave a violent shake of his head. "No. Someone else will go."

Simon gripped Alex's shoulders and stared into his taut face.

Guntram nearly snorted, wondering if the two were going to kiss.

"We have a few hours to make arrangements," Simon said.

"To settle your affairs you mean," Alex said bitterly.

Simon let his hands drop and turned to Guntram. "Go to your men. You'll have access to the house, the dining hall, baths. Don't try to enter the gardens or make a run for the gates. You can tell them everything. We have nothing to hide."

"Madeleine?" Alex said softly behind Simon. "She's not going to understand."

Simon didn't turn. His gaze held Guntram's as he spoke. "I have letters written, and something I will ask of you. For now, I would watch her fly."

Guntram waited until the mage had left, then turned to Nicolas. "I'll need weapons."

Nicolas snorted. "I'll take you to the arsenal, but I don't know what you'll find effective against demons."

"A sword," Alex said, sounding distracted. His gaze was still on the door where Simon had disappeared. "Decapitation works best."

Guntram smiled, steel and muscle—his favorite sort of fight.

As Gabriella drew closer to the Master, she slowed, surprised because the vegetation inside the pool was thicker than she'd first thought. His fingers curled again and she took a deep breath, descending the tiled steps and settling her hand inside his.

His palm was hot, the surface hard. He helped her into the water, and her feet met a soft, sandy bottom. The water was warm, but no warmer than a natural pool. She lifted her gaze, feeling suddenly shy now that she stood so close and by her own choice.

His expression didn't invite, didn't give a hint at his pleasure that she'd obeyed. Instead, he watched as though waiting for something, wanting to see the expressions slide across her face.

The thought that he waited for something had only crossed her mind when she felt something slither around one ankle.

Gabriella gasped and tried to jerk back her foot, but the thing beneath the water wrapped around her, anchoring her there. She shot him a glance filled with alarm. "Do something!"

A smile pulled at one corner of his mouth, but he didn't move. He let go of her hand.

She pulled her foot again, and whatever surrounded it constricted. Then another thin tendril shot upward, sliding around her calf and wrapping around her knee. She peered into the water and caught sight of a dark green vine, the end shaped like a leaf, but thicker and rasping against her skin like a tongue. As she peered down, another vine shot out of the pale sand beneath her feet, and then another; winding quickly around her ankle as they tugged her legs apart.

The demon laughed softly as her arms flailed to grasp his shoulders in panic. His arms closed around her, and he laid her back on the uppermost step.

She let go of him and set her hands on the edge of a step,

gasping for breath. At the sight of his mouth, one corner curling, rage shot through her. "Bastard, make them let go." Vines sprang from the water and twined around her wrists, drawing her arms wide. Now she was spread-eagled, lying across the steps, her body—her sex—exposed. She expected him to gloat.

Instead, his head fell back suddenly, and a long groan tore from his mouth.

She glanced down to find vines entwining beneath the water, one wrapped around his cock, another encircling and laving his balls.

But he didn't look concerned, merely orgasmic.

His heavy-lidded gaze lowered to hers, and she took his cue, relaxing against the tiles beneath her and letting the vines prying her apart do their work.

As soon as she surrendered, the tension eased, and the vines surged between her legs, tickling her inner thighs, stroking between her buttocks, at last sliding along her folds. "Sweet Jesus," she gasped.

A dark brow rose.

And she laughed, beginning a slow rise toward ecstasy. "Guess he has no place here."

He muttered something, and the vines ringing his sex loosened. He strode toward her, lowering himself to a knee on the step just beneath her. When his hands settled to either side of her body and he hovered over her, she lifted her head and nuzzled her cheek alongside his; letting him know she was eager for this, burning for it.

Vines continued to wrap around her body, cushioning her back, sliding around her sides to loop around her breasts and plump them up. He tapped a nipple with a fingertip and a slender vine inched toward it, surrounding the distended tip and tightening deliciously. Then he lowered his head and tongued the end that peeked from the center of the tight ring.

Gabriella's whole body quaked. Spread as though she'd been tied to a rack, something she'd experienced a time or two, she prayed for him to discern the excitement building inside her.

His head reared back, canting, staring into her eyes, and then a small, wicked smile stretched his lush lips. Vines exploded from the water, shooting upward, and he leaned away. One vine quivered, then descended, lashing her belly, her inner thighs, with just enough speed and strength to sting but leave only reddened skin—not a welt.

Gabriella cried out, her hands straining against their bonds, her belly beginning to dance with electric quivers as creamy pleasure filled her channel and trickled down her inner thighs to float away in the pool.

The lashes continued. Tongues tightening, hardening, flicking at her flesh, never the same spot. The leaves twisted, knotted, then lashed at her like the strokes of a cat-o'-nine-tails. Gabriella gasped, her body releasing endorphins that sent her into a haze of euphoria. Her fists curled; her head tilted back.

Then she felt a fingertip slide from between her breasts down her belly to her mound, tracing through her thatch. The leafy tongues followed and slipped between her folds, pressing them apart to tap her clit.

She was close to exploding, sliding deeper into an orgasm so strong and fierce that she rebelled. "No!"

Her eyes slammed open, caught his heavy-lidded glance, and she knew he had no intention of retreating.

A vine lifted in the air above her, coiling around and around, the end whipping like a whirligig, then stretching into an oblong shape. Her breath caught as it dove between her legs, sliding between her folds and pushing deep into her body.

Afraid for a moment, she held her breath, trying to close her legs against the invasion, but the bundle of twisting vines inside her pulsated. The leafy tongues caressed her inner walls, twisting tight and then expanding, then repeating the motion over and over until her belly undulated, and her eyes slid shut.

Whipping vines tapped her breasts, her abdomen, her thighs, stung her lips and nipples, striking without pattern but warming her skin an inch at a time, until the heat inside her curled around her womb, became too much—and not enough.

Her eyes shot open, begging him silently to end it. At a single wave of his hand, all the vines, save the ones cushioning her body and wrapped around her ankles and wrists, slipped back beneath the water.

Gabriella drew short, shattered breaths, staring as he came over her, his hands plunging beneath her bottom, lifting her. His cock, ringed at the base with a single vine, prodded between her slick folds and then sank inside, pressing upward until he was fully lodged inside her.

With all her walls breached, decimated by the frightful, sensual torture, she shivered, silently welcoming his invasion. However, his cock—hot, thick, and pulsing inside her—remained still. She raised her head and bit his shoulder, clamping down to hold him.

Soft, pleased laughter shook his chest, and he began to

move—nothing tentative or exploring about his strokes. His cock drove deep and hard, thrusting with precision and strength, her inner walls stretching so suddenly that she felt the burning pinch. *Perfect.*

Her orgasm exploded, arching her back, shuddering through her splayed limbs. If she'd been free she would have writhed in anguished ecstasy. Instead, all she could manage were shattered groans against his skin. Her teeth gnashed, drawing blood, and he punished her for the injury, hammering harder, driving her breath from her lungs until she grew lightheaded and released him. Her head landed on a tiled step as she lingered in the lush aftermath, her body lolling on the tide of his own exploding pleasure, drifting toward darkness . . .

She awoke and found herself lying on his chest as he rested on a step, her legs spread over his hips, his cock hardening again and still deeply embedded inside her. She raised her head slowly to meet his strange golden eyes.

His hand lifted to her face. Fingers tucked sticky locks of her hair behind her ears. "You will call me 'Bel' or 'Lord' when others are with us," he said slowly in a deep, rumbling bass that vibrated through her chest.

Gabriella swallowed and lifted her breasts off his chest. Her nipples tingled and were tight and hot. "So you can speak English."

His shoulders shrugged. His gaze swept her chest, then slowly met hers again. "If you were from some other place in your world, we would speak another language. You will have no difficulties communicating here."

"Why didn't you let me know that before?"

"I didn't want to hear you beg to be returned."

The deep rumble of his voice vibrated through her body. Her sex clasped his cock. "Will you?" she said, struggling to keep her tone even when her breaths were quickening again. "Will you return me?"

A muscle flexed along his jaw. "Never."

And with his sex stirring inside her, she wasn't all too certain she wanted to leave. At least not yet. This place frightened her, but so did he. *Deliciously so.*

# CHAPTER 4

Alex stood at the edge of the training field where stadium lights burned brightly enough for the kestrel to play. He watched from the garden as Simon lifted his arm to send her skyward again.

The relationship between Madeleine and Simon had always been the most poignant he'd ever observed. Simon waited eagerly every month for the full moon, which freed the kestrel, transforming her into the human woman who'd captured his heart long before anyone he knew had been born.

Seemingly, she was content with the arrangement. Her radiant smile greeted Simon each full moon, her gaze never straying from his tall frame. She spent long hours in his bed. Wherever they went, they touched, her small hand cupped inside Simon's.

At the end of the moonphase, Simon's happiness retreated, held at bay for another month while he tended the kestrel like a precious pet.

In her bird form, Madeleine wasn't sentient, but she was affectionate toward her master, never straying from her perch but calling to him as he passed.

She would be devastated when she awoke and discovered he wasn't there. Alex didn't know how he'd console her.

"I should be the one to go," Nicolas said softly as he stepped beside him to watch the star-crossed pair. "Chessa will have you to care for her and the child. I'm expendable."

"No one is expendable." Alex cut a look to the side. "Besides, she'd never accept me in your place. She's made it perfectly clear that you're her mate. She loves you. And do you really think Mikaela would be happy with the arrangement?"

"Do you think Miki would know she ought to be unhappy?"

Alex gave Nicolas a glare. "I won't bring another woman into our relationship. It's too new. And I find myself . . . satisfied."

Nicolas lifted an eyebrow, but didn't comment. He cleared his throat. "Still, we need the mage more. I should go."

"I know it's hard. I'd go in Simon's place, but he knows what's coming. He'll find a way to come back to us. He has to."

"And if he doesn't," Nicolas said slowly, "don't you think he's prepared you well enough to survive without him? You have all the memories of every one of your ancestors. Didn't they give you any wisdom at all?"

Alex grunted. "Don't be an ass. I'm just like you." He allowed a tight smile to curve his mouth. "Only more evolved."

Nicolas's white teeth flashed. "And you won't disintegrate into dust when you bite it."

"Are we going to compare the size of our cocks next?"

"Don't have to. Chessa has already said she couldn't tell much of a difference."

Alex clapped Nicolas's shoulder. "She's being diplomatic to save your pride."

They both chuckled at the thought of the stubborn vampire ever learning to curb her tongue long enough to show even a little tact.

"We should leave them alone," Alex said, steering Nicolas from the field.

"So much has happened—and it's only been one night."

"I know." Alex paused, and then mentioned what worried him most. His stomach tightened. "I wonder if they'll run into Inanna."

Nicolas's eyes darkened. "Pray that they don't. She'd use them to serve her own purpose. She must never come back."

Alex watched Nicolas from the corner of his eye and cleared his throat. "I haven't asked how you feel about that. Inanna did turn you."

"She turned me, as well as my sweet wife, and she talked Anaïs into committing suicide when the Devourer impregnated her. I have no soft feelings left for her. But I know her better than anyone." Nicolas's upper lip drew into a snarl. "She'll want vengeance."

"She can want all she likes." Alex scoffed. "Her sister rules that realm, and Irkalla has plenty of her own reasons to make sure Inanna remains disappointed."

"I swear you're sounding more like Simon all the time."

"Wise?"

"Pompous."

Alex snorted, another smile creeping across his face. "We should check on the wolves."

"Are you afraid they'll try an attack from inside the compound?"

"No," he said thoughtfully. "I trust Guntram."

Nicolas arched an eyebrow. "Because he gave his word?"

"Because he's in love with Gabriella. He won't risk losing her forever to satisfy his thirst for my blood." He shook his head. "Not yet, anyway."

With a final glance into the night sky at the kestrel tipping her wings to glide on a breeze, Alex left the field, heading through the edge of Inanna's fragrant garden. At the door of the barracks, they passed several members of the security force who'd been assigned to watch over the wolves housed in their barracks.

"Any problems tonight?" Nicolas asked the first man he passed just inside the door.

A shudder shook the man's shoulders. "Other than wolves stinking up the place?"

Alex leveled him with a quelling stare.

The team member straightened his shoulders. "No problems, sir," he said, correcting himself. "Everything's quiet."

"I'm sure you'll keep it that way," Nicolas murmured. "Their leader?"

Alex and Nicolas followed the young *Revenant*'s gaze. They found Guntram in the barracks' arsenal, running his fingers across the serrated blade of a military knife. His lips twisted into a snarl when he spotted them.

"Have you found everything you need?" Alex asked.

Guntram's gaze lifted to Alex's for a moment, then went back to the knife, but not before Alex noted the derisive curling of his upper lip.

"I want a word with you," Guntram said, sliding the knife into a sheath on his belt. "Alone."

Nicolas stiffened. "That's not going to happen."

Worried Nicolas and the wolf might come to blows again, Alex gripped his friend's arm. "Go to Chessa. There's nothing more for you to do here."

"I'll be outside," Nicolas said between his teeth.

"Nic, she's damn close to dropping that baby, and you haven't spared her more than a few minutes all night. Go to her. Guntram won't kill me." His gaze shot to the warrior. "He tried it once. He knows it's not that easy."

A scowl furrowed Nicolas's forehead. "You've met before? Something else you didn't think I needed to know?"

Alex smiled at Guntram, whose mouth was firming into a straight line. "Long story. I'll fill you in later. *Go.*"

Nicolas opened his mouth to say something else, and then closed it. "Later." He aimed a warning at the *were* and left.

Alex strode toward Guntram, then took a seat on a folding chair beside the gun rack. "You wanted to talk."

"I know what you are," Guntram said. "And that you're the same Born she tried to murder."

Alex almost smiled at Guntram's terse delivery. The man didn't waste words. "It was a long time ago. In Germany. She thought I'd betrayed her."

"You had another lover. You did betray her."

Alex shook his head. "I seduced a demon to get something that had been stolen. It was important."

"A wolf would have found another way."

"Because you're loyal to your mates?"

Guntram nodded sharply.

"Vampires don't value fidelity," Alex said, keeping his tone even. The more time he spent with Guntram, the more he wished they weren't standing on opposite sides. Here was a fiercely loyal man. Gabriella was luckier than she knew.

"Why should I trust your word of honor if you don't know what honor is?"

Alex took no offense, and relaxed, meeting the other man's glare with his expression clear of any answering animosity. "Fidelity isn't prized out of necessity," Alex said quietly. "Our kind must feed—on blood, on lust. We can't fill our appetites in a monogamous relationship."

"So none of you remain true to their mates?"

Alex thought of his mother and father, the only blood mates he'd ever known to foreswear sex with anyone else. "It's not unheard of," he admitted.

"But it's inconvenient."

"I suppose you'd see it that way."

"Gabriella is better off without you."

"I'm sure right now that she would agree."

"When I bring her back," Guntram said, his expression turning to stone, "I won't stand aside to let you have her again."

"Are you going to claim her?" Alex asked, not responding to the unspoken challenge. Guntram's fierce passion was interesting given Gabriella's equally fierce independence. "She's sworn since the day I met her that she'd never take a wolf mate."

Guntram's gaze slid away. "If I return with her, I won't give her any choice."

Alex smiled. Guntram would do it to ensure her safety. Or

at least that's what he'd tell himself. And having Gabriella mated would certainly remove a fly in the ointment, from his perspective.

"Guntram, if you want her, I can help."

For Gabriella, the passage of time was measured by the pounding of her heart as blood pumped through her body in a heavy, wanton beat. Her skin, tender still from the lashing she'd received by the vines, was hot and exquisitely sensitized to every caress of the Master's hands and lips. Her reddened nipples never receded, remaining hard and distended. Her clit stayed engorged and throbbing. She restlessly scissored her legs, craving friction to heat her core.

He'd carried her to the bed, water streaming from their bodies, and laid her in the center before coming over her. Just as she'd envisioned, she'd watched him over his shoulder in the mirror as each movement of his shoulders and back animated the dragon tattooed on his back, making the wings rise up and down and the tail undulate with every flex of his buttocks. He'd fucked her again on the bed, without preliminaries, thrusting straight, powering so hard her lungs expelled air in harsh gasps.

Feeling languid, boneless, and drifting toward sleep, she moaned when his large hands parted her again, and she gazed down between their bodies, watching as he smoothed over her skin, his burnished hand caressing pale, pink curves.

For the first time, she noted the ring he wore on one hand. A raised crest with a six-sided star, a large bloodred cabochon at the center and small multicolored jewels studding each point of the star—all sitting atop a crudely made setting that looked forged from brass and iron. Light reflected off the center of the cabochon, and the smooth stone seemed to glow for a moment until he moved his hand again and the illusion faded.

She quickly lost interest in the ring when his hand slid down her belly and cupped her pussy. Two fingers eased inside her, and she sucked in a breath that hissed through clenched teeth.

"Have I hurt you?" he asked, his raised brows showing no particular concern, only curiosity.

"No, but your fingers feel cold inside me."

"That's because your woman's channel is hot." Long, thick fingers swirled inside her. "And wet. I find I'm very, very thirsty."

She shivered at the intimacy that had grown quickly between them, emphasized by their soft whispers and reinforced by the steady sundering of her inhibitions. Even the gauzy fabric he'd drawn down around the bed deepened the feeling that they were the only beings who existed on this plane.

Her breath caught at the dark promise in his eyes as he slid down the bed and settled his torso between her thighs. When his head dipped toward her sex, a thin, ragged moan slipped between her lips.

His gaze met hers again. Black pupils dilated until only thin streaks of gold framed them, and then his tongue flicked out, longer than she'd expected and indented at the tip. The flicker touched her clitoris, stroking it, and her back arched instantly. Another flick and he stroked between her folds, prodding her entrance to lap at the cream sliding down to greet his wicked demon's tongue.

She caught a glimpse of herself in the mirror and almost

didn't recognize the creature lying there with her thighs splayed. Her hair was matted, her eyes overlarge, her mouth red and stretching as she moaned.

His head, circling between her legs, was dark; his thick hair slicked back. Powerful shoulders, bracketed by her thighs, tensed and eased as he plied her with sinuous rasps of his long, slick tongue.

Her body followed his movements, her hips lifting and falling, letting him coax her into full arousal again. When had she surrendered everything to him? When had her plot to seduce him completely devolved until she was the one enraptured? Trapped by her own sensual nature and his natural domination, she'd folded easily. *Too easily.*

She dug her fingers into his scalp and pulled his hair, trying to pry him from her cunt. However, his tongue thrust more insistently inside her, reaching deeper, sliding, fluttering until it found the bundle of nerves a third of the way up, the rounded knot of her inner pleasure center.

Her body vibrated, quivering hard at his internal caresses. He touched nothing else, concentrating his efforts there until her moans grew thin and broken.

When her release spiraled out of control, her thighs clamped his shoulders hard, and she tugged at his hair, fingers clenching in time with the strongly pulsating caresses that squeezed up and down her vagina.

A low, throaty groan emanated from his mouth still locked against her sex, and she shivered at the sensual satisfaction she'd given him.

Then he withdrew his tongue and sat on his haunches between her legs, holding out his hand again, fully expecting her to acquiesce.

*Again? Sweet fuck, will he ever be satisfied?* Just the thought of this powerful demon's insatiable appetite for her flattered her ego, suppressing the alarm jangling at her conscience. She forced herself to hesitate, invocating her proud core to resist, while ignoring the part of her that was dying to surrender and bask in the lush desire he'd created.

One dark brow arched; his eyes narrowed. Remembering where she was and with whom, she gulped down her fear and slowly lifted her hand to place her palm against his.

His fingers clasped hers hard and dragged her upward to her knees.

They faced each other, both breathing hard, his mouth gliding into a smile that made her quiver anew, this time with dread. "What do you want from me?" she asked, her voice overly loud in the stillness surrounding them.

"Your surrender would be a nice start."

"I've done everything you wanted."

Dark eyes flashed. "You've been playing at obedience."

"My actions aren't enough?"

His fingers slipped to her wrists, encircling them like steely cuffs, and her heart pounded harder against her chest. "You think you can toy with me, that I can be fooled into complacency."

Gabriella bit back a groan that he'd read her so well. Had her expression given her away? She wasn't accustomed to schooling her features or her mouth. "Can you read my mind, then?"

"I can read the defiance and pride in your eyes. You betray yourself in so many different ways." Drawing both of her wrists together, he raised them above her head and reached for some silken cords dangling inside the curtains.

Knowing what he had in mind, she began to struggle, jerking hard against his hold, but to no avail. He quickly looped the silk around her wrists, binding her. Raised onto her knees, any tugging pulled on the silk, which constricted her wrists. "It hurts. Untie me."

"You only hurt yourself. Cease your struggles."

Faced toward the curtain now, she glanced over her shoulder. "I don't like this."

"Liar. Your skin is flushing." He inhaled deeply. "Your scent ripens. You crave to be overwhelmed and mastered by a man."

He knew! Mortification heightened the flush creeping across her cheeks. "You've got me all wrong."

"I don't think so. Otherwise it wouldn't have been so easy to draw your hand to that mirror. My love, it only took one look."

Gabriella turned from his self-satisfied expression, fighting the very thing he'd discerned about her. Her entire body was flooding with anticipation, melting from the inside at his commanding tone.

She felt the mattress dip behind her. Felt the heat radiating from his skin as he came between her bent legs and his chest snuggled close to her back. "There is no shame in surrendering," he murmured against her hair.

Which was true in a way. The shame that had painted her whole life with dark, violent colors was deeper than the sexual need he'd discovered . . . and details she'd never shared with anyone since the day she'd made those responsible pay for her pain.

Her submission was just part of her nature, and a facet she'd learned to control by swallowing down her pride to engage in brief liaisons and rid herself of the edgy anxiety that filled her from time to time. With human partners, she could play at submission. Fill the well of her needs, then slip back into the mantle of her rank and kind without anyone knowing—no one who mattered or could use her weakness against her, that is.

Only with Alex had she ever seriously considered surrendering all.

No human could control her or fulfill her. She'd played at it, sharing her secret liaisons with just one of her kind, but Guntram was like a loyal dog and had never used his knowledge to wrest away her power. And in his way, he had stood guard over her, protecting her from herself.

Surrendering to a demon now was unthinkable. But fighting his unnatural charisma was taking all her energy. Somehow, she had to find a way to prevent him from enslaving her to her own pleasure and need.

For just a moment, she considered transforming and biting through her ties. She'd love to see his eyes widen with fear when she turned on him. However, she still didn't know the full extent of his power and strength. And for now, the only advantage she held was the truth about herself.

Hands glided down her back to her buttocks. His fingers curled beneath them and parted her. His cock's blunt crown slid into her crevice, raking up and down, and she sucked her bottom lip between her teeth, because she knew he'd decided to inflame another part of her body.

His fingers bit into her tender flesh, his thumbs swept closer to the small entrance and pressed it open. Again, his cock nudged, centering there, and then pressed inward.

Her buttocks flexed as she tried to pull away, tried to

squeeze them together to repel him. This act was the ultimate in submission—the most intimate, the most demeaning when accomplished through force.

"I don't want this," she hissed.

"Shall I prove that you're lying?" he whispered next to her ear. His mouth dropped to her shoulder, teeth and lips scraping across skin, sparking nerve endings, which crackled and fired, sending darts of pleasure south. She was doomed by her own sensuality.

She shivered at his seductive promise and the underlying hint of menace, and then moaned with relief when his cock shifted, sliding forward to dip into her pussy—just the head, just to wet it, because again, he pressed against her back entrance, this time sinking the crown inside her.

Then his hands let go of her ass and came around her hips, one raking over her stomach to palm a breast and gently massage it, the other sliding between her legs. Fingers plunged into her pussy; his thumb toggled her engorged clit until her body shook, rocked by his skill and his relentless pursuit of her submission.

When his cock thrust upward, she dangled on the cords, her body going limp because she no longer controlled it. Her resistance had been all for show, a front that quickly crumpled as ripples of dark pleasure spiraled inside her.

The demon surrounding her, penetrating her, would make good on his promise to master her. Every endless caress and thrust bound her more tightly in this oppressive realm. Already, she craved his cock, his fingers, his lips . . .

He thrust up again, sliding deep inside her ass. Her ring eased around him, until he was slamming her body down his cock, fucking her relentlessly over and over while he fingered her, until her orgasm exploded, taking her breath, leaving her hanging on the cords and controlled by the hands holding her in a bruising grip that continued to work her up and down his cock.

As her rhythmic convulsions clasping his cock and fingers waned, his motions shortened, sharpened, jerking her body with his powerful thrusts, until his breathing rasped like sandpaper and his body stiffened. Then, giving a muffled groan, warmth filled her as he emptied his passion inside her.

Wrung out and listless, all resistance overcome at last, she wilted against him. He untied her hands and laid her on the bed, clasped close to his shuddering frame.

As she snuggled close to his chest, she silently prayed. Rescue had better come soon or her free will would be turned to mush and her mind consumed with hunger for this dark god. Alex might abandon her here, and she knew deep in her heart that the Master would never let her go.

Guntram was her only hope.

# CHAPTER 5

Sleep eluded Guntram. He lay stretched on a narrow cot in a windowless, monk-like cell, waiting for the evening to arrive—waiting for his "hosts" to leave their beds and summon him.

The wait was interminable. He'd checked on his men, who slept in shifts, not trusting the promise their captors had made to do them no harm. Guntram worried about their safety should something go wrong in the dark realm. If he didn't come back with Gabriella, Alex would have an even bigger problem on his hands. Guntram knew the smartest thing for the vampires to do would be to make the entire team "disappear" rather than release them to carry the tale back to their clan.

However, his wolves' fate didn't weigh heaviest on his conscience. They'd been handpicked by him, knew the risk they'd faced when they'd snuck into enemy territory. They'd face death the same way he would—fighting for every last breath but resigned to their fate. They were all warriors, and their destiny was to sacrifice for the good of the clan.

No, his heart wasn't burdened by their fate. Instead, he worried about the woman again. Gabriella wasn't a warrior, although she'd fought many battles. She was a woman at her core. She ought to have been covered long ago, filled with cubs, cosseted and pampered as any breedable wolf was entitled to be.

Her abduction was as much his fault as Alex's. As a male, he had the duty to protect a female, whatever the means, including taking her and forcing her to his will. Since she'd never accepted a mate from within her own rank, she'd lost the right to refuse a lesser suit.

His protection had enabled her to continue to remain free. His backing had given her a false sense of security. She'd kept her status as alpha of her pack, kept her wealth and her autonomy. Long ago, he'd stopped wondering why she refused to follow her natural path. She'd grown into a goddess in his mind, and as long as she craved her freedom, and more, because he didn't want to see her covered by another male, he'd silently given his support.

Even to the point of watching over her when her heat grew so intense that she had to alleviate the cramping desire by seeking trysts with lesser creatures. Hovering outside motel rooms and sex-club dungeons, knowing what she did with men she didn't give a damn about, hadn't lessened his desire for her.

He'd denied his own urges, shoving them deep inside. She'd damn near made a eunuch of him.

If Alex was to be believed, the last thing she wanted from him was everything he'd ever offered her. She didn't want his protection—she wanted him to prove his physical strength was greater than hers, wanted him to prove he was even more determined to have her than she was to refuse his suit.

The formula for breaking through her icy reserve was simple. Demolish every argument, every show of resistance. Restrain her if need be, never let her get the upper hand—but do it "respectfully."

Guntram had snorted when Alex added that caveat. How did one "respectfully" conquer a woman?

With his body tightening with arousal at the thought of Gabriella spread beneath him, her eyes glaring daggers while her body moistened and heated, Guntram sat up and swung his legs to the side of the cot. A one-fisted rub wasn't going to cure what ailed him. He needed action, needed to break something, put a fist through something hard to dull the sharp edge of his longing.

Like an answer to a prayer, a knock sounded at the door. *At last.*

The blonde Born, Natalie, stood outside his door with a dark, burly *Revenant* who kept close to her back. Her mate perhaps? By the glower on his face, he knew Guntram had thrown her to the ground.

"You ready?" she asked.

Since he'd slept in his clothes, he nodded. "Just let me get my gear," he said, going to the corner where he'd propped the sword he'd selected and the knives he would strap to his belt and inside the top of his boot. A thin and supple steel garrote had already been threaded through a seam of the black cargo pants he'd been given. The handles appeared like toggle adornments at his belt and at the edge of one deep pocket.

He followed the couple down the corridor and through the open barracks, where his team stood in a single rank as he passed, hands fisted over their hearts. At the very end, he halted in front of Udo. "Stay vigilant," he said softly.

Udo snorted. "Just bring her back. I'll make sure the team doesn't get too lazy, living here in the lap of luxury."

Guntram gave him a tight smile and moved along, following Natalie and her mate out of the building and through the darkened gardens to the main house. Inside, he was brought to a salon just off the black-and-white-tiled foyer on the first floor. Alex, Nicolas, and Simon were already inside, along with a red-haired woman who sat quietly beside Alex. Her green eyes widened as she watched him enter—Alex's phoenix, Guntram surmised. A small falcon rested on Simon's raised arm, rubbing its head against his cheek.

*Odd, the pets these bastards keep.*

When Simon spotted him, he gave a last caress to the bird's feathers and handed it to Alex, whose face grew taut. Perhaps the bird was more than a pet or the mage had a very strange fetish.

Guntram took the seat Natalie indicated on a small wine-colored sofa opposite Alex and Simon. When the others chose seats far away from him, he smiled. He'd made use of the showers, so he knew wolfscent and dirt weren't what put them off. "Are we going to have tea before we leave?" he asked edgily.

Simon's lips twitched, but Alex's eyes narrowed as he

transferred the bird to his knee and leaned forward. "Your journey isn't going to be like serving in any war zone you've ever fought in. A little discussion might save your ass."

Guntram shrugged. "Give me a map and a compass, have the old man stay behind me, and we shouldn't run into anything I can't handle." The words should have been pure bluster, but Guntram felt them all the way to his soul. Nothing was going to get in the way of finding Gabriella.

Simon picked up a paper bag sitting on the coffee table between them and dumped out the contents. Two crystals, both dark brown and cloudy, clattered onto the table. They were wrapped in silver wire and hung from black cords.

Guntram bit back the quip that leapt to mind about dressing for the occasion, but Simon's brooding expression said the crystals were more than an adornment. "One for each of us?" he asked, keeping derision from his voice.

"Put it on and tuck it under your shirt," Simon said. "Don't ever take it off when we're inside the dark realm."

Guntram lifted it and curled his fingers around the crystal in his palm. It warmed unnaturally fast inside his hand. He opened his fingers and peered at the stone and discovered that it was actually clear with a brown-black cloud floating beneath its polished surface. "It's enchanted."

"The stones will hold the horrors at bay."

"It's a shield then?"

"Not the sort you're thinking. We may still meet corporeal foes we'll have to battle, but you'll be protected from true hell."

Guntram's hand gripped the stone. Annoyed with Simon's doublespeak but impatient to begin the search, he held his tongue. "Is there anything else, or can we leave?"

Simon's chest lifted around a deep breath and his features tightened. "I need you to trust me," he said, his deepening tone no doubt meant to convey earnestness.

Guntram gave him a wary glance but let him finish.

"I know I haven't given you a single reason to do so, and you have plenty of reasons of your own not to, but I give you my word that my first priority is to bring Gabriella back. She's important to all of us. We don't need a war between the nations. Not when an accord will be vital to all our interests in the future."

Guntram smiled, showing his teeth. "I don't care why you do this. And I don't have to trust you. I'll be watching. So long as you get me inside, I'll follow your lead."

Simon nodded slowly, his expression easing only slightly. Then he gave Alex a level stare. "The promise I extracted from you . . . don't waiver."

Alex's chest rose. "Don't make it necessary."

The two men stood and embraced. Simon gave one more glance at the small falcon and then lifted his chin to point toward the door. "I have everything ready in the council chamber. Follow me."

Guntram followed closely on Simon's heels, his heart beginning a steady thrum like a drumbeat. The journey had begun.

As hours past, spent endlessly screwing with the Master, Gabriella came to the conclusion that some sort of magic had to be at work here. She wasn't tired, but was never fully satisfied. Her lover only had to give her a glance with his strange, gold eyes and she was hot and wet for him. Her pussy burned, and even now her sex throbbed and moistened.

The satin beneath her was still damp in spots. From the water that had streamed from their bodies when he'd brought them both here, and from the arousal and cum that kept her body well lubricated throughout the decadent afternoon.

Her body felt only mildly sore. Odd, considering how explosive their matings had gotten. Demons, it seemed, trumped vampires for stamina.

They'd just finished another frenzied coupling, and their bodies were coated with a thin sheen of sweat. They'd fallen apart, letting the air cool their skin. Staring into the mirror above the bed, she skimmed his body, noting the masculine sprawl of long, muscled limbs and the cock he stroked absently in his hand.

His gaze met hers in the glass, and his lips curved.

"When we aren't with others," she said, turning her face toward him. "What do I call you then?"

His lips twitched. "Master."

Her nipples prickled. Did he insist because he was the Master of the Demons or because he knew of every one of her proclivities? "Don't you have a name?"

His hand roamed upward, scratching his belly. "Not one you would know."

"Try me."

"I am called Marduk," he said, holding her gaze as though searching for a flicker of recognition.

Something in her memory stirred. Maybe a story she'd heard long ago. "I've heard it. I don't remember where. I'm sorry."

"I'm forgotten." Something entered his voice, slipping beneath his grim expression, but it faded quickly before she could determine if it was anger or sadness. "Once I was viewed as a hero in your realm, not a demon. I fought a great battle alongside the Mesopotamians, and ever after, they worshipped me. They told stories about how I fought a great battle against evil creatures, then created the world from their remains. They built cities in my name and worshipped me as a god."

"Do you miss the adulation?"

His lips twisted, and she could have sworn he looked a little embarrassed. "I miss walking among humans. But the attention went to my head. I began to believe it was my responsibility to save humankind. A friend, someone I admired, asked me to take his place here. I was never meant to stay so long."

"Did you leave behind many broken hearts?"

His smile slipped. "One."

The silence stretched, and she knew he wouldn't continue his story. "Don't you want to know my name?"

When his response was only an amused quirk of an eyebrow, she gritted her teeth in irritation. "I'm Gabriella," she said evenly. "I thought you might like to have a name to assign to the woman in your bed now."

"Gabriella," he repeated, so distinctly and softly the word felt like a caress.

She cleared her throat, not wanting to fan the heat that flared so easily between them. "Is this hell?"

"For some. But not necessarily the hell of Christians."

"I have to admit that so far, it's not what I would have expected. That first place, the hall with the demons feasting—that was more what I imagined. But your chamber here . . . you . . ." She stopped because the last thing she wanted to do was give him praise, however pleased and bonelessly relaxed she was.

"If you obey me in all things," he said, reaching over to lift a lock of her damp hair, "you will never know anything other than pleasure."

"I'm not big into obedience," she said, although it was only partly a lie. Submission was a game for her. The only way she could find her pleasure. However, obedience as a rule was something she demanded of others.

"Perhaps you haven't found your true master," he murmured.

"You think you're him?" she said, anger beginning to warm her.

His features hardened, darkening as shadows deepened around his eyes and beneath his sharp cheekbones. He wound the lock around his finger until it tugged her scalp. "I know what you need. I will provide it."

"Because you want me happy?" she snarled.

"Because I want you unharmed."

Gabriella didn't need his constant reminders of the dangers lurking beyond the door. "Happiness isn't important?"

"You will be satisfied, endlessly so. It will be enough."

The way he said it, as though from personal experience, provoked a moment's sympathy, which she crushed ruthlessly a moment later. The Master himself was pitiless, and she had no doubts he'd use her womanly feelings to his advantage if she let him. "That's enough for you? Satisfaction?"

"I serve my purpose. So shall you."

"And my purpose . . . I'm guessing . . . is to satisfy you?" Gabriella's eyes filled with her frustration. "Tell me, can't you find other women to give you service here?" she bit out.

He dropped the silky lock, which remained coiled against

her shoulder. "Of course, but my appetites are not easily appeased. And I've had a steady diet of demon whores and the damned," he said, some strong emotion tightening his voice. "I would taste something . . . pure."

Gabriella sat up, clutching the cover to her breasts. Not for modesty's sake, because that was long gone, but because she was beginning to shiver. "I'm . . . not . . . pure."

His lips curved in a thin-lipped, almost reptilian grin. "You aren't chaste by any stretch of the imagination. But you are living and untouched, for now, by the evil that permeates this place."

"Do you think I can stay that way, living here?"

"I will protect you, but you must never leave this room, this tower, unaccompanied. The cost would be too great."

"What would happen outside that door?"

His expression tightened more, but he didn't respond.

"You won't tell me? You'll wait until I find out for myself?"

"If you obey me, you will never know," he said, enunciating each word as though she were dim-witted.

Gabriella drew a deep breath, frustrated with the conversation. She needed clues to what she'd face when she escaped. "I won't always be such an easy conquest. You're new. You intrigue me. *For now.* But I'll get bored eventually. And you won't be able to keep me in this cage. I don't belong here. I'll want to return home."

"You followed your curiosity here. Your arrogance brought you to me. You won't be bored. Neither will you be alone when I am not here." His face hardened. "You'll be entertained, prepared for each time I enter this chamber, brought to a fever pitch but left wanting. You'll beg me for release each and every time."

"You're an ass. Those creepy vines won't continue to do it for me."

The sudden easing of his expression into amusement infuriated her. He knew something. And then she felt it. A touch that slid along her skin, like flanges cut from velvet, across her back and over the tops of her buttocks.

She reached behind her and rubbed her skin, trying to knock away whatever invisible thing was stroking her, but it wasn't solid, and kept working on her skin beneath the hands that frantically tried to slide them away. "Quit playing with me. You're hardly a man if you have to use tricks like these to help you get a woman horny." Suddenly, she was on her back, staring into his tense face.

"This isn't a game," he said, coming over her. "And I have concern for your pleasure only so far as it enhances mine. Worry when I stop caring whether or not you find your own release."

She shoved at his chest, but he was too heavy, his muscled frame bearing her deep into the mattress so that she couldn't move, couldn't strike.

"Xalia," he said softly.

A musical tinkling, soft and fluid, approached. "Bel," came an eager whisper from just beyond the curtains.

"I would watch you love her."

Then he rolled away and tossed the curtains upward, and Gabriella caught sight of the creature and gasped.

She had waist-length black hair and pale green skin, like an apple's. Shaped like a human throughout her torso, she was as slender as a young girl. Her face wasn't unattractive—despite the color—with even features, a very large mouth, and deep-set leafy-green eyes, also with narrow, vertical pupils. Her breasts were high, firm little mounds with puffy, dark brown nipples. Her labia were smooth and gleaming.

Gabriella's breath caught, whether from fear or curiosity she couldn't have said because she couldn't stop studying her. When her gaze snagged first on her hands, then her feet, her eyes widened, because they were overlarge, the fingers and toes long and spindly. Around her wrists and ankles were bracelets and anklets with small golden bells.

Gabriella cast the Master a panicked glance. "Please. I don't want this."

"You will learn discipline. My needs are all that should concern you. And for now, I prefer to watch."

Gabriella swung her gaze back to the creature, but she was no longer standing at the far side of the bed. When her gaze searched the room, she felt the end of the bed dip and watched with horror as the creature came over the edge, head lowered between her shoulders, crawling like a spider.

Gabriella rolled off the bed, running the moment her feet slapped the tile. But she made it only a step and learned to her horror that although the creature was smaller, her strength was immense. She pulled Gabriella against her, holding her wriggling body easily, and then carried her back, kicking and flailing, to slam her onto the bed.

Then Xalia was on top of her, her arms extending to hold hers down, her long feet curling around Gabriella's legs to keep her spread beneath her warm, smooth body. Mons pressed to mons, Gabriella licked her lips, fighting panic.

The pale green head bent toward her, her expression so solemn with eyes so sad that Gabriella relented and laid back, her breath catching on a sob. "You would have me raped for your pleasure," she said, breaking with the creature's sad gaze to spear the handsome demon beside her.

"I understand how abhorrent that would be for you," he said quietly. "I promise that is not what shall happen."

Gabriella shook her head. "I can't . . . with this . . ."

"Xalia will be your companion. It is entirely your choice whether you want more. But she is skilled—and obedient. Let her serve you."

"Then *she's* to be my jailer?"

"I prefer 'companion.' She will bathe you, dress you. Sing to you if you like. Her voice can soothe even the worst penitent."

Gabriella quivered with outrage, but kept her expression free of anger. "Can she get off me now?" she said evenly.

"Xalia . . ."

The creature sighed and climbed off sideways, crab-like, then dropped off the bed to walk around to the Master. His hand petted the top of her head, and then slid along her cheek. Her eyes, adoration gleaming, closed.

Gabriella wondered about their relationship and knew he must have made use of his precious servant. The thought somehow didn't revolt her. Again, arousal tightened her pussy.

Disgusted with herself, she sat up. "You mentioned I could dress."

"After she bathes you."

And since she was sticky and smelled of sex, she nodded. "But only if the plants in your little bathtub leave me alone."

His smile wasn't reassuring, but rather than lose another battle, she rose from the bed, following Xalia to the pool. The water felt like heaven as it enclosed her body. The plants remained deceptively still.

She sat on a lower step and let the water lap beneath her breasts while the green-skinned woman gathered towels and jars of soft soap. When Xalia lathered up a cloth and began to stroke her back, Gabriella gave herself over to the soothing motions, her eyelids dipping. "You can't keep me here forever," she said softly. "I will escape."

"You will try." Marduk lowered himself to the top step. "But only once. I would spare you even that."

"Spare me?" Her smile was a grimace. "You sound as though you care."

His expression softened. "Despite what I am and where we are, I am not a monster."

She opened her eyes and gave him a baleful glance. "Please, spare me. You dragged me here against my will."

"Your despair called to me."

"Don't even try to wrap it all up like you were doing me a favor. I don't belong here."

One dark brow arched. "You are so certain? Did you not conspire to commit murder?"

She stilled, her gaze flashing back to him and locking for a long charged moment. "That was long ago. And I suffered for that mistake. Besides, the attempt failed. He's forgiven me, and I made amends. I gave him aid."

"You gave him aid, thinking you would win his favor, that you would win concessions and perhaps become his wife."

Gabriella didn't like that he knew her motives. "How do you know all that? Can you see into my world?"

"We have a new resident—someone eager to complain about her treatment in the other realm and tell stories to entertain us. Even now, she'll be lobbying to have you turned over to her to punish you."

Gabriella shivered. “Inanna.”

“Do not worry. She has no status here except what her sister confers. Thus far, Irkalla has been content to see Inanna suffer. Inanna’s husband, Dumuzi, was given her leash.”

Mention of the demon they’d expelled, the Devourer, sent a chill shivering down her spine. “They both know I’m here?”

“Of course,” he said, shrugging as though he didn’t care. “Although I have been with you since you arrived, I am sure Irkalla’s spies have been busy. She will ensure that her sister and her brother-in-law know.”

“Is that why you think I’ll stay here? Because I fear them?”

“Of course not. You are a fierce warrior in your own right. But they are not your greatest fear.”

All this talk of fear filled her with an uneasy impatience. She didn’t dwell on her fears, had never allowed herself to dwell too deeply on them. “Is it you? Are you the one I should fear?”

“No, my love, but you will discover it,” he said matter-of-factly. “And I will be there to soothe you afterward. Then you will be content to remain with me.”

Xalia’s hands replaced the cloth and slid over the tight muscles of her shoulders, massaging them.

Gabriella didn’t want to enjoy the other woman’s touch, but couldn’t stop the deep sigh of pleasure that eased from her. Her eyes closed as the long, spindly fingers curved over her shoulders and slid down to massage her breasts. “I don’t understand this place,” Gabriella said, ignoring her body’s reaction to the soft, slick fingers sliding over her nipples. “The people in the hall where I arrived—they sat with demons.”

“They are the dead,” he murmured. “And they entertain the demons, who feed on them. They pay for their sins for eternity . . . unless they earn favor.”

"That hall is so different from the rest of the fortress. It appears stuck in the Middle Ages, and yet this feels more ancient."

"Time, architecture—they have no real meaning. Lord Malphus built the fortress and the palace according to our queen's preferences. Her preferences were flavored by her birthplace, Sumer. The Hall of the Dead, where the newest arrivals are kept, isn't of any interest to her. Malphus appreciated the ruggedness of the medieval keeps, therefore he built it according to his own tastes."

Gabriella wrinkled her nose. "Malphus. I'm confused now. Everything here originates from the time before the Christians, but Malphus was one of the fallen angels."

"This fortress is but one destination. Did you think nothing else lies beyond the sands?"

Tired of trying to get her mind around something she knew she was better off never fully understanding, she changed the topic. "What will I do with myself when you aren't here?" she asked, even though she had an inkling from the casual way the other woman stroked her skin while she cleansed her. They both expected she'd succumb to the pleasures offered. "I'm not accustomed to inactivity. I'll go mad."

"When you want to stretch your legs, I will take you to the desert."

She opened her eyes to meet his dark gaze. "I can't go for a walk by myself?"

"You will not want to be unaccompanied. As much as I would protect you, even spare you, I think it is a lesson you will have to learn." His head canted, listening to something she couldn't hear, and then he rose, giving Xalia a long, silent gaze.

"You're leaving me?" Gabriella said, then bit her lip. She'd sounded . . . clingy, womanly.

"I have duties," he said, his expression shuttering. "And calls to make upon our rulers."

"Can't I come with you?"

"Not yet. I want the excitement of your being here to die down first. They will be curious. Some lustful to touch and taste you. I must make sure they honor my protection."

Gabriella watched him go, and then slid a sideways glance at her companion.

"Do you want to play?" the creature said in an oddly girlish voice, her hands closing around Gabriella's breasts.

Gabriella's lip curled with disgust. "Is sex all that you think about?"

Xalia's smile was guileless. "It is what I am made for."

"Just bathe me," Gabriella bit out. "That's all I want from you."

As Xalia continued gliding her soapy hands over Gabriella's body, heaving a disappointed sigh, Gabriella contemplated donning her wolfskin to subdue Xalia and attempt an escape. But it was too soon. No doubt the Master would have others watching the door to report if she attempted an escape.

No, she'd take a page from Guntram's book and wait and watch. The opportunity would come. Somehow, she would find a way back to her world, and then Alex and his vampires would learn the true meaning of "hell on Earth."

# CHAPTER 6

With their expressions grim, the vampires' Security Force members ringed the inside of the conference room, armed with an assortment of weapons and ready for any contingency. Some were dressed in solid black uniforms, some in varying shades of camouflage, but all were wearing the same stoic looks.

Guntram's appreciation for Nicolas's training grew. Not one of the men betrayed misgivings about allowing a wolf to accompany their mage into another realm.

Simon set a canvas bag on the conference-room

table, and then raised his glance to everyone assembled there. "You should draw swords now. If anything comes through, destroy it."

"Remember," Nic said, his glance sweeping the room. "Take the head."

Guntram eased his hand to the hilt of his own weapon, but stepped toward Simon, whom he'd follow once the portal was activated.

The mage untied the twine enclosing the bag and reached inside to draw out a metallic stand shaped like the talons of a large bird or reptile. Then he drew out a round object wrapped in quilted fabric. When he stripped away the covering, he placed a black crystal ball atop the claw base.

Guntram grimaced, uneasy with evidence of more of the sorcerer's trappings. Crystal talismans, crystal keys, crystal balls—all just fucking rocks, made strange and dangerous in Simon's hands.

Simon caught his expression and gave him a little smile. "Don't worry, my friend, I do know how to use this." The last thing he pulled from the bag was a rolled scrap of parchment paper, yellowed and frayed with age. He placed one corner of the parchment under the metallic base and smoothed the rest flat. Then he stood back and lifted his gaze to Guntram. "Ready?"

At Guntram's sharp nod, Simon picked up the crystal and held it cupped in one palm. Reading from the parchment, he began to chant in a language Guntram didn't understand. It was melodic, rolling, like water burbling in a stream.

The first thing Guntram noticed was the hair on his arms lifting as though the air around him had become charged with static electricity. Then the air began to move; softly at first, barely noticeable, like a breath or soft sigh. It built in intensity until it gusted and swirled, lifting the heavy curtains at the windows and pulling at Guntram's hair.

Guntram gazed around him at the men with their swords drawn, their expressions set. They'd seen this before. So, he quelled his own unease and turned to Simon again. The orb resting on his hand had begun to glow as though a small flame flickered inside it—softly at first, like fire licking at kindling. Then suddenly, the flame burst, filling the crystal, and finally, exploding like glass shattering into silvery shards, shooting outward and expanding to brighten every corner of the room.

Guntram blinked, blinded momentarily. When he opened his eyes again, the rays bursting from the tiny star-like mass bent at sharp angles. The angles softened, curving, lapping over one another until they formed a solid circle, spinning around and around the edge of the blinding light. Then the center of the circle began to dim and shimmer, the surface rippling like a vertical pond.

"We go now!" Simon shouted, because the wind inside the room was rushing past them. "Grab the bag from the table and step through the circle, Guntram. I'll be right behind you."

Guntram grunted and grabbed the bag. Then, without bothering to give the room and its occupants a final glance, he wrapped his fist around the pommel of his sword and ducked through the portal. For a second, his body felt stretched then compacted. Air whooshed from his lungs.

On the other side of the portal, he stepped onto solid ground and glanced back. Simon followed on his heels. The light emanating from the ball blinked out.

Bright spots danced in front of Guntram's eyes, fading

slowly. It was pitch-black where they stood. "We should have brought flashlights," he grumbled.

"They wouldn't have worked here, anyway. Just wait a moment until your sight adjusts, but I would advise that you start stomping your feet."

Something chirped beside his left boot, and then the sound was repeated over and over. The hairs on the back of his neck prickled as the sound rose to a noisy chorus. He lifted his feet, stomping in place and cursing softly to himself.

As his eyes adjusted, he made out small figures scurrying across the dark floor, lit like fireflies, but with a blue fluorescent glow, lighting up one at a time—spiders, hundreds of them, and all scurrying toward them and beginning to sidle down the sides of what appeared to be a tunnel or a cave.

"Move," Simon said, shoving him forward. "They're meat eaters and will swarm us if we stand still. They can strip a man to his bones in minutes."

With the spiders providing scant light, they forged ahead.

"Give me the bag," Simon said behind him.

Guntram handed over the canvas bag, and Simon tucked the crystal inside it, still moving forward. They'd only gone about thirty feet when Simon grabbed his arm to stop him and bent to stow the bag behind a rock. "Can't be caught with this." Then they were off again, the walls of the cave thickening with glowing spiders of all sizes.

"Are they poisonous?" Guntram asked, brushing his shoulders and head as spiders fell from the ceiling.

"Just hungry, but they don't like external light. We don't have much farther to go."

The tunnel turned and suddenly they were poised at an opening that overlooked a vast desert lit by silver moonlight, tall dunes rippling in the distance like waves on a sea as wind shifted the sand.

"This isn't the room in the mirror," Guntram muttered, hoping like hell they hadn't landed in the wrong place.

"Be glad it's not," Simon said, staring out. "We wouldn't have made it five feet inside the hall before the hellhounds tore us apart."

"But Gabriella isn't here."

"Don't worry. We're just outside the fortress. We'll have to make our way back inside, but this is the safest route to avoid detection."

Guntram glanced down, guessing they were about a hundred fifty feet off the desert floor. "You didn't think to bring a rope?"

"We won't need it. We're climbing up. The fortress's curtain wall is above us."

Guntram aimed a glare at the mage. "I'm not a damn goat."

"But you are an agile wolf," Simon said, smiling. "The edges of the stones are worn and curved. We'll find hand- and footholds. You've done this before."

He shook his head. "I beg to differ. I've never scaled a wall in my life. Explain."

Simon clapped his hand on Guntram's shoulder. "Guntram, I'm a time traveler. I've lived this before—with you. Believe me, this is the least of the challenges we'll face."

Marduk strode into Irkalla's private rooms, knowing that he entered a den of vipers.

Where his own chamber was sunlit and airy, Irkalla's was necessarily dark and filled with shadows, the air thick with perfume and incense. Lushly upholstered sofas, hassocks, and woven rugs ensured that every surface was soft enough to provide for her pleasure.

In the dark, candlelit room, the bloodred fabrics and gilt furniture hinted at her bloodthirsty and avaricious nature.

Marduk had no doubt that Irkalla's consort, the Dark One, and her sister Inanna had been apprised of the capture of the woman now ensconced in his chamber. Already Irkalla's sycophants filled every available seat, and more milled around the entrance as he passed through. All waiting to see whether Irkalla would rail at him for bringing a living creature across the breach without consulting her first.

Thankfully, there was no sign of Inanna. So far, she hadn't been allowed the privilege of attending her sister.

Marduk secretly thought Irkalla feared her sister would poison her, and that she enjoyed dangling incrementally escalating boons to keep Inanna's ambitions in check.

While he pretended unconcern, inside, his stomach roiled. If Irkalla's interest had been piqued, his hopes of keeping Gabriella safe would be dashed. Guilt, an emotion he hadn't indulged in a long time, swept through him. If anything happened, he'd be to blame for letting his boredom and loneliness drag the woman through the mirror.

"Lord Marduk." The voice, soft and seductive, came from behind him.

Forcing a smile, he turned, glancing down to find Irkalla's sharp-eyed gaze raking his body. Marduk relaxed. If she was seeking sex, she wasn't too perturbed with his actions.

Dressed in an opaque golden robe that dragged on the floor behind her, Irkalla radiated confidence and majesty. As always, his breath caught at her beauty. Her black hair fell in a thick, straight curtain down her back. Perfectly arched brows, dark brown eyes, and dusky skin would have pleased even the most discerning man.

But there was also a deceptive innocence to her beautiful features—the slightly rounded cheeks, the dewiness of her skin—that disarmed those who didn't know her better.

However, her figure bore the truth of her licentious nature—full breasts and hips, a narrow waist, and long curved legs. Once upon a time, a mere glimpse of her body could heat his blood, but he was bored. Her self-centered search for pleasure no longer offered him any challenge.

Irkalla held out her hand, and he crooked his elbow automatically, inviting her to slide closer.

Her red lips pouted as she peered up at him. "Little birds are atwitter with news," she murmured.

"How convenient," he said dryly. "I've been occupied or I would have told you first myself."

Her head tilted, and her piercing gaze watched him from beneath the dark fringe of her thick lashes. "And yet you answered my summons promptly. Should I be relieved your little pet hasn't replaced me in your affections?"

"Ma'am, you are first in my heart," he lied easily. "These millennia would have been dismal without your company."

Her fingers tightened like talons on his arms. "I would never remind you of your obligation," she lied, "but it does please me that you remember my many kindnesses."

"I remember more than kindness, lady." Mindful of everyone watching, he bent to whisper into her ear. "My blood quickens at the thought of the pleasures we have shared."

Her cheeks flooded with a rosy hue, and he knew he'd pleased her. He breathed easier.

"I awoke with a fierce hunger, lover," she whispered.

"Your husband did not offer a vein?"

Her lips formed a girlish moue. "You're teasing now. I keep him enthralled, weakened with my love. But my appetite is immense—as is yours. Are you completely sapped?" she said, turning and lifting her heavy-lidded eyes to give him the look that spelled a quick death to his hope for a hasty exit.

Impatience heated his cheeks. His cock could barely manage a stir of interest after the lush buffet Gabriella had offered. Recalling how wetly and tightly Gabriella's sex had clasped his cock, Marduk willed his sex to fill.

In full view of her court, he forced Irkalla's hand from his arm to the front of his trousers, ignoring her sharp gasp at the bold action. "My guest only scratched at my hunger."

Her fingers curved around the ridge growing steadily beneath the fabric. Her happy smile stretched lush red lips. "I find I want you all to myself." No sooner had she spoken the words then her courtiers fled the room, leaving them alone.

Irkalla opened the single golden clasp that closed her robe and let the silky fabric slide off her shoulders to the floor.

Likewise, he held her gaze and removed his clothing, then came to one knee in front of her, bowing his head. "How may I please you, mistress?"

Irkalla's dainty hands bracketed his face and tilted it upward. "I would pleasure you first. I would like to know the many flavors of your new lover."

Marduk felt heat rise on his cheeks again. He hadn't time to bathe before he'd left Gabriella, and the bitch knew it. But he bit his tongue and nodded. "Whatever you desire."

"Come," she said, leading him toward her bed. "I'd have something soft beneath my knees when I sup from you."

He had to keep Irkalla in the dark about his growing impatience with the monarch's possessiveness. With his passions not completely assuaged by his new sex slave, Marduk followed. His cock hardened steadily while his heart thudded dully in his chest.

She stepped up the small riser to the comfort of her soft, down-filled bed, eagerly tossing sumptuous cushions covered in the same bloodred velvet and gold thread to the floor to make room for them both. Not that her large bed couldn't have held another set of lovers—it had, whenever the queen's hungers grew insatiable.

Now, Irkalla's face beamed as she patted the center of the mattress. "Come. Why are you so slow? I've been waiting for you for hours."

Marduk grew still inside, careful not to let her see how much she had disturbed him. *Hours?* She'd starved herself purposely, waiting to unleash her passions on him—as punishment for his actions? As a vicious reminder of where his loyalties would forever lie?

He'd had enough. In her present mood, she'd savage his cock. Tamping down his distress over Gabriella's safety, he decided to deliver a reminder of his own—one that would satisfy both their lusts, but leave her with no doubts about why she kept him as a paramour.

Marduk lunged for her, digging his fingers into her soft shoulders.

Irkalla curled her fingers and raked his chest with her nails, drawing blood, which only excited her hunger more. The teeth at the upper corners of her feral smile extended, her pupils dilated, and darkness consumed even the whites of her eyes.

However, he was stronger, his passions running deeper; he turned her to face the mattress and leaned over, trapping her as she wriggled in his grasp. Mindful of the attendants listening at the door, he whispered harshly, "Is your arrogance so great you forget what I am?"

Her muffled reply was lost among the feathers spilling from the mattress where her teeth had raked slashes in the tucking.

"I've faced forces beyond your imagination. You may be a Born bitch, but I'm stronger. You should fear me. My fire would destroy you."

Her fury ran unabated as she bucked and heaved. He brought his weight down on her and roughly parted her legs with his knees, shoving them wide. At the same time, he drew her arms up behind her; straining tendons forced her to lie still or risk ripping her arms from their sockets.

However, as he well knew, fury fed her passion. Her arousal scented the air.

Her struggles had inflamed him as well, and he aimed his cock between her legs, found the dampness between her legs and crammed his cock upward, halting Irkalla's next muffled shriek.

Fully seated, he leaned close again. "Now that I have your attention, darling, I'm going to let go of your arms. Come up on your knees."

When he dropped her wrists, she slowly brought them to her sides and lifted her torso from the mattress, spitting feathers.

He smiled at her docility, knowing that if she turned her face toward him now, he'd see her features were slackening, softening, the primal darkness in her gaze bleeding away as her sensuality overtook her bloodlust.

Lest she forget this was punishment, he wrapped her long

hair in his fist and pulled back her head. Then he stroked his hips forward, riding her flanks; pounding her buttocks with sharp slaps as her moist center melted around him.

The first fluttering ripples of her orgasm caressed his shaft, and he rewarded her with a flurry of thrusts that built heated friction against her inner walls. She danced on his cock, her bottom shivering, jerking, until at last she howled and grew limp in his grasp.

Marduk lowered her to the bed, pulled out and turned her, proving his lack of fear by rolling to his back, pulling her thighs astride his hips, and plunging upward to spear her with his sex again.

Irkalla, her face reddened, her lips bruised and bitten, trained her moist gaze on him. Then she braced her small hands against his shoulders and began to rock forward and back. "Do I please you?" she asked in a subdued whisper.

"Not yet, love," he said softly. "Would you like to taste my passion for you?"

Her entire body trembled, and she nodded.

Gripping her slight waist, he pulled her off his cock and shoved her down the bed. Then he caressed her face with both hands and aimed her mouth over his cock.

Her groan as she suckled him vibrated against his sensitive head. He petted her, combing her hair with his fingers, raking her scalp and tugging her closer.

Her jaws widened, gliding down, her teeth carefully shielded behind her lips, coming off him to lick the length of his shaft, swirling her tongue along his rigid length, and then diving beneath to mouth his balls.

She painted him with the moisture of her mouth, suckling

his balls one at a time and laving them richly, her soft mouth tugging and building a sensual tension he felt all the way to his toes.

His thighs tensed, and he raised his knees slightly to dig his heels into the mattress. He pumped his hips upward, stroking at air until she ceased her teasing gobbles and returned to his aching shaft.

Her soft hands surrounded him, gliding up and down, pulling the foreskin down the shaft and up. Her lips kissed his tip, rubbing over the crown, her eyes closing as her tongue lapped a bead of arousal from the slit.

"I taste you. I taste her." Her sharp-eyed gaze speared him. "She's not human, milord."

"What does your clever tongue discern?"

Her nose wrinkled. "Wolf."

He smiled at her as though grateful for her cleverness, but he'd known the moment he'd pulled Gabriella over his shoulder and smelled her skin. It's why he'd entered the bath. To entice her to join him and wash away the scent before anyone else noticed.

"Shall it be our secret?" he said. "See how long it takes for her to reveal her nature?"

Irkalla smiled and opened wide, sliding down his cock with more conviction now that she'd given him something he hadn't commanded. She thought she'd taken back control.

He let her think it while he took his pleasure from her. While she was consumed with greedy lust, she couldn't think beyond her own arousal. Keeping her on the edge had been a strategy he'd employed throughout their long relationship.

From time to time, Irkalla needed reminders like these that

he was one demon who would never accept a leash—even one as rich and pleasurable as what she offered. She didn't respect anyone willing to reside under her dominion.

And while he played at paying homage to her rank, they both knew who ruled the relationship. He had only to give her a single fierce glare and she became wet. When he placed her in stocks and whipped her, she trusted him enough not to fear he would betray her, offering a woman's sweet cream for the powerful arousal his domination provided.

Gabriella was similarly affected. For now, she remained submissive only because she was uncertain of her fate. When she grew more confident, he would have his work cut out to prove his mastery.

Irkalla hadn't offered him a true challenge in eons. Excitement over the thought of the battles to come with Gabriella hardened his balls to the point of bursting.

Irkalla murmured around him, her mouth suctioning harder. She mistook the source of his growing excitement, which amused him.

His fingers dug into her scalp, forcing her to take him deeper. He thrust hard against the back of her throat, heard her soft choking sounds and smiled. "Open your throat. You'll swallow my seed, mistress."

Irkalla's hands tightened around the base of his cock, squeezing hard as she pumped up and down. Her mouth caressed his shaft, her tongue swirled down his length. Her throat opened and closed, swallowing around him, caressing the crown, and then opened again to take him deeper.

Holding her hair in his fist, he pumped his hips upward, slamming down her throat until his balls exploded and ropes of semen spurted into her.

She swallowed greedily, moans vibrating around him until she'd wrung every last drop.

His hand loosened on her hair, and she lifted, coming off his cock to tilt her face toward him. "Please," she begged.

And because she was the perfect supplicant, he widened his legs and cupped his balls and cock, lifting them away. "Drink, love."

Her face dove between his legs, her tongue skimming over his inner thigh up into his groin. Then she pierced him, and blood began to flow from the twin wounds she'd made.

Again, his cock filled even as blood streamed out of him, enticed by her vampire's allure into full-blown arousal. He needed her to cast for him, needed her to supplant his natural need for the woman in his chamber so that he could please the creature filling her belly on his lifeblood.

For as long as Irkalla believed he loved her, the woman he'd decided would fill his lonely heart would be safe.

# CHAPTER 7

Guntram reached down to offer Simon a hand, grasping it and heaving him over the edge of the parapet. Ducking down, they huddled for a moment with their backs against the crenellated wall while they caught their breath. They sat hidden by the shadows cast by a huge moon hovering over the tall dunes in the distance.

The climb up the sandstone wall had invigorated him, allowing him to expend some of the pent-up energy his worry and frustration had built up. As always, the physical challenge left him feeling relaxed despite the danger pressing closer, making it easier to think.

Wiping his sweaty face with his sleeve, he took stock of where they sat.

The walkway at the top of the fortress was approximately ten feet wide and stretched the length of a long curtain wall. No guards were within sight or scent—not patrolling the walkway or stationed in the tall parapets at the corners of the fortification, which seemed odd. Why build a wall if you didn't have enemies ready to invade?

"Where do we go from here?" he whispered to Simon, who was taking a little longer to catch his breath.

Simon reached out and gripped his forearm, then dragged himself up. "We'll head to one of the towers and make our way down to the city streets."

"Are there no guards?"

"Not the sort you're expecting, I imagine," Simon murmured. "Guards patrol inside the city. *Anzu*-birds keep watch from above—and occasionally the *lillum*, especially nasty creatures. Keep an eye peeled toward the sky." Taking another deep breath, he shoved away from the wall. "Come, we have to keep moving."

Crouching to keep their heads below the top of the wall, they hurried down the wallwalk to the nearest tower. Guntram paused at the doorway, peering down the dark, spiraling stone steps. Simon gave him a shove from behind. "Keep moving. We'll have no problems until we're inside the fortress."

Guntram took him at his word. The mage had been right so far. Ducking, he entered the stairs and felt a hot breeze whipping upward, evaporating the rest of the sweat beading on his forehead.

Stealthily, they hurried down the darkened tower toward the street, with Guntram wondering all the while about a fortress free from watchful guards. Unease crept along his spine. Guntram didn't like surprises, and wished he'd had more time to learn about the terrain and the dangers lurking before he'd come.

At the bottom of the steps, a doorway opened directly onto a city block. Pausing again, he hugged the door frame and peered up and down the narrow cobblestone street, not unlike those he'd walked in medieval townships. The smells that assaulted his nose were familiar as well: urine, feces, decaying bodies. He wrinkled his nose in disgust.

However, it was the sounds of the place that sent a chill up his spine. Low, mournful wails and cries rose in the air. Crackling crunches emanated from darkened doors and alleyways—like bones being ground by powerful jaws.

"Don't stop now," Simon said, shoving him again.

They kept close to the outer curtain wall. On the opposite side of the street were doorways leading into multistoried houses and establishments. Huddled on stoops and in corners were lumpy bodies dressed in ragged, filth-encrusted clothing.

Simon darted across the street to one doorway. Guntram followed.

Simon pulled a leather bag from a pocket and extracted two gold coins, purchasing smelly robes from two men huddled close whose dry-eyed gazes didn't see beyond the shiny coins.

Guntram grimaced when Simon passed him one of the robes, but didn't hesitate to pull it on to hide his clothing. Now, they looked just like the rest of the pitiful creatures hiding in the shadowed doorways.

Then they were off again, Simon keeping his back to the wall, his gaze lifting to the star-filled sky above the darkened streets.

That's when Guntram heard it—a loud, piercing roar and the flap of huge, feathered wings.

They darted toward a stoop, melting into the shadows as they watched one of the winged creatures with the head of a lion and a powerful eagle-like body swoop down, pluck a woman from a doorway, and disappear into the sky again.

Guntram shuddered at the screams that faded into the night.

Simon darted out again, Guntram on his heels, and they ran, turning a sharp corner and coming to a doorway. Simon rapped on the wooden door with three quick and one single heavy knocks in succession.

Footsteps scuffled on the other side, the door cracked, and a single eye peered outside. Then the door flew open, and Simon slid inside.

Guntram glanced once more around the alleyway and slipped in behind him, closing the door. The smell of offal from the street didn't penetrate the room. Something he noted gratefully.

Simon and an old man embraced, and then held each other at arm's length. The old man's eyes teared up. "Good to see you, old friend."

Simon's smile was tight but genuine. "Ninshubur, we need a place to rest until tomorrow night."

"You must stay with me. I can't believe you're here," the old man said, his voice breaking. "I thought the knock was a trick my mind was playing."

"It's been a long, long time."

"Longer for you, no doubt," the old man said, grinning. Finally, he peered beyond Simon's shoulder. "Come deeper inside. You must eat. Then I'll let you rest. I can only offer pallets. My circumstances have fallen since last we met."

Simon nodded. “Inanna has much to answer for.”

“I should never have aligned my fate with hers.”

“You’ve heard that she has returned.”

“There’s little else buzzing around the palace. Irkalla’s crowing. But please, sit. Then you must tell me everything.”

Guntram glanced around the room furnished only with two chairs, a table, and a shelf-like bed. At least everything looked clean. After the refuse in the streets, he felt as though the scents permeated his skin. He dragged the robe over his head and tossed it next to the door.

“Not here,” Ninshubur said, when Guntram would have taken one of the rough chairs. The old man led them through a doorway at the back of the room, and into an apartment. At the light of a candle, Guntram’s eyebrows rose.

Rich mosaic tiles decorated the floor with images of the sun, moon, and several constellations. The walls were painted a deep midnight blue. A sumptuous bed with the mussed covers thrown back betrayed where the old man had been when they knocked. An ornate table of dark wood with a tiled top stood in one corner. Chairs with upholstered seats surrounded it.

Ninshubur must have noticed Guntram’s bemusement at the contrast between his outer room and this chamber. “I smuggled in some of my furnishings before I was banished from court,” he said, rheumy eyes twinkling. “But I must keep up outward appearances or become a target for thieves. No one knows about this room.”

Guntram grunted and dropped into one of the comfortable chairs at the table. As the elderly man bustled about, serving them bread, cheese, and wine, Guntram fought the same restlessness that had plagued him for days. His fingers drummed the table.

"Relax, Guntram. There's nothing more we can accomplish," Simon assured him. "We'll find her tomorrow night."

"Will she be well?" he asked, wishing the time-traveling mage would share some of what he already knew.

"She hasn't come to any lasting harm."

Guntram's gaze sharpened at the ambiguous response.

Simon cleared his throat. "It won't be easy to extract her from her current circumstance."

"But she has come to no . . . lasting harm. Has she been raped, then?" he asked quietly.

Simon's tight smile didn't calm his fears. Gabriella was a proud woman. To be taken by force would be worse for her than death. But he could tell Simon wouldn't say any more.

Resigned to cool his heels again, he drank down the beverage Ninshubur set in front of him. The drink was sweet, like fermented honey. He drained it and slapped the cup on the table.

Ninshubur laughed. "You'll have a headache come morning."

"But I'll sleep well." He had a feeling he'd need all the rest he could get.

Gabriella stood on the balcony. Moonlight painted the barren landscape stretching as far as she could see in shades of silver and gray. Marduk had been gone for hours, and she'd chased Xalia away after she'd been bathed and dressed, and candles around the room had been lit. The demon girl gave her a major case of the willies despite the fact she seemed harmless and sincere in her wish to serve her. Gabriella hoped Marduk never invited her to join them in bed.

She'd pleaded exhaustion, wanting time alone to thoroughly explore the room, which she had to no avail. There was nothing she could use as a weapon and no hidden accesses. The pool's drainage spout was too narrow for her hips to ever fit through, as was the pipe servicing a toilet. The only way out was through the door, which was locked, or out the window. But the drop was a long one to the desert floor, and besides, she didn't think she'd find a way home there. Her escape route had to be somewhere inside this fortress. Perhaps through the mirror in the hall, if she could access it like Alex's from this side before the hellhounds or the dinner guests ate her.

If there was another way out, she'd find it, but first she had to gain Marduk's trust so that he'd let her out of this room. Then maybe she'd find an ally, someone she could bribe, but with what?

She shuddered, remembering what Marduk said about how valuable a live creature from the other realm was. Maybe she'd have to trade favors or blood for information. Unless Guntram found her first.

Closing her eyes, she prayed. Something she never did. She hadn't needed prayers before, having always relied on her silent protector to keep her safe. But she prayed now, and not just for herself. Guntram would be out of his depth here. He might be a fearsome warrior, but he needed a sadistic sort of cleverness to maneuver here.

Still, thoughts of him wading into a fray on her behalf, his strong features tight and feral, warmed her heart. Again she wondered why she'd resisted her attraction to him. A man willing to lay down his life for a woman, a man willing to see her happy above his own self-interest was worth more than foolish pride.

And she knew without a doubt he'd be just as single-minded when seeing to her pleasure. His powerful body had always drawn her lustful gaze. He'd never been shy about letting her see his reaction to hers. Shifting from wolfskin to human form after darting through the forest when she'd tried to outrun her heats, he'd always followed, basking unashamed in moonlight.

His low, fierce growls as he'd narrowed his gaze when she'd sauntered naked among the males had been more than a warning for them to keep their distance. His turgid cock spoke volumes.

Once, she'd pushed him beyond his iron control.

*"You shouldn't tease them, Princess," he'd said after chasing the others off.*

*Resting against the trunk of a pine tree, she'd raised her arms above her head, pretending to stretch, enjoying the way the crisp air spiked her nipples. "Why? I have you to protect me."*

*His gaze swung toward hers. "You shouldn't tease me."*

*"Why are you so serious, Raven? They know I'll never let them have me. It's only a game we play, circling each other."*

*"For you perhaps. But the stakes are high. One might get ambitious."*

*She'd eyed him, sweeping his body, noting the tension in his shoulders and fisted hands. Then he'd faced her, and again, her breath caught at the strength of his arousal. He was right. She shouldn't tease him. It had to be painful to restrain himself. After cutting out the other competing males, his nature demanded he cover her.*

*"You've never even asked me. Not once," she said softly.*

*Guntram's square jaw tightened. "I serve your pleasure, Princess."*

Even now, the memory of the heat in his glance seared. Guntram was faithful to her beyond his self-interest. He would come for her.

However, she couldn't afford to wait. She needed to find her own escape. Needed to find someone to bribe.

And maybe Marduk was the least scary thing inside the fortress, and she'd have Jabba the Hut to try to seduce. Gabriella grimaced.

There was too much she didn't know about this place, and she was hesitant to discover it on her own. His warning about finding "true hell" wouldn't let go of her imagination, and she envisioned herself standing on glowing embers while demons stripped away her flesh.

It looked like the only way out of this room for now would be with her captor. The sooner she convinced him she'd accepted her fate, the better. Only she hoped like hell he'd provide her with something more substantial to wear should he take her somewhere.

The harem-girl getup Xalia had provided marked her as a sexual playmate. The thin linen skirt went only mid-thigh and was tied around her hips with gold braiding. More gold braid framed two peek-a-boo mesh cups, which constituted the bra. Two bows were the only things holding her clothing in place. Worse, she hadn't been given any footwear. If she made a run for it, she'd have no choice but to do so in wolfskin.

The sound of a door closing drew her back into the room. Marduk stalked inside, his stiff posture radiating displeasure.

Her heart skipped a beat at his appearance. She wished he wasn't so handsome and virile. He wore the same black clothing she'd always seen him in, but now she knew what it covered. Just the memory of watching his back and powerful buttocks stretching and undulating above hers was enough to make her wet.

His black expression gave her pause.

"Something's happened?" she asked, not sure whether it was a good idea to draw his attention to her when he was in this mood or not. But the sooner she figured him out the better.

His gaze met hers, his scowl deepened. "You're to appear in the great hall tomorrow night."

She suppressed a shiver. Part of her was elated that at last she'd escape this room, but another part knew his tension had a reason. "That's a bad thing?"

"Irkalla's curious about you."

"Again, I'm not seeing the problem. I'll meet her and it'll be over."

"She wants to parade you in front of her sister. Inanna has been trying to ingratiate herself with the court."

"And you think Inanna might try to make problems for me."

His nod was curt.

"Can she take me from you?"

"Not without a battle. Not overtly, but they can play games with you." His gaze softened. "I promised you that I'd see you came to no harm in my care."

Gabriella did her best to suppress the thrill his comment gave her. Protectiveness in a lover, even when she didn't intend to keep him, was a turn-on. "I'll be careful not to incite her," she said carefully.

He shook his head. "You don't understand."

Gabriella shrugged. "Then help me. Tell me what I face."

"Irkalla rules the Dark One with seductive arts, which she wields like weapons. Her appetite is voracious. If she wants to draw you into the games, offer your service to the wrong mate . . ."

She remembered the varied forms of the demons in the hall, and her stomach churned. "They can have me?"

"I serve Irkalla. I enjoy favor because I please her."

"You mean you have sex with her?"

"Most demons bow down to me," he said, without acknowledging her question. "I have been given dominion over them. But those within the inner circle are immune to my special powers. I curry favor with the queen to keep my enemies in check."

"So you're as much enslaved as I am."

"By choice. It makes living here less complicated."

"All right, I'm still not understanding how being paraded into that circle will be dangerous for me. What sorts of things might I be asked to do?"

"Irkalla has a knack for finding one's greatest pleasure and greatest fear. Let's hope she takes a shine to you." He glanced around. "You sent Xalia away?"

Gabriella knew the subject of her appearance in court had been dropped. Her gaze slid away from his. "I preferred to wait for your return . . . alone."

Marduk held out his hand. This time she didn't hesitate, striding forward to slip her hand inside his. His gaze slid down her body. "You look lovely."

She couldn't believe it when she started to preen. Dressed like a whore, and yet she felt no shame—only a fierce pleasure at the approval glittering in his eyes. *Fuck, I need to get out of here.*

Scratching sounded at the door.

"Food has arrived."

As soon as he spoke, her stomach growled. His lips twitched, and she lifted her shoulders.

It had been hours since she'd arrived, and she was starved. She let him lead her to one of the legless sofas as low tables were carried inside and set before them. A trail of servants, all appearing human—so, presumably the dead—filed in with small covered dishes. No cutlery or plates were set out, but the silver covers were whisked away and linen napkins draped over their laps before the servants left.

She was relieved to recognize most of the meats by their scent. Flat bread, vegetables, and flowers soaked in honey rounded out the meal. A silver chalice of wine and a beaker of water were set before them. Not understanding the etiquette, she waited for him to begin eating then followed his lead as he ate with his fingers, plucking slivers of meat from the trays. He ate casually, his gaze barely straying from hers as she began to feast.

His expression relaxed, and he smiled at her gasps of pleasure when she tried to the honeyed flowers. "Roses are your favorite."

"I've drunk rosehip tea, but never eaten the blossoms. They're yummy."

"You enjoy your food."

"Of course. Don't tell me they have anorexics in hell."

He shrugged. "I think an appetite for food follows an appetite for life."

"You get a lot of chances to observe that here?" she said around a mouthful of food. "Life, I mean."

"The dead who are favored enough to escape damnation

make the motions. They eat, make love, but there's no real joy in it."

"But you have those like Irkalla and her bitch sister. They're Born vampires and very much alive."

"It's possibly why I allowed myself to be attracted to Irkalla."

"And you're a demon, right? As the Master of the Demons," she said, "you're alive."

"Not in the same way. We don't have that inner fire, that same vitality. We operate on hunger rather than love."

Gabriella drew her brows into a frown. "I don't operate on love."

"Love for life, for adventure then. You brim with fire."

She canted her head. "Do you think that by touching me, capturing me, that you can capture some of that fire?"

His glance slid away. "When I walked in your realm, I loved a woman. A human. Her hair was the color of fire. Her passion for life was fierce. I abandoned her long ago, but I remember how it felt to hold her and make love with her."

"So I'm a substitute for the woman you left behind?"

"You're nothing like her."

"In a good way or bad way?" she said, letting a smile curve her lips.

He lifted one dark brow. "Are you fishing for a compliment?"

Gabriella wrinkled her nose at him, enjoying the conversation. "Maybe I'm just trying to figure out if I'm doomed to disappoint."

"Are you worried you will not please me?"

She hadn't been. Not until he said it. But Marduk wasn't

quite the monster she'd expected. Not that she thought for a minute that he wouldn't lash out in a heartbeat if she defied him, but she sensed he was simply lonely. Suddenly, not measuring up, disappointing him, meant something to her. And not just because it would harm her campaign to cozen him into trusting her.

"I think," she said slowly, "that I've come to understand that I need you. So the last thing I want is to fail to meet your expectations."

Marduk wiped his fingertips on his napkin and raised a hand to her face. His palm cupped her cheek while his gaze bored into hers. Again, she hoped like hell he couldn't read minds, because she thought her will might be crumbling.

"Already, you please me greatly." His thumb slid beneath her chin, then over it. The slight pressure from it teased her mouth open.

He bent toward her and pressed his lips to hers, and Gabriella melted against the plush cushions of the couch, her meal forgotten. Pleasure exploded, trembling on her mouth where he brushed her lips in drugging laps, his moustache and beard gently abrading her skin, setting fire to her body. Her nipples beaded against the soft mesh; her pussy dampened the linen skirt beneath her.

He leaned over her, pressing her backward until she lay deep in the cushions. She parted her legs, opening to him as he came down on her, one foot on the floor, a knee nudging between her legs, pushing up the skirt and rubbing against her sex.

His breaths deepened, seeping into her mouth. His tongue, tasting of honey and roses, plunged into her mouth, lapping along hers, curling to rim her teeth, then licking her lips and tugging them. When he pulled back, she rose to follow, not because he hurt her, but because she wanted more.

His hands smoothed around her bare waist and pulled at the bow behind her. Her bra loosened, sliding sideways, and he dove for a breast, nuzzling aside the fabric and rubbing his chin, his lips, and then his tongue over the sensitive peak.

Her belly undulated, her hips lifting to rub harder against his knee, but it wasn't enough. She pulled his dark hair, forcing his head back. "Please, Bel, Lord . . . *please* . . ."

His low, rumbling growl set her pussy pulsing. He stripped away the bra. "Hold out your hands."

Gabriella lifted them, pressing her wrists together, and he bound them with the bra and stretched her arms above her head. She writhed on the sofa, still pressing her pussy against his knee. It wouldn't take much more for her to come.

He tugged the braid at her hips, unwrapping her skirt as though opening a present, pushing apart the fabric to bare her sex.

She'd left a wet spot on his dark trousers. They both stared at it, and his eyes narrowed and his chest rose faster. He untied the top of his pants, exposing his long, thick cock, and she put a foot on the floor and raised her hips, inviting him to slide his cock inside her.

His eyes closed, his hand gripped his cock and rubbed up and down his shaft, and then he wound his other hand in the braid at her wrist and pulled her up.

She followed, letting him turn her to face away. He draped her over the back of the sofa on the soft plush cushions. She widened her legs, bending low, standing on bent legs on the sofa cushions while he rose and stood behind her. In this awkward position, she couldn't look back, couldn't see what he was doing, but she felt his hands cup her buttocks, felt his mouth drop kisses on one globe and then the other, felt his fingers cupping her sex from behind and swirling inside.

Her legs quivered, and she tried to draw a deeper breath, but the edge of the sofa bit into her diaphragm and she could only gasp, growing lightheaded as he continued to finger her, thrusting into her and drawing down more moisture.

Then he leaned against her, his cock prodding her entrance. He had to be standing behind her. She could imagine how he looked hovering over her quivering frame, and she was helpless to prevent anything he might do.

Fingers traced the crease between her buttocks. His cock circled on her cunt, just the blunt, rounded head pressing inside. Her pussy contracted—a sexy kiss that left his crown slick with her juices. Air hissed between his teeth.

He parted her buttocks, thumbs digging between, and she knew where he was looking. God, would he just fuck her? She tried to thrust backward and force his cock deeper, but he pulled away. She moaned at the loss.

Now her whole body trembled and jerked with slight spasms, tension winding tightly inside her. His cock glided around her opening, then stroked downward, nudging her clit. A thumb circled on her forbidden entrance, rimming the sensitive mouth.

"What do you want, love?" he whispered.

"For you to take me," she moaned.

"Is there anything you would deny me?"

"Nothing. Just please come inside me."

His hands stilled. His body withdrew. "Xalia, come."

Gabriella's belly knotted. "No, no, no . . . I sent her away . . ."

"She's never far away."

Bells tinkled, drawing closer. The cushions between Gabriella's spread legs sank. Soft hair brushed against the apex of her thighs, and then a warm, moist mouth pressed against Gabriella's open sex.

Gabriella lifted up, sending a frantic glance backward. Xalia sat on the couch, facing the Master, her hands wrapped around his cock but her head disappearing between Gabriella's legs. Her mouth suckled Gabriella's sex and stroked the cock thrusting between her hands.

Gabriella met the challenge glittering in the Master's eyes and clamped her jaw shut, facing forward again. She wouldn't freak out, wouldn't complain. She'd told him she'd do anything. And the things she felt—spread open for him to enjoy, being pleasured by his little slave's mouth—were almost too pleasurable to bear.

Xalia's breaths bathed her wet sex in small, excited gasps. Her lips pulled at Gabriella's labia, her tongue stroked into her entrance, then scraped downward, glancing over her distended clit.

Gabriella groaned, and her legs trembled again. When her demon lover's hands clamped on her buttocks and his cock came at her again, pressing past Xalia's tongue, Gabriella was past caring that two inhuman creatures were taking her. The rasping tongue lashing at her clit and his thick, hot cock felt divine.

His strokes sank slowly inside her, tunneling deep, past tissues still hot and swollen from their earlier rounds of lovemaking. It didn't matter, it didn't hurt, she was so wet, so hot, she was quickly unraveling.

His hands went to her waist and another set parted her buttocks, and then long, slender fingers wrapped around the globes and slid between. When Xalia's slight, soft fingertips entered her ass, curling, stroking deep, Gabriella couldn't have protested if she'd wanted to. She was close, edging toward an orgasm so explosive her legs turned to rubber. But Marduk held her upright, slamming her toward him, rocking her against Xalia's mouth, the motions dragging on the fingers stroking inside her.

More fingers pressed inside, stretching her, and she knew he was watching the long, pale green stems torturing her ass, because his strokes were becoming sharper, stronger, charged with his growing excitement.

Her breasts chafed on the soft sofa, her nipples ripening, the tips elongating. Her skin was getting hotter, her cunt clasping, creamy arousal churning inside her, making the sounds of his strokes wetter, nastier—the way she liked it.

When Xalia's lips closed around her clit and suckled it hard, Gabriella's back arched and a thin, keening wail broke as a wave of wet, hot heat poured over her body. The Master's strokes slowed as she came back down, draped over the sofa back, limp and sated.

Xalia moaned against her sex, but let go of her clit, pausing to lick it with long brushes of her slippery tongue as the last shivering convulsions waned.

Then the two beneath and behind her left. Bells trilled toward the pool then returned. A soft cloth cleansed her intimately, and then large hard hands lifted her up.

Held against her demon's chest, she raised her bound hands over his neck, and snuggled her face into the corner of his shoulder as he strode toward the bed.

Xalia pulled back the covers. The Master laid her in the center, and then aimed a glance at Xalia, who grinned with delight. Gabriella didn't have the energy to grow alarmed, simply accepted the tug on her tethers that once again stretched her arms upward. Another length of braiding, ripped from her linen skirt, was tied between her hands and looped around an iron spoke in the ornate headboard.

She couldn't gather the energy to complain. If they wanted to play, they'd have to do it while she napped.

It wasn't until something was latched around each ankle that she pried open an eyelid to peek. Thick leather bands encircled her—bands with hooks on the outside. When ropes were tied over opposite sides of the canopy above and then tied off in the hooks, she came fully awake.

She'd been trussed up like this before. Spread for the pleasure of a Dom who'd liked keeping her helpless while he stroked her skin with a flogger and fucked both orifices with a strap-on and his own cock.

Now, she wondered what a demon might do. And just how depraved she was to hope his skill trumped her Atlanta master.

# CHAPTER 8

For Gabriella, time slowed and nerve endings honed painfully sharp as her arousal was slowly stoked over and over to a fever pitch. Lying with her hands tied, her legs raised and spread, added a scary, thrilling edge to the play. They could do anything they wanted and she was completely helpless to stop them.

What they wanted, apparently, was to drive her slowly crazy. She'd expected a sexy flogging followed by something deliciously rough. Instead, they were trying to tease her to death—driving her to the edge and then retreating, waiting until her blood cooled and her arousal faded before torturing her upward again.

They'd taken turns lapping at her pussy, one dipping downward to lick and suckle her quivering folds while the other held her sex spread open and rubbed her clit. Each time she'd be so close, her breaths growing ragged, but then they'd sat back, stroking her belly and her legs while she'd thrashed her head and cursed them.

She'd tried hiding her response, holding her breath when her orgasm approached, forcing her body to remain still, but they'd known. Her pussy pulsed; her silken fluids drenched the bedding beneath her.

Now Xalia's hands moved in soft, liquid swirls as she smoothed oil over her skin, anointing every inch of her chest, belly and legs, soothing her with the steady motions.

Gabriella smelled like a head shop, redolent with oriental incenses like patchouli and sandalwood. Her skin gleamed pale and golden in the candlelight.

When Xalia stroked the oil between her legs, starting mid-thigh and gliding deeper, she glanced against her outer labia and then slid away. *Sweet fuck, would they ever let her come?*

Gabriella began to fight her ties in earnest. Her head thrashed on the pillow, the muscles of her arms and legs tensed and jerked until she tired and relaxed limply against her restraints. Defeated again.

The Master watched, lying on his side at the end of the bed, his gaze on her open sex as Xalia tortured her with gentle caresses.

Gabriella could only stare raptly when the green face descended toward her sex and a dark tongue lavished her folds with wet strokes that teased the edges, then lapped between and at last prodded her entrance.

She thought she'd go out of her mind when Xalia's long,

slender digits fingered her asshole and plunged inside. She had no intentions of complaining, not when Marduk's eyelids dropped and his nostrils flared as the aroma of her arousal strengthened. Maybe this time he'd be tempted beyond control to end it.

But he sat up and clapped his hands.

Gabriella's gaze swung to the door.

A man, dressed in a short linen skirt similar to the one she'd worn, entered the chamber, carrying a flanged implement. By the deference of his downcast eyes, she guessed he was a servant. *Another sex slave?*

Leanly built and youthful, he had a sculpted nose and jaw, thin sensual lips, and gleaming brown eyes. His chestnut hair was long and tied back in a leather thong.

Xalia crowed with delight and pulled away, sitting cross-legged on the bed beside the Master, who promptly began to finger her slick green labia, his gaze locking with Gabriella's. They sat as though preparing for a performance.

The young man in the skirt knelt on the edge of the mattress and lowered his head. "May I pleasure the supplicant?"

At Marduk's nod, the younger man raised the flogger and tapped Gabriella's inner thigh.

She didn't react—purposely, because she craved a serious whipping. After the tender torture, she wouldn't let loose until her skin and sex stung. Setting her lips into a straight, stoic line, she didn't blink at the anemic lashes he delivered.

Gradually, Marduk's man applied more force, gauging the increasing violence of his strokes by a careful inspection of her face, still expressionless, and the telltale thickening of her labia as she grew more and more aroused. He touched her with his fingers, impersonally plucking at her cunt, before sighing and applying another round of stinging lashes.

Gabriella noted the color flushing his cheeks, the erection pulsing beneath his clothing. When her gaze lifted to his face, although he didn't meet her eyes, she noted one corner of his mouth curved. There was arrogance in this slave. Her belly tightened, and she bit her lips to still a tremble.

"Stripe her," Marduk said softly.

Just the sharp, precise delivery of those two words was enough to make her wet.

Then the flanges landed in several sharp strokes in succession, crisscrossing her inner thighs and belly. When a flick grazed one nipple, she cried out. Her eyelids dipped as a dreamy euphoria captured her at last.

The man halted, pulling her back again, and sent a sideways glance to Marduk, who nodded, and then he continued.

Gabriella's body began to quake as her skin turned pink and small welts rose on her skin. Every inch was covered, her nipples receiving more than their share of attention, but the tips were completely aroused, elongated, her breasts quivering.

How she wished he'd apply a flick or two to her pussy, but she guessed Marduk would save that for last, because he knew that was all it would take to make her come.

Marduk gave the man another nod.

The flogger fell on the bed and the servant bent from the side over Gabriella's pussy and tongued her open sex.

Shock held her still, arresting the orgasm he'd so carefully built. His tongue and lips licked and sucked, every fold and crevice cleaned. She glanced sideways and caught a glimpse of his arousal tenting the thin linen.

Her gaze came back to Marduk.

The dragon lord smiled like a cat.

Gabriella blew shallow breaths between pursed lips and jutted her chin upward, pretending the mouth lapping over her sex wasn't making her pulse leap.

All the while the slave whipped her and ministered to her sex with his mouth, he'd kept his gaze from meeting hers directly.

But she caught a fleeting glance. His brown eyes softened. And then he straightened, cupped his hand and slapped the center of her spread thighs.

The sound was lush and wet—succulent. He did it again, and Gabriella groaned, straining again at her bonds, wishing she had the leverage to undulate her hips because her arousal had spiked hard and was constricting her channel, rippling up and down as her sex clasped and relaxed.

She missed the cue from Marduk, but knew one must have passed among the three watching her, because the servant bent over a breast and began to suckle while he parted her folds with his fingers and Xalia slid her long fingers inside Gabriella's entrance. Three fingers at first that curved toward the ceiling and scraped the inner pleasure center, making her belly leap and quiver.

Xalia laughed softly, and pulled out her fingers, cupped all four together and slowly pushed them back inside, pausing to curve her thumb toward her palm and then shoving inward, her slender fist working its way inside Gabriella, who gasped at the sudden stretching.

The sounds Gabriella's body made embarrassed her as Xalia began to pump in and out of her moist, greedy cunt-mouth. But Gabriella soon didn't care. Her groans intensified as her body shuddered and jerked, nearing the edge of her climax. She feared she'd burst into tears when it happened because they had her body and nerves stretched beyond their limits.

Her eyelids slid closed, and she gulped for air. Then the ties around her ankles loosened, and the ones around her wrists, but she was too far gone to move. Not until the hand and mouth pulled away and she was hauled against Marduk's solid chest did she open her eyes. Marduk lay back and urged her over him.

Then the servant crawled behind her and pressed her down atop Marduk's chest. His hands parted her buttocks, and his cock pushed against her back entrance.

She groaned, but again couldn't form a word of protest, because her mind was blown, her body quaking with need.

The slave's cock slid up her ass and she was grateful for the burning that had her pussy tightening hard around Marduk's cock. When her face was pressed against Marduk's neck, Xalia straddled their bodies. Gabriella could only guess what was happening above her by the moist sounds of a mouth sucking on wet pussy.

The four of them writhed together and apart, moving slowly, inexorably into a dark pleasurable rhythm.

The scents of their arousal and the thick fluids the men summoned from the women, the smell of sweat and musk, was aphrodisiac enough. Gabriella was completely overwhelmed, whimpering against Marduk's chest until he lifted her face. "Come for me, darling," he whispered, his gaze dark and gleaming.

Gabriella's mouth opened wide and a keening cry tore from it in a long, shrill wail. The arousal coiled tightly around her core unraveled in an instant.

The servant plunged hard into her ass; Marduk's hands shoved her forward and back on his cock until the lusty heat was too much and she began to sob.

The cock in her ass slowly withdrew. Xalia and the servant left the bed and padded toward the door. Marduk rolled Gabriella beneath him and continued to stroke his massive cock inside her in slow, drugging thrusts that soothed and excited until she felt another orgasm tremble through her body.

When it eased, she was clinging to him, her arms and legs wrapped tightly around his torso. His fingers wiped the tears from her cheeks. He bent to kiss her, and then he, too, withdrew from her.

He left her on the bed, her legs sprawled open, too weak to worry about her modesty or self-respect. He'd plundered both.

When his strong arms lifted her from the bed and carried her to the pool, she was barely awake. She lay across his lap as he bathed her.

"What do you think of my protection now?" he said softly.

Her eyelids fluttered open, her gaze locking with his. For the first time, she saw the man inside the demon. Her lips trembled and her eyes filled. Warm approval and acceptance, even a little affection gleamed in his golden gaze.

"I'm undone," she said, surprised to find her voice so hoarse.

"I will give you everything you desire."

"But not the one thing I crave most."

His jaw tightened. "You are mine. I won't ever let you go."

Guntram awoke at the soft scrape of Ninshubur's feet across the tiled floor as he scuffed toward the outer chamber. Without windows, Guntram guessed it must be morning. He was in no hurry to move. The affects of the mead had worn off long ago, and he'd been lying in the dark, thinking about Gabriella and getting hard. Again.

What was it about her that made him as uncontrolled as a boy? Other women, other wolves had pranced around him, trying to tempt the *raven*, but he'd never succumbed.

And Gabriella knew. Her eyes would gleam with amusement at the females' efforts to draw him into sex, and especially at their inevitable disappointment.

Once, when he'd accompanied her on a trade mission in North Carolina, their small band had taken to the forests to shake out their fur and run.

*The moon had called them, full, bright, hypnotic. They'd run until their chests heaved, then collapsed next to a river, lying on a bed of fallen leaves while their heartbeats slowed and their breaths deepened.*

*Gabriella had shifted, pulling the others into their humanksin, her female musk a heady perfume that called to their heated bodies. While the others laughed, not nearly as sharply aroused because they never denied themselves a willing partner, he'd felt the familiar tightening in his loins at her easy sensuality. She seemed to mock his celibacy, tempting him to act on the primal impulses that compelled them to seek a willing mate.*

*Gabriella bent to cup water in her hands and drink, as immodest in her current form as she was in wolfskin, offering a view that had him gritting his teeth. His gaze flicked over her bottom, over her slick sex.*

*She glanced over her shoulder, her golden brown eyes twinkling, and laughed.*

*And why wouldn't she? He'd grown hard. Lying still, he tried to tamp down the sudden lust that gripped him.*

*"I don't mind, you know . . . if you want to ease yourself."*

*For just a moment, his heart skipped a beat. Was she offering herself to him?*

*"I like to watch. It's only fair, since you've watched me so many times."*

*He tightened his lips and looked away, into the intersecting branches blotting out the ripening moon above them. Her teasing could sometimes feel like a cruel barb.*

*"Guntram," she said softly. "Please." She reached out to him, her fingers sliding along his cock.*

*He clamped his hand around her wrist and pushed her away.*

*She bit her lower lip, and her gaze dropped. "I'm sorry."*

*Guntram lay there, aching, his cock burning where her fingers had glided along his length, and he couldn't fight the impulse a moment longer. He clasped his cock inside his fist and stroked himself, watching her expression.*

*Her gaze was greedy, sparkling with excitement as his strokes quickened. Urgency built in his loins, cramping his balls, and he pumped harder, not trying to quiet the slapping sounds he made as he worked himself.*

*When his cock burst and semen spurted in thick, white stripes, he lay trembling.*

*Gabriella's shortened breaths made her large breasts quiver. She licked her lips, then reached over and dipped her fingertip into one glistening stripe and brought it to her mouth.*

Sharing that moment had been the closest he'd ever come to having sex with his goddess. The memory haunted his dreams, engendering visions of what it would have been like to take her in that bed of leaves with the rest of their small pack watching.

Ruthlessly, he gripped his cock and stroked himself to

orgasm, not caring that Simon had to hear every moment of his anguish. When he was done and lay gasping in damp sheets, he covered his eyes with his forearm, trying to blot the memory from his mind. Today, he needed focus, needed to be strong and vigilant.

Scuffling footsteps reentered the room. Light crept beneath his arm and he pulled it from his eyes to find Ninshubur carrying a candle.

"We should go out for a while," Simon said from his pallet, yawning and stretching his arms over his head. "Find our bearings." When his gaze met Guntram's there was compassion in his face.

Guntram sat up, turned on his pallet, and wrapped an arm around one bent knee to hide his wet belly. "I'm tired of following you and waiting for you to cue me what to do. How about you just tell me what to expect today?"

Simon raked a hand through his hair, then gave Guntram a nod. "All right. We're going to find a way into the palace, in particular, Irkalla's chambers. She hosts nightly feasts."

Guntram's lips curled in disgust. Understanding the nature of vampires, he didn't have to think hard to figure out the nature of the feasts.

"We'll find Gabriella in the middle of it all. Tonight won't be a rescue, but you will let her know that one is under way. Your job is to get close enough to pass along the message."

Tonight, he'd see Gabriella, and discover for himself whether she'd been harmed. "What will you be doing?"

"Distracting anyone who's watching you."

"How will we get inside?"

Simon grinned. "Why, we're walking through the front door."

* * *

Bright light streamed into the Master's chamber, softened only by the mesh curtains closed against the morning sunlight.

Gabriella cracked open her eyes and listened, but heard no footsteps, no breaths or faint heartbeats. She inhaled through her nose, but found only the stale aroma of sex and Marduk's fading musk.

She was alone.

Gingerly, she sat up, grimacing at the small intimate aches. Her head spun with the images that flitted through her mind of all the nasty things she'd done. Her hand smoothed over her skin, feeling raised welts still hot to the touch. A glance downward assured her they weren't all that visible—were no longer red—just shallow stripes of raised flesh. She pinched one and groaned, loving the way the pain induced a heady arousal that rushed beneath her skin, flushing her, heating her sex.

"I'm such a slut," she whispered.

And she was no closer to finding a means to escape. Already, her master's attentions were beginning to fill her head with thoughts of what a life here with him would be like.

However, she wasn't a bird like Simon's kestrel, which could be forever happy inside her golden cage. She was a wolf. Her innate pride and independence would eventually rise up to nip her in the ass. As attractive as the demon was, she couldn't forget what he was or where they were. Reaffirming her goal, she dropped her hands away from her hot skin and rose from the sumptuous bed.

She bathed quickly in the pool, keeping an eye out for movement from the sandy floor, but the vines behaved. Perhaps they only responded to the dragon's urgings. She ruthlessly thrust aside a niggling disappointment and finished washing her hair and body with the potted soaps Xalia had left behind.

Because even the shredded skirt and bra had disappeared, she walked nude to the balcony and brushed her hair in the sunlight until it and her body were dry.

By the time she'd finished her ablutions, she was bored and pacing inside the chamber, an edgy anger growing along with her hunger. Silently, she railed at how quickly Marduk forgot all about her when he wasn't thinking of his own pleasure.

She walked to the door, pressed an ear to the wood, but heard no sounds outside. Trying the latch, she found that this time it depressed. She cracked open the door and peered into the stairwell.

It was empty.

Thoughts swirled inside her head. She knew it was risky, but she longed to stretch her legs and needed to at least try to gain her freedom. And because she hadn't clothing or shoes to make an escape, she backed away from the door, shook out her hair, and let the change come over her.

Her shoulders drew back, her head fell forward, and then she dropped onto her hands and knees, barely suppressing an excited howl as hair sprouted over her skin and bones crackled and reformed. When she straightened on all fours and shook her fur, elation filled her.

She nosed open the door and sprinted quickly down the winding staircase, down to the bottom and out the door into the cobbled street.

The melding aromas assaulted her nostrils, but she inhaled deeply, catching an elusive and familiar scent. She bent closer and drew in the scent, quivering when she recognized it.

Guntram was here! She dropped her nose to the ground, found another spot where his fading scent remained, then took another a long stride farther down the street, ignoring the gasps of people darting from her path as she rushed forward in her eagerness to find him.

Then she heard shouts and the heavy *whomp* of large wings and raised her nose from the trail she followed to see a winged creature swooping down. A thick golden ruff of fur surrounded its leonine head. Golden brown feathers cloaked its wide-spread wings, but it was the lion's paws, outstretched, claws extended, that made her heart skip a beat.

She whirled and headed the opposite way from Guntram's scent, away from the demon bird rushing toward her. She ran hard, her lungs burning, felt claws rake her tail and changed direction again. When another swipe at her flank turned her again, she realized the creature was herding her, but she was panicked, couldn't take the time to think, because the thing was just above her.

Then she saw the open gates, saw the desert stretching in front of her and darted outside, flying down the grooved and graveled track to the bottom of the ridge where the fortress perched and ran for the dunes stretching as far as she could see.

The flapping grew fainter; the creature's rumbling roar rose above her as it returned to the fortress.

She was outside with a wide-open expanse in front of her, and she was free.

Marduk's heart lightened as soon as he entered his chamber. Her scent, freshly bathed, hovered in the air. "Gabriella," he called out.

There was no response. He walked to the bed and flung back the covers, walked to the pool and peered into the corners beneath the branches of the trees, peered into the bottom as his heart skipped a beat, but she was nowhere to be found.

He heard a footpad behind him and whirled, but his heart fell to his toes at the sight of Xalia, wringing her hands.

"Where is she?" he said, keeping his voice even.

"Gone," Xalia said tearfully.

He froze. "Xalia, you had only one duty. You know where she is. Tell me now."

"She went outside. Shifted into a wolf. She was too fast for me to follow."

"She overpowered you then? That's how she got out the door?"

Xalia's glance fell away. "She's been pretending to love you. Pretending she's happy. I left the door open to prove it to you."

Marduk didn't trust himself to touch her. He set his fists on his hips and towered over her, making her quake at the sight of his fury. "Where did she go? And don't tell me you don't know. I won't believe you."

"An *anzu*-bird followed her through the streets. She escaped into the desert."

Marduk's body vibrated with horror. He walked toward the balcony, scanned the horizon but found no trace of her. She was out there, alone. He'd have spared her the truth if only she'd been willing to let him guide her.

He shouldn't show her any mercy, should let the lesson she was about to learn be imprinted on her mind. Then she'd never attempt to escape him again. When her body cooled from her rush to freedom, the nightmare would begin.

If she'd escaped the jaws of the *anzu*.

For her own good, he should let it happen, but he remembered how sweet her cries had sounded as she'd whimpered in his arms the last time he'd taken her in the night. Remembered, too, how warm his chest had grown, how deeply he had slept.

He stripped on the balcony, aimed a glare at Xalia, telling her silently to await his return. Then he stepped off into the air, transforming before he fell to the ground.

# CHAPTER 9

Gabriella ran as far as she could until her lungs felt ready to burst, then settled at the bottom of a dune and scratched at the sand, digging a hole to back inside and hide from whatever else might follow her from the air.

Only as her blood cooled did she begin to worry. She had no water, and hunger rumbled in her belly. Worse, she hadn't a clue how far the desert stretched or if there was an end, a place beyond the hot, golden sand.

She'd have to wait for darkness, climb to the top of the tallest dune and have a look around. One thing she knew—she couldn't go back. Marduk would be furious she'd escaped.

She settled her muzzle atop her front paws. Happy at least that she was alone and had time to think about all that had happened, away from the enticements of her captor. She'd almost succumbed to his seduction, had been close to surrendering. She'd felt her will bending, nearly breaking beneath his sensual assault.

A shadow passed over the sand in front of her, so large it sunk her surroundings into dusk-like darkness.

She raised her head and watched a black cloud blot out the blazing sun. Odd, since there hadn't been a cloud in the sky when she'd watched from the balcony of Marduk's chamber. Then a distinct chill arrived on a breeze, and the blazing, empty desert blurred before her eyes.

The fur on her back lifted; her heart began to pound slowly. Something wasn't right. Then she remembered Marduk's warnings and knew she was in real trouble.

"True hell" had found her.

*Gabriella blinked, then glanced down. She was no longer a wolf lying in a sandy den. She was in humanskin and clothed in a white shift. Her bare feet curled against cold, damp stone. Looking around her, the bare stone-block walls and arched ceiling above her head seemed familiar. She stood in the foyer of a stone keep, a tall oak door in front of her.*

*Voices carried from beyond the door. She slumped toward it, her ear at the crack. Inside, familiar voices whispered. Voices she hadn't heard in centuries.*

*Mother? Father? Dear God, where was she? And when?*

*"She's just a child." Her mother's voice quavered.*

*A deep snort sounded. "She bled. She's a woman now. It's our way."*

*"They'll savage her."*

*"She'll survive. And she'll have a mate to protect her."*

*"It's too soon. Please, husband. Let me lock her door. We'll wait until her next season. She has a right to know what is expected. I haven't had time to prepare her."*

*"You've coddled her. She should have known long ago."*

*A wolf howled in the distance, drawing Gabriella's attention from the heated conversation in the other room.*

*And suddenly she knew where she was, and what night this was, and her blood ran cold. "Run to your room and lock the goddamn door!" she screamed inside her mind.*

*But the girl she'd been didn't hear. Heated excitement of a sort she'd never experienced before flooded her young body, moistening the place between her legs. She wondered if it was blood. Her menses, or so her mother had explained when she'd provided the rags she would use to protect her clothing. But it had ended a fortnight ago.*

*It was too soon for that to happen again, and the moisture was too hot and thin. Something else was happening.*

*Another howl, another voice, called to her, inviting her to run.*

*She ignored the conversation in the hall and ran on light steps to the tall wooden doors at the entrance of the keep and pushed them open. At the top of the steps, she shed her clothing, wanting to join the wolves, her playmates, in the forest.*

*Her mother's shriek sounded in the distance behind her, but she was already shifting, already running for the gate, her heart beating happily as she entered the forest.*

*Freedom awaited her there. Whining howls erupted around her and she called back, letting them know where she was as she raced toward the stream. Her pack's special meeting place.*

*Rabbits and deer would be feeding. A hunt would ease the tension coiling inside her body these past few days. She entered a clearing and halted, not recognizing the wolves that waited there.*

*Not her pack. Lone wolves. Ones her mother had warned her about. She began to back up, preparing to whirl and run the opposite way, but another blocked her path.*

*Low growls emanated from the two largest wolves in front of her, one a speckled gray, the other pure black. Teeth bared as the two males faced off, until the gray leapt, jaws opening, and he took the black to the ground, rolling in the leaves and dirt.*

*She backed up, knowing she needed to escape because the other males weren't watching the fight. They watched her. And were slowly closing in.*

*She felt a cold nose nuzzle beneath her tail, and whipped around to snap, forcing him to jump back, but when she faced forward again, the black was on his feet and approaching, his head low to the ground, his eyes glinting in the darkness.*

*The other wolves continued to close in, and she began to quiver, knowing her escape was closed.*

*Frozen in place, terrified by the vicious flair of his nostrils and the length of white fang he displayed, she could only watch in horror. He came close, his nose sniffling along her sides, under her tail, his tongue lapping out to lick her there.*

*She folded down her tail and bent her back legs to escape him, but he nipped her flanks and she danced to the side, trying to evade his attention.*

*She understood his purpose now. Sensed on a primal level that the males had gathered because of her heat, because of the scent of arousal that carried on the wind, summoning them.*

*If one covered her, conquered her, she'd be his. Mated. Despite what her mother thought, she knew that much about their ways. If she was dominated, pierced and locked by his wolf's knotted member, she'd be his.*

*And she wasn't ready. She'd have preferred meeting her future mate the way her human friends did. She would have preferred knowing something of his temperament, and whether he would expect her to be meek, like her mother, or let her be bold, as was her nature.*

*How she wished she'd heeded her mother's words. The black wolf lunged at her, rolled her to her back and over again, and then as she lay crouched on the ground, he mounted her from behind, his front legs framing her body and holding her, pinning her in place.*

*Then his mouth clamped down on her neck, and he began to rut, pushing against her.*

*Panic gripped her and she bent her head toward the dirt, trying to ease the painful grip he had on her neck while she clawed the ground with her front paws and tried to crawl from under him.*

*She whimpered and yelped as his penis pushed against her entrance and he began to pump swiftly, trying to enter her.*

*Gabriella squirmed, panic deepening, knowing she had only moments before they were locked together and his seed spilled into her womb.*

*She crawled forward again, trying to escape, but he gripped her sides harder, his teeth sank through her fur into her neck. She had only moments before it would be too late.*

*She opened her mouth and howled, ignored the teeth at her neck, and turned her head to slash at his withers.*

*He yelped, his grip loosened.*

*It was enough. She bucked and dragged forward, crawling from beneath him, then turned quickly to leap at his back and savage him.*

*Her fangs sank into his back, a fang hooking into his spine and he wobbled, and fell flat against the ground, whimpering. Then she whipped around and faced the rest, her fur lifting off her neck and back, her growl as low and deadly as she could muster.*

*The gray, his coat speckled with blood, approached next.*

*She didn't wait for him to attack. She lunged, fangs bared, with a harsh keening cry eerie to her own ears.*

*Their chests slammed together, their jaws slashed at fur and flesh, until he staggered away and lay on his side, blood spraying from his mouth rhythmically with every breath that rattled from his chest.*

*The other wolves circled her restlessly, growling ominously.*

*But she was maddened, filled with bloodlust for the band of brothers. Blood surged throughout her body, aided by a heart beating fiercely with fear and fury.*

*Then the sounds of other wolves rushing through the forest neared.*

*She stood above the jerking body of the black male she'd bested, waiting for her own pack as they filled the clearing.*

*When they'd halted, chests quivering and breathless, she pulled on her humanskin, uncaring for the blood slipping down her legs or for the myriad of slashes to her sides, neck, and flanks. "The one who would have mated with me is dead. I have the right to rule myself."*

*One by one, her pack transformed. Her father and mother stared at the carnage around her, at the blood soaking into the leaves and pine needles cushioning the forest floor. At the blood staining her pale skin.*

*Gabriella held her head high, but her body quivered and she knew she wouldn't be able to maintain her proud stance much longer.*

*Her father's jaw tensed. His eyebrows lowered until dark shadows deepened the sockets. "Do you know what you've done? That was Ulfric's son you murdered."*

*"It wasn't murder," she said, her voice tightening.*

*"You're a breedable female. I sent out the call to the neighboring clans myself. I wanted the best, the strongest of their males to take you."*

*"You did this?" her mother said softly. "Without warning me?"*

*"You're a woman. My bitch. Keep your opinions to yourself. Don't you see the damage you've already done? You let her think she was*

*as strong as a man, as important. If you'd been a better mother, we wouldn't have this wolf's blood on our hands."*

*Gabriella stared at her father, at the man who'd seemed proud of her strength and intelligence. But now she realized those qualities had only interested him because they made her more attractive when he'd offered her for mating.*

*"Take her back to the keep," her father said without sparing her a glance. "We'll have to send word to Ulfric and see what will satisfy him for the loss of his son."*

*"They will want her blood! Please," her mother said, grabbing his arm and pleading.*

*"Perhaps I should offer yours as well," he said, shaking her off his arm and turning to head back to the keep.*

*Gabriella stayed frozen until hands gripped her upper arms to pull her after her father. She dug her heels into the dirt, jerked against their firm hold, but to no avail. She couldn't let them take her. Ulfric would kill her. But only after he took what his son was denied.*

*Her mother's gaze locked with hers, and she gave her a single slow nod.*

*Gabriella sank to the ground, and jerked free of their grips. They bent to pick her up, but she scooted backward, lowering her head to her chest and let the change come over her again.*

*As a wolf, she lunged at one pack mate, slicing at the muscle at the back of his heels, then whipping toward the other and snapping at his hands, severing two fingers. Both men howled and fell to their knees. Gabriella gave her mother one final glance and raced into the forest, knowing she'd never see her mother or her home again.*

From one moment to the next, Gabriella was once again in the desert, but in her woman's form, her body stretched on burning sand. She lifted her head and tried to will her body to change again so that her thick fur would protect her from the fierce rays. But she was too weak. Too thirsty.

She was going to die here. Still, she'd rather be here than back inside her nightmare. But if that was the best that hell could dish up, then she wondered what all the fuss had been about. So, she'd relived her worst nightmare. She'd survived and prevailed, then and now.

Then another huge, engulfing shadow crept across the sand toward her, and her eyes widened. *God, not again.*

The sand beyond the fortress undulated like a lover's curving back, dunes lifting and falling, swept from side to side by the sighing wind.

Marduk searched the ground beneath him, frantically seeking some sign of her passing, but the wind had obliterated her tracks.

Not until he saw the *lillum*, circling like vultures, did he release a deep, relieved sigh.

He flattened his wings, diving toward the ground beneath them, then pulled back to settle on the ground beside Gabriella.

Three female *lillum* landed opposite Gabriella's writhing body, folding back their black wings. Aya, the leader of their small flock, stepped forward, her toe touching Gabriella's buttocks. "Is she precious to you, Master?"

As always, he was careful to hide his interest. "*If I treated her well, do you think she'd flee to the desert to escape me?*" he said, sending the message with his mind.

Her face, as shiny and dark as obsidian, was split by a smile. Long black fangs slid from beneath her upper and lower lips to interlock. "Can we taste?"

"*She's weakened. Why not wait until later, in Irkalla's chambers?*"

"Our queen will likely drain her beyond use for us. It's been so long since any of us tasted of the living."

"*Aya, take your drink, but only a sip. She must appear tonight, and I have to make her presentable.*"

As the *lillum* surrounded her, bending their slender, dark forms over Gabriella, Marduk suppressed his revulsion. Lilith's children were among the oldest demon hybrids in this realm. Their appetites and minds were primitive and rapacious.

Aya rolled Gabriella to her back. Gabriella's eyes remained open but unfocused, no doubt still in the thrall of an escalating nightmare. He'd warned her what would happen. Yet, if he touched her now, wakened her from her dream, she'd have another nightmare to add to the one currently gripping her mind.

So he left her in that other world while the three demons bent over her neck and both wrists, their black incisors sinking deeply as they supped. Wings stiffened as their voices seemed to intertwine and become one, in a high, ululating tone that pierced his ears.

"*Enough*," he said softly.

Their disappointed sighs sounded deceptively soft and girlish, but their heads rose, blood drenching their lips. Then they spiraled straight into the air, laughing as they darted toward the fortress.

Marduk studied Gabriella, noting the quivering breaths, her widened eyes. When he pulled her from hell, she'd have little relief once she caught sight of him. Still, this was all part of the lesson she must learn. She might have continued to think of him as just another man—easily led by his desires.

Now, she'd think twice about defying him again. He reached out and touched one taloned claw against her hip.

Gabriella sucked in a deep breath, her eyes blinking as she returned. Her face turned toward him. Then her mouth opened around a long, shrill scream.

She rolled from under his talon, then froze.

He knew she was sunk again in the dark time. He touched her again. "*Only when you are with me, when I touch you, are you free of hell.*"

She remained rigid beneath him, her face turning to peer at him over her shoulder. "Marduk?"

"*I will take you back.*"

Her eyes filled slowly, and fat tears rolled down her cheeks. "I can't stay here. With you. I want to go home."

"*You accepted my invitation.*"

"You compelled me to touch that glass."

"*If you hadn't been ready to leave, ready to be seduced, you would never have succumbed to my lure. Come, you are tired and thirsty. Let me care for you.*"

She broke with his gaze and stared ahead of her. "I'm afraid of this place. Of the terrors it holds. I don't know how to go about making a life for myself."

"*So long as you obey me, you have nothing to fear. I will protect you. Provide for you.*"

"I'm afraid of needing you," she said in a soft, broken voice.

Heady satisfaction filled him. If she feared it, then she was tempted to surrender. "*Climb onto my back, darling, but never let your touch leave my skin.*"

She swiped at her tears, leaving streaks of dirt staining her cheeks. Her lips curved downward, but her hand lifted to the top of his leathery claw while he pulled it up to help her rise. She came shakily to her feet, her eyes wide as her gaze swept his dragon form. "I saw your aura before, when I looked into the mirror. I knew what you must be in truth, but . . . you're more beautiful than I could have imagined."

Marduk's mouth opened, stretching back. He was pleased she wasn't frightened of him in this form. That she found him "beautiful." "*Climb onto me. We must head back and prepare for Irkalla's feast. Another day I will fly with you here if you like.*"

Her head lowered, not responding to his suggestion, but she smoothed her hands over his shoulders and stepped on the edge of his wing, which he held rigid until she was seated on his shoulders.

Then he lifted his wings and flapped downward, ignoring her gasp and the way her hands found purchase on the ridged scales at the back of his neck. He lifted into the air, soaring, and turning slowly back toward the fortress.

He felt her lean forward, scanning the ground they flew past and heard more gasps.

Beneath them lay bleached bones of creatures large and small, half buried in the sand that hid, then revealed, them as the wind surged. The desert was a graveyard for demons, and she might have remained among them if he hadn't found her in time.

As the setting sun burned brightly at the horizon, they rushed toward the fortress walls. He tilted his wings, aligning his body with the narrow street outside his tower door and set down.

She climbed down without encouragement. When she turned back, he was once again in his human form. As naked as she was. Her glance slid over his body, snagging on his growing erection.

Her body reacted to the sight, her posture easing into a feminine stance, with thighs clamped closed and breasts lifted. Her nipples tightened, peaking instantly.

He hid a smile and held out his hand.

She slipped hers inside his and turned toward the door. But she stumbled and stared straight ahead at the people who'd climbed down from their stoops to catch a glimpse of the dragon and his woman.

Her gaze clung to two men in particular, who seemed equally frozen until one of them grabbed the arm of the taller individual and pushed him toward an alleyway.

Marduk wondered at Gabriella's fascination, but she shook herself, turned to give him a tight smile, and entered his tower without saying a word.

Fierce elation swept through Guntram as Simon hustled him through Ninshubur's front door. Gabriella was alive and apparently unharmed. Dwelling purposely only on that one fact for the moment, he drew in a deep, relieved breath.

As soon as the door closed behind them, he whirled. "We've found her." He felt like embracing Simon and dancing, so great was his relief. Thankfully, he remembered himself, and the fact he didn't particularly like the mage, and managed to restrain his joy.

The arrival of the enormous red dragon had sent people into the streets to gape. His skin, covered in bright red scales rimmed in black, glistened in the bright sun. The large wings, cloaked only in a fine reddish brown down, spread so wide they touched the buildings on both sides of the street until they folded inward. His head, as broad as an elephant's, was long and bluntly shaped, the nostrils large and flaring. The eyes, a deep gold with elliptical pupils, stared unblinking at the crowd that milled before him.

The tail itself was long, tensile and bordered along the end with raised, spiked scales that looked sharp enough to cut a man in two when snapped like a whip, which it did until he settled.

As fearsome as the dragon looked, the sight of the woman, naked and disheveled but riding fearlessly astride the dragon, had caused even more of a stir.

Guntram's own mouth had gaped for all of a second. When she'd slid to the ground and the dragon shifted into a tall, dark man, his body had tightened in denial. Her trust as she'd placed her hand inside the man's had been telling.

His stomach had churned, noting the way her expression and demeanor softened toward the demon. He'd wondered if he was already too late to save her.

Only when her gaze had collided with his had he felt relief.

She'd started, her eyes rounding, but before he could signal her, Simon had shoved him toward the door.

"Who was she with?" Guntram asked, his body tightening again, ready for action, ready to pound the man who'd dared touch her into a bloody pulp.

"The Master of the Demons." Simon turned away.

"But she seemed safe," Guntram continued. "Is he her captor?"

"I was afraid this would happen again," Simon said, ripping his filthy robe over his head. "Guntram, his involvement makes this tricky."

"Why? Who is he?"

"He's an ally. Of sorts. But if he's claimed her, if he feels affection for her, he won't release her easily."

"An ally? *A demon?*"

Simon hurried through the rough apartment at the front into Ninshubur's secret room. "His name's Marduk. Long ago, he was given rule over the demons in the Land of the Dead."

Guntram followed, becoming frustrated since it seemed he had to pull the information from the mage. "I'm confused then. I thought Nergal and his consort Irkalla ruled here."

"They are the first order of rulers, but the Master of the Demons controls the lesser demons by virtue of a bequest from King Solomon."

"I don't care if God himself ordained the bastard, he's holding Gabriella against her will. She saw me, Simon. Did you see her expression?"

Simon's gaze met his at last. What Guntram saw didn't reassure him. Pity softened his expression. "She seemed conflicted. Already she looks to him for protection. He holds hell at bay for her."

Ninshubur bustled into the room, lowering a wooden latch to lock them all inside. "Did you see her?" he asked excitedly.

Guntram nodded, his stomach beginning to boil again. She was so close; the entrance to the tower she'd entered was just around the corner.

"Everyone's talking," the old man said, his arms filled with packages. "They all know she's living flesh, and that she attempted an escape. The *lillum* found her first. If she's discovered on her own again, she'll be eaten."

Guntram turned to Simon again, ready to shake the answers he wanted free. "This dragon that holds her, you said he's an ally. Can't he be persuaded to surrender her to us?"

Simon's chest rose. "He's been in this realm for nearly three thousand years, since the death of Solomon. No matter that he was entrusted with a sacred duty; he's been corrupted. He's been alone for all this time. Except for Irkalla, who's as vile as her sister, he's had no one. He won't be persuaded."

"So we must take her."

Simon nodded slowly. "First steps, friend. We have to let her know we have a plan to free her."

"And do we? I'm assuming we can't just enter the tower and walk up to her door."

"There are watchers set around his chambers. Some of them are Irkalla's because she's jealous. Some are ones he's set in place to keep Gabriella safe. We'll have a chance to talk to her tonight when she appears in Irkalla's court."

"Why can't we take her then?"

"Too many will be watching. Only one of us can approach her without raising suspicion. You must find a way to get close. Make sure she wants to be freed."

"Of course she does. Why would she want to stay in this place?"

Simon's mouth formed a small, tight smile. "Tell me, Guntram, hasn't Gabriella always craved a master?"

Guntram thought back to what Alex had told him. Gabriella needed a strong mate, someone to overwhelm her and still make her feel safe. Had the dragon fulfilled that need? He ground his jaws together. His heartbeats evened. Now, he could think. "Tonight's feast, then. That's where she'll be. The entrance to the palace is guarded. How will we get past the sentries?"

Simon lifted his brows and gave them a wicked waggle. "I'll have no problem passing. We're going to waylay one of her courtiers. While you truss him up, I'll assume his form.

You'll already be in disguise as my slave. Let's just hope that Irkalla is so consumed with keeping Marduk from Gabriella that she doesn't decide to give my new slave a test run."

Guntram grimaced. "I'm assuming when you say slave that I'm going to be served up as a sexual playmate. I don't play."

Simon quickly extinguished the grin stretching his lips. "Keep vigilant. Try not to look too fierce. That will only get you more attention from every woman there."

Guntram barely suppressed a growl. The only woman whose attention he craved was serving up submission to a dragon. How could a lone wolf compete with that?

# CHAPTER 10

Gabriella's body vibrated with excitement.

And not just because Marduk used his hands and lips to bathe away the dirt from her body. Sitting astride his lap, impaled on his thick cock, she snuggled close to his chest to hide her expression.

Marduk poured water over her shoulder, then smoothed his lips along the curve. "You understand now why you can never leave this tower alone?" he asked, his tone solemn.

A shudder racked her, dragging her down from the exultant high she'd experienced at seeing Guntram and Simon Jameson among the crowd who'd watched them arrive. She didn't want a reminder of what she'd experienced in the desert—her nightmare, relived time and again, but changed, the horrors deepening with each recurrence.

She hadn't won the battle against Ulfric's son the last time and had suffered his rape. If she'd had to live it again, what more would have happened? Would the wolves have ripped her apart? Or all taken turns?

Marduk's arms wrapped around her, and he murmured against her hair, "I will keep you safe. What did you learn today?"

Gabriella nestled deeper in his embrace. "That your touch keeps the nightmare at bay."

"My touch, this tower. All are enchanted. You're safe here."

"But I'm not dead. Why do I experience hell?"

His shrug didn't satisfy her curiosity. She leaned back to give him a frown, but the movement forced her deeper on his cock. It twitched inside her. Her lips pouted. "Not fair, talking this way."

"I never claimed to fight fair, my love."

Her breath huffed out. "Don't call me that."

"But you are. My love. *Mine*."

"That sounds so . . . primitive. I'm a modern woman. I own myself. And I can choose lovers without getting sticky with emotion. I *fuck*."

His hands grasped her hips and moved her up and down his shaft. "Perhaps in the past that was true. But at your core, you are warm, yielding . . ." He drew a long, slow breath and pushed her back down. "You're a woman, Gabriella. You've been in need of a man to satisfy your cravings and to rein in your passion."

"I don't need a man to hold any reins. I'm my own master."

"But you do crave to submit, don't you?" When she scowled his lips curved. "How can your fierce independence and your need to be mastered coexist?"

She shook her hair back and the wet strands fell against her shoulders. She ground down his cock, squeezing around him, a subtle reminder that she was an equal combatant in this intimate battle. "I don't know. But I've kept myself free of controlling males all my life. And I should warn you that the last to try to take me by force choked on his own blood."

His smile deepened beneath the neat black moustache that framed his lips and dipped down to a narrow, devilish beard. That smile, so smug and self-assured, infuriated her because her body betrayed her every time.

Already lush heat bloomed inside her, causing her vagina to pulsate and ripple.

His smile froze, his nostrils flared, and she couldn't stand it a second longer, leaning closer to slide her lips across his, coaxing them open with a glide of her tongue, then moaning as he slid his inside her. Their mouths warred, their heads pressing forward, grinding as their bodies heated. Her hips ground down, then slipped forward and back to rub her clit against the base of his cock.

His hands didn't fight her movements, just caressed her bottom, cupping it, lifting and rolling it, and then fingers sneaked between her buttocks and glided down.

She gasped when he touched her sensitive entrance, groaned when he dipped a thick fingertip inside, then crashed her hips against him, rising higher and higher because she couldn't wait another moment to come.

Her orgasm crashed like the waves of water that churned

between their bodies as she rode him. Cream and froth bathing her inside and out. But she quickly realized she was doing all the work, and that her hard-bodied demon was only watching, biding his time until her pleasure receded.

His lips had thinned to a narrow, straight line. His eyebrows were drawn into a severe scowl.

He'd let her take her pleasure, but the lesson she hoped he'd forgotten had only begun.

Her body shivered now, not from residual fear or the relief at seeing an old friend coming to her rescue, but from the arousal that shouldn't be climbing so quickly inside her again.

When her motions stilled, he lifted her off his cock, then slapped the water with his open palms.

The dark, terrible vines emerged from the beneath the sand, wrapping around her arms and legs, her torso, even threading through her hair to hold her still. When she opened her mouth, another looped itself around her head, wrapping twice. And because she couldn't bear the thought of them entering her mouth, she clamped her lips shut, letting them gag her.

Her eyes widened on him, not understanding the anger that radiated from his taut body. He'd been so tender, bringing her to the water to wash away the sand, soothing her with soft murmurs and caresses as she'd lain against his chest.

For a moment she'd forgotten what he was, that he wasn't really the man standing in front of her. He was a dragon, a cold-blooded predator. And she'd crossed him. What punishment would he visit on her now that she was restrained and completely at his mercy?

Because she didn't want him to know she was frightened, she wriggled against her bonds, screaming at him from behind her gag.

Bells tinkled, nearing, and Gabriella shot daggers with her gaze as the tinkling was muffled and his little sex slave entered the water. But there was more than one splash behind her as Xalia and whatever accompanied her joined them.

Xalia swam around in front of her, then stood, coming so close her small green breasts pressed just below her own. Xalia's eyes were moist. "You should not have run." Then she lifted her hands and snapped her fingers.

A pale figure glided beneath the water around her, too fast for her to make out its shape. It circled the pool, swam between Marduk's spread legs, between her own. Its skin was soft and sleek, like a dolphin's.

Her body began to quiver. Xalia bent slightly, tapped Gabriella's breast and waited as a vine encircled it. The nipple grew engorged, the tip reddening as the vine constricted. Then a thin tendril crept to the nipple and ringed it, constricting so tightly, so deliciously, that Gabriella couldn't suppress a moan.

Xalia's lips twitched, then flattened again. She tapped the opposite breast and waited until it was wrapped. Then she sank beneath the water, parted Gabriella's folds with her fingers, and held them while the vines slid between her legs, trapping the folds open.

Every part of her was framed, opened, but for what? Gabriella lifted her gaze to Marduk, unable to hide her growing unease. His features were tight with a malevolent cast that shocked her. Here was the demon who'd been hiding inside the handsome man all along.

"Dagon," Marduk said, his tone even.

Xalia's expression became soft, almost delirious. As she leaned to the side to peek around Gabriella, her breasts grazed Gabriella's ribs.

Marduk's expression clearly showed his displeasure as he stepped out of the pool. Over his shoulder he said, "Xalia, make sure she's made ready in time."

Marduk slung clothing over his shoulder and left the room nude. The silence he left behind was punctuated by Gabriella's short, rasping breaths as she waited for a glimpse of the creature standing right behind her.

"Leave us." The voice was soft, almost tender in its delivery.

Gabriella jerked and the vines tightened.

Xalia's lips pouted, but she withdrew to sit on the upper step of the pool.

The vines clamped over Gabriella's mouth fell away.

"Lord Marduk's call was as unexpected as it is rare," whispered the soft male voice behind her. "What have you done to upset him so?"

Gabriella pressed her lips together, rather than rail at her treatment, which was her first instinct. But he stayed silent so long, her own impatience had her blurting, "Does he only have to say your name to summon you?"

"As I am bound to him, yes."

Something cool and slippery glided down her back. "And you do whatever he commands?"

"When he issues a command, yes."

"Did he issue you a command regarding me?"

"Do you think you're important enough to consume even that much of his attention?"

Gabriella gritted her teeth at the sarcasm in his tone. "Important enough for him to tell you to get your ass here, apparently."

The water between her feet began to burble as though boiling, but the temperature didn't change. Disturbed because she couldn't look down to see what was happening, she ground her jaws tight. No way would she let him know he'd frightened her.

After a few moments the water grew still. "Did he send you to punish me?"

A soft snort gusted against her ear. "Is that what you think? Do you deserve punishment? It might explain his sour expression when he departed."

"If not to punish, then why did he ask you to come?"

"I think he did not want to be the one to cause you pain."

"Is your cock that enormous?"

Laughter gusted, warming the back of her neck. "That's the first thing that came to your mind?"

"My pussy's spread. What am I supposed to think?"

"You are so quick to jump to conclusions."

"Then you are here to render punishment? Why don't you just get on with it?"

His hands caressed the notches of her hips and his body pressed against her back and bottom. He was nude, his erection fitting snugly against the crevice of her ass. "If it was punishment he intended, he would hardly ask me to be the deliverer."

"Why's that? Are you the demon of boredom?"

He withdrew and stepped around her, and her breath caught. He was as beautifully pale as Marduk was dark. His eyes were the color of the sea, his skin as luminescent as water struck by sunlight. His hair was blond and fell in wet curls to his shoulders.

The expression he wore was slightly bemused. "I am considered many things, but never boring. I have power over water. On Earth, I frightened sailors, who thought I was a sea serpent."

Instantly, she relaxed. He hardly seemed a malevolent entity—just miffed at being marginalized. "You're a merman, huh?" The water burbled again, but she no longer feared he'd poach her. "I'm to be prepared for presentation to Irkalla's court. Is that why you're here?"

One corner of his mouth quirked upward. "You are quick. I'm here to adorn your body with the trappings of a slave."

Gabriella formed her lips into a disgruntled moue. "I'm not a slave. I recognize no man as my master."

"But you shall be marked as such." He cupped his empty hand, then opened it, palm up. Lying in the center was a slender golden ring from which a polished amber-colored stone dangled.

"You're going to pierce my ears?"

His smile broadened. The thin tendril-like vine encircling one nipple constricted and she knew where the ring was going to be inserted.

He broke the solid ring with a sharp snap of his fingers, then held it to the reddened, protruding nipple. With just a twist, it pierced her, the break closing immediately. Besides a small sting, her breast seemed intact, no blood appearing around the wound.

Not so bad, she said to herself, staring straight ahead as he produced another identical ring and pierced the opposite nipple.

The vines dropped away from around her breasts, blood flowed into her breasts and she heaved a sigh of relief. When his fingers tugged on the circles, she didn't flinch, but she did feel a tingle of arousal.

He dropped to his knees in front of her, his head just above the water, and pierced her belly button with a larger ring, then strung thin gold chains from both nipples to the one at her belly and added another to encircle her waist. When his fingers stroked between her folds, only then did she grow concerned again.

"Easy," he whispered. "I must arouse you to finish this."

Xalia giggled from the steps.

Gabriella had forgotten the little green demon, and gave her a sharp glare, which only managed to increase her mirth.

"I wonder where he will attach the leash," Xalia said, giggling again.

Gabriella hadn't thought that far ahead, but if Marduk thought she'd be led around by her clit, he'd better rethink that plan.

However, the thought of Guntram seeing her like that didn't have the same effect. She thought she might enjoy seeing his face redden, his body hardening as he fought the urge to drop his gaze when he followed the thin chain downward.

Dagon fingered her diligently, then curled his finger to rub her clit. "A little shy, are you?"

It was Gabriella's turn to snort. The last thing she was going to admit out loud was that she required rougher handling than he offered to turn her on. His head bent, submerging, and his tongue laved the hood protecting her clitoris. He pulled it between his lips and suckled, drawing harder and harder until her toes curled into the sand. A sudden pricking pain caused her pussy to contract, but that was all the response he drew from her as he slid the last ring into her body. A final chain was linked to her bellybutton ring and fastened to the ring piercing her clit, and then he stood.

Dagon moved close, his warm-blooded body heating her front. "Do you require punishing?" he murmured.

"You tell me," she said evenly.

"You've been disappointingly obedient."

Gabriella was all right with that. Her battle wasn't with this blond Adonis. She had far scarier things in store for her this night.

The vines dropped from her body, and she swayed.

He caught her against his chest and her nipple rings dragged across his skin. A warm tingling caught her breath.

Dagon lifted one brow. "Since they're so new, you'll be on the edge of arousal all evening. Punishment enough for one such as you, I think."

Gabriella shook off his hands and turned, deliberately keeping her head up rather than give him the satisfaction of watching her stare at his work. The new "adornments" excited her. She'd never considered being pierced before, but realized she would have enjoyed having a lover insist. Her glance swept Xalia, who still wore a delighted grin. Her nipples and pussy were bare. Why had Marduk singled her out? Did he really intend to lead her about by the rings as Xalia had hinted?

She grabbed a linen towel from the stack and dried her body, ignoring the other two who were swimming toward the deeper end. When both of their bodies sank into the water, she watched for a minute, curious, but they only played, swimming like seals beneath the surface.

She hadn't thought Xalia was a water creature too, but maybe she simply had amazing lungs. Shrugging, she picked up a brush from a basket filled with toiletries and strode toward the balcony. As she stroked her hair, letting it dry slowly in the hot breeze, and enjoyed the heat the gold rings trapped, stinging her nipples and clit, she realized she couldn't wait to see Guntram's reaction.

Gabriella was honest enough with herself to admit she was confused about how she felt about both men. On one hand, she'd never been so relieved to see anyone in her life than Marduk when she'd woken up in the desert. That he was the most exciting lover she'd ever had was also true. He frightened her, but no man had ever mastered her so thoroughly. His brand of lovemaking was addictive.

And yet, she'd never been so happy as she had been when she'd caught Guntram's scent. Her stalwart warrior, her *War Raven*, had entered hell, braving death to rescue her. That he was so loyal filled her with warmth. They shared so much history, and he'd given her the freedom to be herself. Although she'd never given in to the urge to act on her attraction, she had been tempted.

The sight of his nude body, fresh from a run with the pack, never failed to stir her. The heat in his gaze when he stood proud and straight while she inspected him told her the attraction wasn't one-sided. If he freed her, she wondered if he would expect more from her.

For the first time, she considered what it would be like to be mated to such a man. He wasn't the same sort of wolf her father had been. Perhaps surrendering her mantle to him wouldn't be so horrible after all.

Gabriella remembered the first time she'd met him. In her small pack she'd gathered to form her new family, she'd had only two males, who had fought constantly. That evening, they'd stopped at an inn to eat and rest, and she'd overheard them arguing.

*"She's a girl!" one drunkenly bellowed. "One of us should cover her. Then all that gold will be ours."*

*"One of ours, you mean," the other snarled.*

*"We could share. She's more than enough female to satisfy us both."*

*"You're talking of raping her?"*

*"It's not rape. It's our way. And she knows it, too." His voice dropped conspiratorially. "Why do you think she keeps herself armed in her sleep?"*

*The other grunted. "How do you propose we take her?"*

*"Can't while she sleeps. She'd slit our throats."*

*"Then when we're traveling. Her horse could be spooked. Spill her from the saddle. And before she can catch her breath, we'll have her."*

*"Then what?"*

*"We find ourselves a place, our own territory to rule. Maybe get ourselves a couple more brood bitches . . ."*

*Gabriella had heard enough. She'd already paid them up front for the next month's service, but she'd cut her losses now and sneak away while they drank. With luck, she'd be long gone by the time they noticed, and her scent too faded for them to track.*

*Her mind made up, she'd turned—and bumped into a wall of hard muscle. Her gaze shot upward in alarm.*

*The expression of the warrior in front of her was frightening in its intensity—grim, tight. His nostrils flared as he inhaled her scent.*

*Another wolf? Were they conspiring together?*

*His chin lifted toward the men she'd been spying on. "What do you intend to do about them?"*

*"What concern is it of yours?"*

*"You're a woman. Weaker by nature. Perhaps I don't like the odds."*

*"Or maybe you're in with them."*

*His lips curled derisively. "I'm a better judge of character than that."*

*Her cheeks warmed. The two men had been the best she could buy. Lone wolves were reluctant to be led by a female. "If you're not with them, then stand aside."*

*"Are you going to run?"*

*"Whatever I decide to do, I wouldn't tell you."*

*"They'll follow. And if you give them too much of a fight, they'll kill you."*

*"And you know this because you'd do the same thing?"*

*His eyes narrowed with deadly intent. "I'm not that dishonorable."*

*"I meant no insult. But I really do need to stretch my lead. Out of my way."*

*Still he didn't budge, his chest scraping along hers as he breathed. "Perhaps I could offer my sword. We'd travel together, set up camp, and wait for them."*

*"So that you can lull me into trusting you and have the job done before either of them arrive?"*

*"The job?"*

*"Have me covered and claimed so that you can take my wealth for yourself."*

*He snorted. "For one thing, I don't think you're so stupid as to carry all your wealth with you. For another, I told you, I'm not like them. If I give you my word I'll not harm you, even to claim you, you can trust it."*

*"I should take you at your word? What assurances do you offer?"*

*"None. But you're smart enough to reason out that they will dog your steps until they find you. So, unless you kill them, you will always be looking over your shoulder. And one more thing, if we kill them both, you will only have the worry of facing down one wolf, should I turn out to be other than what I've said, rather than two. Better odds for you."*

*However, gazing into his stern features and standing chest to chest with him did nothing to relieve her fears. His steely glance didn't waiver once as she swept his face for hints of his thoughts. But he gave nothing away. His stillness as he suffered her inspection seemed to calm her own body, then her mind.*

*This man was worth a half dozen of the bastards she'd hired. And what choice did she really have? He could take her now before she had a chance to draw her own weapon. Further, if he was telling her the truth, this was a man who could help her build the force she needed, if he could be convinced to stay with her beyond this task.*

*She'd squared her shoulders and drawn a deep breath. "Your horse?"*

*"Outside. Tied to the post."*

*"Mine's in the stables. It will need to be saddled."*

*"I already took care of that."*

*"What?"*

*"I know who you are. It's why I'm here. I studied you all as you arrived, and knew you'd be needing my help sooner or later. I bided my time."*

*A strategist. Something else she needed. The man was growing more attractive by the moment. "Just so you know—I'm not seeking a mate."*

*"Nor am I. I'm a mercenary. I prefer to be free to leave whenever I choose."*

*Only he hadn't. As she'd huddled under blankets next to the fire he'd built, he'd stalked the two men, who snuck into her camp. They'd been dead before she'd had a chance to flip back her blanket.*

He'd won her respect for his skills that night, but over their long acquaintance he'd won so much more. She loved him. Perhaps not a romantic kind of love, but he was a solid man—of body and conscience. His blunt, canny observations and skill at battle had earned her respect. His steadfast loyalty and selfless devotion to her needs had earned her affection.

"Let me brush your hair," Xalia said softly.

Gabriella blinked, hoping her expression hadn't somehow betrayed her straying thoughts. "I can manage on my own. I'm not helpless."

"Would you deny me the pleasure?" Xalia's expression was guileless.

Feeling like an ogre, Gabriella gave her the brush. Xalia resumed the soothing strokes.

"How long have you been with Marduk?"

Xalia's laughter trilled. "I served the previous Master. So, a very, very long time."

Time had little meaning, Gabriella guessed, when one's days were spent doing the same things, over and over.

"Are you sore?" This came from Dagon, who stepped into view and knelt at her side to finger the rings at her breasts.

"Only mildly so," she said.

"Do you enjoy them?"

Gabriella couldn't hold back her grin. "Is this your function in life? To pierce women's sexual organs?"

Dagon laughed, which set Xalia giggling. "Only when I'm very, very lucky. I think Marduk didn't know whether to spank you or kiss you when he returned with you, so asking me to do the honors was just a way for him to save face."

Gabriella snorted and then shared in their laughter. The thought of Marduk confused about what to do with a woman was just too funny.

# CHAPTER
# 11

So what was he? That Dagon you sent to stick me?" she asked, clinging to Marduk's arm as they made their way toward the palace, purposely keeping her conversation light and constant, just to prick at him with high spirits. "Was he really a merman?"

Marduk grunted, but didn't respond.

She wondered if he was annoyed because he'd returned to the chamber, his arms filled with colorful fabric and jewels, to find the three of them laughing. Hardly the punishment he'd envisioned.

He'd been monosyllabic ever since.

With just a jut of his chin, he'd banished her companions from the room, then held out his hand—a gesture she was starting to despise because she couldn't resist the silent command.

Then he'd lifted his arm, turning her under it, his dark glance sliding over her skin, pausing on every bauble. His thumb had flicked the rings in her nipples, a finger traced the chain to her belly-button ring, which he toggled.

When he'd traced downward, her breath had caught, her eyelids dropping to half-mast, but much to her disappointment he'd skipped the clit ring. "Did he cause you pain?"

"Funny," she whispered, breathless beneath his relentless stare, "it was exquisite."

His lips had firmed; his golden eyes narrowed. His hand had tightened around hers and drew her against his body. His erection had jutted against her bare belly, and her pulse leaped. "Did he take you?"

"Was he supposed to?" she asked innocently.

When he damn near squinted at her through fierce slits, she decided he wasn't in the mood to be teased. Something she couldn't resist. "He aroused me only to . . . prick me," she said, in her best breathy "Marilyn"—which had the effect she desired.

He sank to his knees in front of her and lifted one of her legs over his shoulder. She dug her fingers into his hair . . . for balance . . . while he fingered her clit ring.

Her body responded instantly, and liquid arousal seeped to wet her folds. He skimmed it with a single fingertip and used it to lubricate the aroused knot, rubbing in circles and tapping the ring until she vibrated against him, an orgasm slamming through her too quickly to be truly satisfying.

When she slumped over him, he disentangled her fingers from his hair and slid her leg off his shoulder. When he rose, his cheeks were reddened, his lips moist with her juices. "These weren't meant for your enjoyment."

Gabriella didn't resent her new adornments or the implication they were intended to mark her as a slave. Marduk's reaction had been too delicious. The warm, sexy feeling his unintended lovemaking had left kept her on the edge.

Dagon had been right. Even hidden beneath layers of gauzy clothing, her breasts and clit tingled, remaining engorged because every scrap of fabric, every breath of air that touched her, kept her mildly aroused. She did, however, mind her multilayered harem outfit.

Xalia had dressed Gabriella, fitting a slim short skirt in a ripe berry hue around her hips and tying it together with a jeweled braid. Then a see-through tunic was pulled over Gabriella's head. The tunic was split at both sides, and fastened by a jeweled girdle around her waist. Bangles, all gold and studded with emeralds, sapphires, and rubies, encircled her wrists. A chain with golden bells, very like the ones Xalia wore was fastened around one ankle. A headdress comprised of a gauzy scarf covered her hair and cloaked her face. On her feet, she wore soft silk slippers.

The clothing barely hid her assets; the rings at her nipples merely denting the fabric and emphasizing their existence. The heavier jewelry made her feel as though she was indeed wearing a prisoner's chains.

Beside her, Marduk had forgone his usual dark medieval-style garb. Tonight, he wore only a linen kilt that left his powerful torso and hewn thighs bare. A gold armband surrounded his left forearm, and a crown bearing the same crest as his ring sat atop his dark hair. She'd been attracted to his well-made body from the start. Now, he took her breath away.

And the bastard knew it. While her gaze ate up every inch of him, the corners of his lips curled in a self-satisfied smirk.

Walking beside him through the darkened streets, she stayed close to him, touching him, as he'd instructed, to keep the nightmares at bay. She thought she might have clung like a leech, anyway, because of the slithering sounds that surrounded them. The streets were far from empty. Far from quiet.

Rasping whispers in the dark, low moans, an occasional shriek—she felt as though she was walking through a Halloween fun house, only the creatures hidden in the darkness weren't costumed monsters, they were the real thing.

Only because of Marduk's presence at her side did she remain unmolested.

They didn't have to travel far. Their route had taken them from Marduk's turreted tower set inside the curtain wall through narrow cobbled streets toward the center of the small city inside the fortress. As they drew closer, above the tiled roofs, Gabriella caught glimpses of the inner wall surrounding the palace.

Another full moon shone from the sky, silvering the cobblestone beneath her feet and lending a soft, fairy-tale-like patina to the pale sandstone walls they approached. A barred gate rose slowly on creaking gears to let them enter, but they were stopped by a creature with the head of a bull and the body of a very beefy man, who stepped into their path.

Marduk's hand slid over hers on his arm, but he remained quiet.

The bull-man nodded to Marduk, then turned to Gabriella.

Her eyes rounded as his face drew nearer. It was enormous,

his nostrils flaring; humid heat gusted in her face with his snort. "The Mistress of the Dead demands tribute."

"Tribute?" she said faintly.

"Give him your bracelets," Marduk said softly.

Frowning, she slid them over her wrists and deposited them in the beast's open palm.

The bull-man bowed and swept out his arm. "Enter, lady. May you find joy in Kur-gal this night."

She watched the bull-man's lips move, bemused, but Marduk gave her a gentle shake. "You were staring," he whispered, bending toward her ear as they walked away.

"I couldn't help it. I was talking to a cow."

Marduk chuckled beside her, and Gabriella felt lighthearted again. So, they'd entered the Queen of the Dead's palace—she should have expected a surprise or two.

The gate opened into a flagstone-paved courtyard filled with a lush profusion of fragrant flowers and guests. A fountain burbled in the center where several people sat, some with feet dangling in the water, watching a nude woman turning her face into the spill from a marble penis.

There were scantily dressed dancers in gauzy costumes even more revealing than her own moving among the milling guests, like characters straight from an *Arabian Nights* tale. More creatures like the bull-man at the gate were interspersed among the guests—hybrids produced through humans' crossbreeding with goats, horses, and birds—male and female parts exposed as they roamed. And while clothing seemed an option, so far, this party wasn't the orgy of lust she'd half expected.

"You seem disappointed," he said softly.

She blinked. "No . . . just surprised. I'd expected something less like a frat party."

"That term doesn't translate well, but I'll assume you were thinking that only sex and violence would occur here. We have only reached the first level of the entertainments. We have farther to go."

He guided her toward the back of the courtyard and through another set of gates, guarded by a pair of bored-looking twins—male and seemingly all human. Their gazes sharpened on her, then turned to Marduk, to whom they bowed. "What tribute do you offer, Bel?" they said in unison.

Gabriella quirked an eyebrow, knowing what was coming.

"Your headdress and tiara should suffice," Marduk said, so casually, she knew this was a game for him and he was waiting for her to balk.

Without complaint, she gave the items to the twins and was waved through gate with another, "May you find joy in Kur-gal."

"What's Kur-gal?"

"The name of an ancient Sumerian city, and what Irkalla fashioned this palace to be. She insists on ceremony. The first time Inanna entered these gates long ago, Irkalla forced her through the same ritual as you are going through now. It's now used to acclimate all new guests to her rule."

The gate they passed through opened into a hall filled with tables laden with large round trays of food—roasted lambs' heads sitting in mounds of saffron rice, fruit of every description, round flat breads that the guests tore with their fingers and fed to their companions as laughter and goblets of wine were raised in the air.

"A party and a feast," she said faintly, her heart rate beginning to escalate. "Other than the costumes, this doesn't look so different from the hall where I arrived."

"Here there are no penitents serving their guts to demons as punishment. They won't be bathing in blood anytime soon."

"But there are human dead and demons here."

"These undead have been elevated from the cursed halls through favors they've given to their masters."

"What sorts of favors earn them this reward?"

Marduk took her hand and lifted it to his mouth, drawing her gaze from the tables to his dark, penetrating gaze.

"Does sex earn them rewards?" she blurted. "Is it because they are more attractive?"

"Or more skilled. They also trade in information. Like when a particularly succulent living woman fled my captivity."

"So you don't have to set watchers. All the undead would scramble to be the first to sound an alert?"

Marduk's smile didn't alleviate her unease. "I wouldn't mislead you. You should know you have no recourse but to behave."

She looked around them. There were empty spaces at the benches pulled up to long trench tables. "We aren't staying here either? Will you feed me sometime tonight? My stomach's growling." Then her gaze fell on one of the baked lambs' heads and she shuddered. "But I can wait . . ."

"We will stop in the next chamber to eat. The crowd is smaller. Not quite so loud. And you will meet our rulers."

Gabriella's breath caught when he dropped her hand and turned. She waited for a second, frozen, but the nightmare didn't consume her. Assuming the palace was enchanted, just as his chamber was, she rushed to stay close behind him as he strode to the side of the room and a set of golden doors.

Even before they reached the guards—a rank of identical creatures, all sporting jackals' heads and dressed in short golden kirtles—she was pulling her tunic off over her head. She dropped it into the hand of the jackal-man closest to the doors.

Which left her only with the silken slippers, slave's bracelets and anklets, and the short skirt.

Her breasts with their new adornments prickled as the jackals' gazes swept her nearly nude form.

"Come," Marduk said, grabbing her arm and sweeping past the long rank, ignoring the customary welcome they intoned.

Inside the rulers' private hall, Gabriella's eyes widened. Gold shimmered wherever her gaze rested—on the cutlery, the plates, even the mosaic studded with precious stones beneath her feet. But it was the two figures seated atop a dais stretching along the back of the hall that glittered brightest of all.

Dressed in a silk tunic embroidered in gold thread and wearing a golden crown shaped like a Quaker oatmeal box and more jewelry on his wrists and fingers than she'd started this adventure with, the King of the Dead was a short, corpulent figure. Hunched over his plate, he was seemingly unaware that his queen's rapacious gaze clung to Marduk's frame as he strolled into the room.

Marduk had dropped his hand from her arm, gesturing silently that she must enter after him.

She didn't resent being relegated to the rear. Staying three steps behind him, her head lowered, she watched everything from the corners of her downcast eyes.

All the occupants of the room, save the king and queen, were staring at her.

Gabriella trembled as dozens of demons assessed her body with greedy eyes, lifting noses to catch her scent as she passed. Did they smell life? Or a meal?

Marduk walked directly to the front of the dais and bent at the waist. "My queen," he said softly, giving her a small, tight smile. Then he nodded to the king. "Sire."

When he looked over his shoulder, his gaze compelled her to do the same. She swept into a curtsy, made awkward by the fact her short skirt pulled upward and she didn't really want to flash her ass to the entire assemblage, but her attempt seemed to please the woman, whose wedge-like crown sparkled with diamonds and rubies. "Marduk, I'm so glad you recaptured your little pet."

Gabriella ground her teeth at the woman's tone, sarcasm served in whiskey-laced syrup.

Still, she couldn't help but stare at Irkalla—she was the mirror image of her sister, Inanna; same long swath of raven hair, dusky skin, large, almond-shaped eyes. Her lips were just as lushly formed, but the corners tipped just the slightest bit downward. Was the power she'd amassed in this realm a bitter reward?

"She didn't wander far," Marduk murmured.

Irkalla's gaze studied Gabriella's body, pausing on her ripened breasts. "We're pleased she seems to have come through her ordeal unscathed."

Gabriella felt heat warm her cheeks and breasts. She wanted badly to join the conversation, irritated that they spoke as though she hadn't a thought of her own.

Instead, she surreptitiously studied the other woman's attributes, knowing Marduk had enjoyed them all. And she conceded the comparison—her own sturdy body against Irkalla's lushly endowed frame—didn't serve her well. Irkalla needn't worry when she gazed into the mirror and asked, "Who's the fairest of us all . . . ?"

Her only competition would be her equally beautiful sister.

Dressed as Irkalla was, her station proclaimed in a gold-embroidered silk sheath and a broad, gold collar encrusted with large pearls and bloodred jewels that lay flat against her chest, Inanna didn't stand a chance of outshining her sister.

As Marduk and Irkalla traded pleasantries, Gabriella shifted restlessly. She had so many questions begging for answers. She'd yet to see anything faintly reminiscent of the hell she'd been schooled to expect. This Land of the Dead seemed disappointingly tame. Not that she wasn't grateful that fire wasn't licking her skin. But still. As decadent as the sex had been with Marduk, she'd had darker, more deliciously frightening times spent in human "hells" and dungeons.

Suddenly, the downward curves of Irkalla's lips slowly lifted, and her gaze fell on something right behind Gabriella.

She couldn't resist peeking around her shoulder to see what amused the queen. Her gaze slammed into Inanna's narrowed eyes. The vampire was led by a massively built, handsome man who held the end of a long silver chain attached to a studded black collar. Inanna's chin tilted upward, a proud captive, her completely nude body gleaming with a light application of oil.

Gabriella silently promised to thank Marduk the first chance she got for not humiliating her in that fashion.

Her gaze went back to the man who held the repulsive leash. So, this was Dumuzi's true face? Inanna's husband had apparently shed the skin of the man he'd inhabited last in the other realm, Pasqual.

How had Inanna ever thought to rule him? His body, clothed only in a red kirtle, exuded power and sensuality. His features were rugged, completely masculine. His dark, narrowed gaze landed on Gabriella, and he smiled.

She shivered at the calculating way his gaze dropped to her breasts, then to the tender area just beneath her rib cage. She remembered the way he'd ripped the heart out of Alex's phoenix, his cupped fingers plunging beneath her ribs and hooking upward, only to pull away, holding her still-beating heart in his hand.

Here was a hint of the wicked darkness. And then she wondered about the others at the tables in this hall, so seemingly civilized and well behaved. What sorts of beastly secrets did they carry inside their souls?

She edged closer to Marduk, felt his hand settle on her waist, and trembled with relief, her courage bolstered by his support.

"You're already acquainted with my sister and her husband, yes?" Irkalla drawled.

Gabriella nodded. "We've met."

"Old friends then?"

Inanna's lips tightened, and she gave Gabriella a contemptuous stare at odds with the vulnerability of her appearance. "Never. Do you think I would consort with a werebeast?"

"Now, now, sister," Irkalla said, amusement in her tone. "Lord Marduk might take umbrage to your comment. He's also a shape-shifter, although he never stinks of dog. Won't you join us, Marduk? A place will be made for your little slave, too. Dumuzi, would you like to sit beside them and renew your acquaintance?"

Dumuzi's head lowered, his smile stretching his thin lips. "I would be honored to share your table. And my slave will behave this time."

Inanna's nostrils flared and her lips tightened, but she held the rebuke that Gabriella knew had to be burning inside her. The proud bitch had been humbled here. But Gabriella couldn't work up any pity for the vampire.

Marduk led the strange procession around the end of the dais and climbed up the steps, taking a seat beside Irkalla, whose cheeks flared with excited color. A kneeler, like a church's psalter was placed beside Marduk for her to take. Dumuzi had a chair, but Inanna had her own kneeler, which placed both their heads lower than anyone else's at the table—annoying, but Gabriella wasn't the one who had to make a place for herself in this world. She let the insult roll off her proud shoulders while Inanna's gaze smoldered.

Without any spoken command, servers arrived in front of the table with gold plates and finely crafted chalices to set before Dumuzi and Marduk. Wine was poured; trays of meat, fish and vegetables, honeyed fruits were offered.

Marduk took samplings of all the foods, using his fingers to take bites. After he'd taken several, he offered her tidbits, feeding her like a favored pet.

She didn't mind. When a sliver of beef was placed on her tongue, she sucked on the finger, licking up the warm juice.

His fingertip glided along her bottom lip when he pulled it away, and suddenly she was getting hot again, her eyes closing to relish the sweep of that finger, her nipples tightening, the golden rings offering a pinching sting that stimulated her further.

When she opened her eyes, the heat in his gaze told her he knew exactly what she felt. But he turned his head toward Irkalla to talk, ignoring her now, stoking resentment and a stirring of surprising jealousy, but also a slow-burning heat, because she knew the meal was one long tease and that she'd be sharing Marduk with another woman by the looks of Irkalla's delighted smile.

Then Dumuzi's hand landed on her shoulder, wrapping around the curve and squeezing.

Gabriella's heartbeat slowed to a dull thud against her chest, and she held her breath while his fingers trailed between her breasts and downward, circling in teasing forays just below her ribs.

"Stop playing with her," Irkalla said, laughter in her voice. "She must know Marduk isn't ready to let you have her heart."

"Pity. I've never tasted wolf." His gaze cut to Inanna, who glared at Gabriella. "Perhaps, if you are good tonight, Irkalla will let you drink from the wolf."

Irkalla lifted her hand and a server bolted forward, bowing in front of the table. "What may I bring you, mistress?"

"Something rare for my sister, but something still beating for her master." Her gaze landed on Gabriella. "Have no fears this night. We will all seek our pleasures. Even you."

Marduk remained silent beside her, his lips curved into a wicked smile. The threatening undercurrents swirling around them didn't seem to concern him.

Gabriella relaxed, taking her cue from his easy posture. His fingers fed her another tidbit of meat and she wolfed it down, knowing she'd need her belly full.

The hand still stroking over her ribs climbed upward, cupped a breast, and toggled the golden circle. "So pretty, these little beads," Dumuzi said. "I'd love to see them trembling . . ." His hand slid away. "Perhaps later."

Gabriella clasped her hands in her lap and waited to be fed although her appetite had waned. Whatever came, she'd have to trust that Marduk's influence would keep her safe, however much the others at this table might want to torment her with hints of harm.

The irony that she was placing her trust in a demon didn't escape her. Marduk might have pulled her into hell, but he'd protected her and kept her nightmares at bay.

For as long as it took for Guntram to craft their escape, she'd play along and do her best to enjoy the licentious pleasures offered, but only because fighting would be a waste of energy.

Never one to shy away from sensual adventure, she also admitted that she possessed a ravenous curiosity and had no doubts this night would be filled with new experiences.

# CHAPTER 12

Guntram eyed the iron gate they'd have to pass through to get into the palace. A large half-bull, half-human creature stood unmoving beside it, gripping a wicked-looking spear. "Somehow, I don't think he'll just let us walk through. I hope you have a better plan."

Every step closer to his goal presented a new hurdle. He and Simon waited a hundred feet from the entrance, hiding behind the corner of a building. Had been for over an hour. Long enough to see Gabriella and her "master" enter the palace's gates and disappear inside.

He almost hadn't recognized her. Dressed like a harem slut, she'd clung to the dragon shifter's arm, smiling easily into the man's hard-edged face as though she didn't fear his fierce expression—as though she'd placed complete trust in this man for her safety.

With his stomach churning, he hadn't been able to take his gaze from Gabriella's tall, curvy body. She walked with a sinuous grace, her eyes sparkling.

Even from so far away, he'd caught the heady aroma of her arousal and a desperate fury filled him. He was so close. But was he already too late? He'd told Simon there was no way she'd choose to remain with her captor, but now he wasn't so sure.

Further, Simon's plan wasn't getting them any closer to that gate.

Dressed in their smelly borrowed clothing, they walked in stumbling, erratic circles, pretending to be plagued by invisible horrors like the rest of the lost souls hovering in the street.

Guntram halted and stuck his hands on his hips, eyeing the walls and wondering whether he could simply shift and jump over it.

"Have some patience, Guntram," Simon said. "I'm waiting for the right mark . . . and he's here."

A man strode down the street, nearing the corner, but still out of sight of the guard.

Simon lifted his chin, signaling he'd made his choice, and ambled forward, headed directly for the tall, golden-haired creature, who was dressed in a white toga-like garment. The creature's skin seemed almost translucent in the fading light.

"Dagon," Simon called softly.

The man's head turned, blue eyes narrowing. "Do I know you?"

"No, but we must borrow something from you."

"I don't think so," the demon said, pushing past him.

"Hold him," Simon said calmly.

Glad for an excuse for a little violence, Guntram leapt for the demon, taking him easily to the ground. The demon bucked and wriggled beneath him, but Guntram slammed his knee into the center of his back, pinning him and pushing the air from his lungs so that he couldn't catch a breath and shout for help.

"Raise his face."

Guntram grabbed the demon's blond hair and dragged his head upward.

Simon uncurled one palm, revealing a purple powder in his palm, which he blew into the demon's face.

The blond creature's eyes rolled back, and he slumped beneath Guntram. "Dress him in your robe."

Guntram pulled him to an alleyway and quickly stripped the reeking garment over his head and pulled it over the man's still form, yanking up the hood to hide his face.

Standing only in his trousers and military boots, Guntram watched as Simon knelt beside the demon and glided his hand over his still face. Then he lifted the same hand and slid it over his own. Simon's body transformed, shifting into an exact copy of the unconscious man.

"That's disturbing," Guntram murmured.

The full lips of Simon's borrowed face curved. Then he slung the bag he'd carried from Ninshubur's home onto the ground beside the demon's still form. He dug into it, pulling out a leather mask, which he tossed at Guntram. "Put this over your head. No one knows you here, but the mask will mark you as a player in tonight's entertainment. We should have no trouble entering now."

Guntram pulled the mask over his head.

Simon tossed him a small jar next. "Rub this salve into your skin. It will mask your scent. We can't have anyone making you as a wolf."

Guntram slathered the oily salve over his skin, wrinkling his nose at the scent of almonds, lavender, and sandalwood. The demons around them might not identify him as a wolf, but they might wonder about his preferences.

Then he followed Simon in his new skin around the corner and toward the gates of the palace.

The bull-man bowed, demanding tribute. Simon pulled a strand of perfect pearls from a leather purse at his belted waist.

Had he taken them from the demon or produced them from the air? Guntram didn't think much was beyond his companion's capabilities, but let the thought go because they were through the door and entering a courtyard.

There was no sign of Gabriella. He mentioned it.

Simon grimaced. "You hardly thought it would be that easy."

They passed a fountain and a woman bobbed from beneath the surface of the water to spit a stream of water on his feet as he passed. Guntram spared her a quick glare, but she merely laughed. "What's next?" he asked, his shoulders bunching with the need to release some more of the frustration he'd been storing up for hours. "Other than finding her tonight, what do you hope to accomplish?"

"As I told you yesterday, you must get close enough to tell

her we're arranging her escape. If you can, ask her for the identities of her master's companions so that we can approach them and find one willing to help us."

"Do you really think any of them would cross him?"

"Some will be jealous of the attention he pays her."

"So, a girl."

Simon shrugged, dropping his voice as they approached a set of twins at another gate. "I know you're worried about her. And you have good reason, but we can't take her from here. Too many guards. Too many layers of protection. The first thing you have to find out is whether she's willing to leave."

"Do you really think she might want to stay?"

"Some find their dreams answered in this place. You saw her. Did she seem afraid for her fate?"

"She might have been acting or just making the best of a bad situation," he said, hoping like hell it was true.

"You won't know for sure until you talk to her."

"How will I approach her?"

Simon smiled and slapped his back. "You're part of the entertainment—entertain."

Guntram cursed softly, following behind Simon as he bartered to get through the next set of gates. Again, he found no sign of Gabriella or the tall, dark demon who'd escorted her here.

Once inside the gilded hall, he and Simon hovered at the doorway. At last, Guntram found her, sitting beside the demon at the head table. From the waist up she was nude, and she was leaning against the demon, who absently fed her slivers of meat from his own plate like a dog.

That she wasn't baring her teeth at the outrage was telling.

That she sat so still, so calmly beside her master bothered him even more. Gabriella was a vibrant woman, always animated. She seemed subdued, and yet she wasn't tethered, wasn't even wearing a collar to restrain her. Her gaze never left the man beside her. Had he mesmerized her? Or had he seduced her, taking her will?

She appeared unharmed, as beautiful as ever, but lacking that hint of inner fire he'd always admired.

Simon grabbed his arm. "Come. We aren't staying here. When they're finished eating, they'll head to the dungeon. Let's get there ahead of them."

Guntram dragged his gaze from her, submerging his doubts, and followed again while Simon offered another tribute and entered a corridor that ended in a steep stone staircase.

The staircase led down into darkness unrelieved by any source of light. The air was warm and humid. The scent of sex and musky sweat was carried on a breeze that swept up the steps, providing an intoxicating trail into the depths beneath the great palace. They passed the last layer of the palace's stone foundation and continued down a hollowed cavern.

Guntram's eyes adjusted to the darkness as he descended. "With all the rooms above, Irkalla chooses to play in a cave?"

"Caves are nescient. Places where life is birthed. Where sins are hidden."

"Where screaming won't call attention?"

"That, too, I'm sure. She may have a very open marriage to Nergal, but she chooses not to flaunt her indiscretions."

The steps ended, and crude torches in sconces were mounted on the wall, lighting a long passage that Guntram had to hunch his shoulders to traverse. Built to Irkalla's height, no doubt.

Thankfully, it was a short passage and opened into a room not unlike some of the dungeons in the sex clubs Gabriella liked to frequent. Sumptuous carpeting covered the floor. The black stone walls were unrelieved except for the hundreds of candles burning to shed light around the room. Tall candelabra were situated to cast light into the shadowy center of the room. Legless sofas, little more than Persian bolster cushions, and pillows filled the center of the enormous space. A long equipment rack stretched along one wall, filled with floggers of every length and material, whips, cat-o'-nine-tails, masks and blindfolds, and ropes.

"Choose your equipment now. Those who are invited will be coming soon. Choose your space or a room along that corridor. Whatever you think will intrigue your princess."

Guntram followed Simon's gesture toward a row of cells with iron bars—viewing rooms for sexual performances. He passed one with chains and manacles set into the stone wall, then another with a rack. When he found a cell containing a platform with padded steps, he slowed and entered it. The platform allowed a supplicant to kneel over a padded bench, buttocks pointing toward the back wall. The player in this drama would be the center of attention while he applied whips and floggers to the supplicant's ass. If he decided to fuck her, their faces would be viewed, but little else.

He chose this room knowing Gabriella would enjoy a sexy spanking from an anonymous master. He strode back to the main room, chose his implements from the display rack and returned. All the while, he mused at how ironic it was that his long-held wish was about to come true. He'd entered Gabriella's fantasy world and might just get the chance to provide her the pleasure of punishment she needed to achieve sexual release. If all went according to plan, he'd reveal himself while she was still bound to the bench. Then at last, he'd take her, *cover her*, and make her his own.

First, he'd need her to be mindless with desire. But he'd had centuries of studying her, watching over her while she'd lost herself in passion with others. By the time she understood what was happening, it would be too late for her to change her mind. The deed done.

It didn't matter that there would be no witnesses to bear the truth of their mating to the pack. If she chose to deny him later, at least he'd know the truth.

For the first time since he'd entered this damned place, Guntram was fiercely glad to be there. Tonight, the Wolfen bitch he'd longed for would at last be his.

Gabriella followed Marduk, holding her questions, her tongue stilled by the look he'd given her when his queen had finally finished her meal and risen.

Irkalla had kissed her husband's cheek and wished him a good rest, quietly offering him his choices of entertainments to be delivered to his chambers.

After he'd left, she surveyed the hall, and all the eager faces turned her way. She'd made quick work of choosing her playmates for the evening. Everyone at the head table was invited, naturally. Then she'd chosen only the most virile and well-hung males and women whose lustful expressions portrayed a feral yet sensual bent. Then she'd swept toward the doors, leading her odd assortment of guests down a long dark stairwell.

Gabriella had followed close on Marduk's heels, aware of Dumuzi's presence at her back and Inanna's malevolent presence behind him. When the party had spilled into a dungeon-like chamber, she'd breathed a sigh of relief that here was something familiar.

"Unfamiliar" would be entering this kind of place with someone she actually knew. When she'd entered clubs like this back in her own world, she'd entered as a stranger consorting with strangers. Here, Marduk's darkening gaze held her, warning her silently that his generosity was limited.

She wished she understood exactly what he might punish her for enjoying, but shrugged. Already Irkalla hovered at his elbow, ready to lead him toward one of the many low couches. He followed, looking over his shoulder only once before turning to the queen to undress her.

The others took their cue from the pair, dropping their clothes where they stood. Gabriella, not wanting to feel any more conspicuous than she already was, untied the short linen skirt and left it in a puddle.

"Your master has abandoned you," Dumuzi murmured, his hand still wrapped around Inanna's black leather leash.

"He's not my master," Gabriella said, then wished she'd bitten her tongue.

Dumuzi's soft laughter drifted around her, raising the hairs on the back of her neck. The last thing she wanted was to invite more attention from him.

"Marduk is very proud," he said, "and covetous. He would disagree."

"Well, his opinion seems to hold some sway here. You'd do well to remember that."

"You were left to play here. Just another playmate to service the members of the queen's court." His intent gaze told her he meant to make use of that fact.

But she didn't want to play with him. Her gaze locked with Inanna's, whose expression was tight. She seemed afraid.

"I'd like to see what entertainments are offered here," Gabriella said with a small, strained smile.

Dumuzi lifted his hand and waved to a servant carrying a silver tray filled with beakers of red liquid. He chose two drinks, offering her one and sipping at his own.

"Everyone's so . . . busy," he said softly.

Her gaze followed his. He was right. All around them there was movement, rhythmic, surging—bodies standing, lying, straddling. Only Dumuzi, Inanna, and herself stood perfectly still, untouched by the fervor slowly building inside the room.

Untouched but not unaroused, she conceded, feeling her own core melt, moisture trickling downward.

"Your master isn't pleased that you're talking with me," he said slyly.

Marduk was seated on a sofa, surrounded by naked women. The queen knelt on the cushion beside him and was sliding her tongue into his ear. Hands stroked his flesh, petted his sex, but his gaze bored into hers.

Gabriella arched an eyebrow, letting him see her gaze land on every one of his companions before meeting his again—her point underlined. She was free to take her own pleasure.

His lips thinned, but Gabriella wasn't afraid of retribution. She looked forward to it.

For now, she stood beside a monster who kept eyeing her chest. Whether he liked the shape of her bosom or was fixated on the heart lying beneath it, she didn't care. He didn't dare harm her.

However, he did dare to move closer, his hand sliding over her hip, then skimming over her ass to give her a squeeze.

Gabriella knew she should move away immediately. Her body was already betraying her. The sounds building around her—low, heated murmurs, soft seductive laughter, moist caresses—had her nipples tightening into erect little points.

And the aromas! Lord, she couldn't take a breath without smelling sex . . . yeasty, musky, sweaty . . .

The urge to shake out her fur and howl was nearly overpowering—and then she felt it, the inner tension that coiled ruthlessly around her womb—and she moaned.

How had she missed it? The cramping that preceded ovulation had passed unnoticed. No wonder she'd been so docile, so content to wallow in the lust her new master had induced.

Was that it? Or had something extra been in the drink Dumuzi had given her? Something to force her into season? But why would anyone bother to go to such an extreme? Sex for the thrill, for the release was always possible for a wolf, but not imperative. At least not outside those days when her body craved seed to procreate. Good Lord, and it was happening now.

She swayed on her feet, feeling the urge to fall to the floor on her hands and knees and back her ass up to the first dick willing to penetrate her.

However, she'd be left unfulfilled. Only a male of her species could provide the ultimate relief. Only their cocks could swell deep inside her and lock within her channel. She'd never done it, never allowed it. Couldn't remain in the company of a male wolf when this blinding need hit her.

She glanced wildly around the room, ready to approach a man, any man. When she glanced back at Dumuzi, his eyes narrowed. His head canted, a faint smile tipping the corners of his mouth. "Are you all right?"

"Fine," she bit out, folding an arm across her breast as

though shielding herself from his avid gaze would somehow lessen her arousal. "It stinks in here. There's no air."

"It's bound to get worse for someone with such a sensitive nose. But you seem uncomfortable. Are you aroused?"

"I'm fine."

"Perhaps you like watching others taking their pleasure. I invite you to watch me taking my conjugal rights."

And because watching was preferable to letting the bastard touch her, she didn't move.

He tugged on the leash he held, pulling Inanna behind him, and approached one of the hybrid creatures, one of the bull-men, whose huge head dipped as Dumuzi leaned close and whispered his instructions.

Inanna's eyes widened and her head shook, her poise destroyed.

Dumuzi wound the leash around and around his fist, drawing her closer, then pulled his hand down, forcing her to her knees in front of him. "Remember how you took me the first time, wife?" he said silkily, his free hand sinking into her thick hair. He flexed his hips forward, his cock sliding along her cheek. "With your mouth after you slipped me your wizard's powder. I'd like to rekindle that memory. Open to me."

He glared into her sullen face, and slowly Inanna relented, opening her mouth.

With his hand wrapped around himself, he fed her his dick, sliding it between her lips. "No teeth," he said, tapping her nose with a finger. "Don't even think it."

Her mouth widened, her lips folding around her teeth. Dumuzi's chest rose swiftly as her mouth enclosed him.

Gabriella's own breaths quickened along her with heartbeats. His cock was lovely—long and thick, with a slight upward curve. Her cunt tightened, softened. Slick moisture slid between her thighs.

Slowly, he fucked Inanna's mouth, giving her shallow strokes and seeming to savor the suctioning of her lips.

For a moment, a look passed between husband and wife, something that caused a wave of prickling heat to sweep over her own chest and belly. His dark-eyed gaze never left Inanna's; her eyes grew liquid . . . with remorse? Or was it a plea for mercy?

Dumuzi's mouth firmed and curved. His strokes became sharper, driving deeper into her throat. A subtle shifting of his feet provided a signal.

The bull-man stepped behind Inanna and knelt. His human hands glided down her sides, clutched her hips and pulled her ass toward his groin. The massive red cock standing against his belly glided between Inanna's buttocks.

The bitch queen of New Orleans was getting ready to service a bull. Gabriella should have felt satisfaction at the woman's plight as Inanna's desperate gaze locked with her husband's, but instead, all Gabriella felt was jealousy.

That massive cock would fill her, stretch her inner walls, and plunge so deeply that it would pound against her cervix. His seed would be useless, but the urge to mate would be abated for at least as long as it took for her heart to slow and her body to ready herself for another partner.

Inanna's buttocks jiggled with the strength of the beast's thrusts. Her voice, muffled by the cock she'd swallowed, grunted harshly. Still, the woman was aroused; white, creamy streaks glazed the bull's cock. Her skin flushed, perspiration glowing.

Dumuzi stroked into her, forcing her take him deeper

and deeper, until she gurgled and choked. And yet her lips gripped him, her head bobbed, taking him, swallowing his cum down when his eyes slid closed and his hips jerked.

When he backed away from her, he stood to the side as the bull-man pushed her head to the floor and gripped her buttocks to power harder and deeper into her.

Gabriella didn't even jump when Dumuzi stood behind her and smoothed his hand over her belly and downward, fingers slipping between her folds. "Watch him fuck her. Would you like to take her place, feel his bull's cock crowd so thick and hard inside, you'll think he's going to split you in two?"

"He'd fit," she bit out, then wish she'd sunk her teeth into her lips, because he knew how excited she was—his fingers were soaked in cream.

His thumb touched her clitoris, then fluttered on it. Not enough to do it for her, but enough to tease. She clamped her thighs closed, trying to halt his exploration, but her muscles quivered, hugging him more than stopping him.

"Bend over. I'll make it quick."

"You're spent. Useless for a little while."

"I have a fist. Broad as that cock you're so fascinated watching."

She whimpered, but still resisted the urge to comply with his demand.

"Once, I was a man," he whispered in her ear. "She sent me here. Gave me to her sister, who transformed me. She murdered our son. I've survived ever since, living for just one goal. To see her punished. To know she's remorseful for destroying my family."

"Do you think I should pity you? You've murdered innocents to feed your appetite for beating hearts."

"I don't want your pity. Just your submission. I will treat you well. I have no grudge against you."

She snorted. "No grudge? Even though I played my own part in returning you here?"

"Alex was responsible. It was inevitable. He actually did me a great service. Inanna hates living under her sister's thumb." His thumb stroked her clit again.

Her body vibrated, but she held firm despite the warmth of the broad chest pressing closer to her back.

The bull shuddered behind Inanna and made a low, growling moan—a sound that made Inanna wince. "If he moos I'll kill him," she muttered, but she sank lower to the carpet, strained whimpers gusting from her, until at last she screamed.

Dumuzi chuckled and removed his hand from between Gabriella's legs. "The moment has passed. I'll find you later."

She didn't know whether to be disappointed or relieved, but took a deep breath.

In control of herself again, Gabriella shook back her hair. She gave the demon a look filled with loathing and strode quickly away, ready to put space between herself and the wicked couple.

When she turned, she bumped into another body, this one clothed. Her hands came up automatically to push him away.

"Gabriella!" Dagon said, his voice sounding somehow off, different.

"You again," she said, trying to recover her poise.

He smiled, humor gleaming in his blue eyes. "Enjoying yourself?"

Not sure what the expected answer was, she shrugged. "Not taking part in the games?"

"Perhaps later. Your master is watching."

Gabriella stiffened. She needed to find some privacy. To regroup. To gain control of the fluctuating ardor roiling through her body—or she might do something that would draw too much attention and reveal her problem. The thought of demons surrounding her, taking turns, was too reminiscent of another heat. She needed a partner. Just one.

"If you're looking to escape the crowd, you might find what you need down that hallway."

She didn't ask how he'd guessed. Didn't want to let him know his instinct had been dead-on. She shoved past him toward the corridor he'd indicated.

Desperate, she escaped down the corridor and discovered a row of cell-like rooms filled with the sounds of more creatures having sex, until she stumbled past one with a lone figure standing in the dark behind a platform, the purpose of which she instantly gleaned. A kneeler. A spanking bench.

And if anyone needed punishment, needed her flesh scoured to erase the shame left by the arousal a demon had built inside her, it was her.

# CHAPTER 13

May I serve you, mistress?" the man standing in the darkness said softly.

She looked behind her down the long, dark corridor, assuring herself that she hadn't been followed. "I . . . I think so. Yes."

He stepped from the shadows, and Gabriella's gaze swept over him. Her lust renewed instantly. His human form pleased her. Bare-chested, thick brown fur covering his chest, he appeared so like Guntram she nearly cried. She wondered what horror the mask hid, but decided she didn't really want to know. Maybe he was handsome—one of the undead humans, just playing the executioner role for entertainment purposes.

His scent was unusual. Beneath a light floral lay an earthier aroma, pleasing to her nose. She stepped inside the cell and slid the barred door closed behind her. "What do you offer?"

"Any fantasy you desire," he said, his voice deep and gruff.

She shivered at his tone, her nipples prickling to attention. Light didn't penetrate the deep, hollow shadows of the mask. She couldn't tell where his glance roamed, and she wondered if she pleased him half as much.

"Would you prefer I take you?" he said, slowly, still rooted to the spot. "Will you submit to me?"

"I think I'd like to be surprised," she replied, surprised her voice sounded so breathy.

"Will you allow me to bind you?" he said, his voice less hesitant, less submissive than before.

Excited by her own powerful response to just his voice, she gave him a flirtatious glance, peering up at him from beneath her lashes. "I'll allow it, so long as you promise not to eat me while I'm helpless."

"Why limit our pleasure?"

Gabriella's lips twitched. "I belong to Marduk. So long as I walk out of here unharmed, you can do pretty much what you like."

"Marduk, the Master of the Demons. Do you enjoy his bed?"

Something in his voice, a simmering disapproval, made her uncomfortable. "I . . . do what I must."

His head ducked, acknowledging the ambiguity of her reply.

Gabriella found herself enjoying this encounter, enjoying

the sight of the man who drew nearer now. When he lifted his hand, his palm turned upward, she didn't hesitate as she had the first time Marduk demanded.

This man's hand was calloused, his palm so large it engulfed hers. He drew her closer, his nostrils flaring. Had he caught the telltale scent of her heat? Would he know what it meant?

"Will he come looking for you anytime soon?" he asked, urgency making his words clipped.

"He's occupied at the moment."

"Then we're alone."

The cage door wasn't solid, but somehow the acoustics of the small chamber softened the sounds from beyond its confines, enhancing the feeling that indeed they really were alone.

He pulled her close enough that the baubles attached to her nipples tangled in his chest hair. The slight tug caused the sensitized tips to swell. She moved closer. "Are you expecting anyone else?"

"I've been waiting for you. I chased off the last demon who tried to enter my cell."

"And he allowed it?"

His lips twitched. "I think I frightened him. I might have mentioned a preference for roasted balls."

Gabriella tossed back her hair, enjoying the humor he revealed beneath his fearsome mask. "And do you?"

"The only thing I wish to warm is you," he said quietly.

Gabriella licked her lips, tilting back her head. "With flame . . . or friction?"

"Do you have a preference?"

"You're teasing me now."

"But you aren't sure."

"Even when things seem similar to what I'm accustomed to . . . I sometimes find myself surprised here."

"Caution is wise."

"Then we should hurry. Marduk is busy at the moment. Why waste another minute?" When he still didn't bust a move, she lifted her hand to cup the curve of his masculine breast. Muscle flexed beneath her palm. "However you want me, I'm yours."

His square jaw tightened, and he nodded toward the bench behind her. "Bend over it. I will ease the tension riding you. Then we'll play."

She didn't ask how he knew. Perhaps all of them knew instinctually. Usually, back in her own world, only wolves sensed her heat. But right now, holding a thought, following a suspicion was beyond her. A heady, powerful swell of arousal held her in its grip. It might have had something to do with the cock encased in his dark trousers and pressing against her belly, which was quickly filling, its size pleasing—not as disgustingly large as the bull-man's, but exactly proportioned for her enjoyment.

Giving him a challenging tilt of her chin, she tugged her hand from his tight grip and stepped away. Then she turned and climbed onto the platform, settling her knees on a padded step and her belly on the platform, the edge of which ended just beneath her breasts. The position made her feel immediately vulnerable, completely feminine. Her ass was presented in exactly the pose a she-wolf might provide her mate for his inspection.

A deep, slow intake of breath was the only reaction she could discern from the man in the mask. He walked behind the bench and silently urged her to widen her stance, pressing against her knees until he was satisfied. Then he walked to one side and lifted her hand and closed leather straps around her wrist, repeating the action for her other hand.

Gabriella felt no alarm, no fear. Although he remained silent, his methodical approach was reassuring. That was, until he made another slow circle around her, and she sensed his body tautening. His head was held lower, his nostrils flaring like a wolf's might to draw in scent and stoke his own desire.

Again, she thought his actions, his demeanor was so like Guntram, or what she would imagine he would be like when deeply aroused, that her body shivered with excitement, waiting to see what he would do next.

He surprised her with fingers sifting soothingly through her hair. She released a little sigh, pressing into his hands until he scratched her scalp, petting her tenderly, like a wolf might do for his mate.

Then he lifted her hair and twisted it, dropping the long rope over her shoulder. His hands smoothed slowly down her back and over her buttocks. Standing now directly behind her, she knew what he'd see in the torchlight. Her sex was swollen, red, dripping with honeyed arousal; the inner lips parting, her entrance pulsing, sucking at air.

A low growl erupted from him, and then lips glided over her labia. "Princess, are you ready to be mine?"

Gabriella froze. "Guntram?" she asked, her voice thickening with emotion, but then she realized what he'd said. She jerked against her restraints, joy and outrage mixing in an explosive cocktail. "Guntram! Release me!"

A soft masculine snort sounded behind her. "Alex said that

I should ignore your pleas. Take my cues instead from your body. I smell your heat, Princess. Even now, your sweet cunt swells and drips honey, begging my cock to fill you."

Straining her head upward, she tried glancing over her shoulder to give him a glare, but couldn't quite turn that far. She rattled the bench with her furious bucking. "You know this can never be. I will never surrender my mantle to a male."

"And you shall never have to," he said, his words clipped. "I intend to take it."

Gabriella shivered at the hard edge of his voice, cursing her own body for the heat that radiated from her womb, tightening her belly and sending rippling shudders down her channel. "Have you come to rescue me?" she said, hoping to turn his mind to the bigger problem.

"Simon and I are working on that. We must retrieve something now that we know where you are."

"I'm watched."

"Also working on that. Let's talk afterward." His rough palms slid down her back, pausing to cup her bottom, then he dropped his hands from her skin.

There was a rustling behind her and the sounds of indrawn breaths. And she knew he was pulling in her scent, letting it enhance his own arousal.

When his lips and nose sank into her folds, she jerked. "Stop it. I don't know what you think you're doing, but you have to remember whom you serve."

"I could never forget. I've protected you, stood guard over you, prevented other males from forcing their suits on you. *For too long.* Did you think I was made of stone?"

His tongue stroked over her folds, and Gabriella's breath

hissed between her teeth. She clamped her jaws shut, knowing soon she'd be begging out loud if she couldn't figure out a way to put a stop to this. "Why now, Guntram? Why press your suit in this place? Would you really mate with me in the midst of all this evil?"

"I have no choice. I'm as bound by my duty as you are to this bench."

"Is that what I am? A duty? Is this only your way of protecting me? Because I'm not seeing it. When you're done I still have to leave with him. I'll still be in his bed, servicing his desires."

"Don't talk about him now," he growled. "We haven't much time, and I have to finish this for both our sakes."

"If you make me pregnant and fail to get me out of here, do you really want your cubs born here?"

"That will never happen. I'd die first."

"And that's supposed to make me feel better?"

Again, his tongue stroked over her, slipping between her labia, prodding her entrance and driving inward to lap at her honey-coated walls.

She squirmed on the bench, fisting her hands and pulling at her ties, but to no avail. She was at his mercy. Just as he'd intended. The thought that Guntram had planned this excited her. That he wouldn't listen to her pleas confused her—but also made her perversely glad.

"Do you know how many times I've stood in the darkness, watching you—smelling your arousal, knowing your pussy melted around another man's cock while I forced myself to remain unaffected? Hundreds of years, I've waited for just one chance to be with you. If I'm to die here, don't you think you owe me this?"

The tightness of his gruff voice affected her like no other ever had. She'd yearned for him to come. To save her. Had she also, secretly, wanted to surrender to *him*, her protector, her personal guardian?

She'd always known he'd watched, and the knowledge had spurred her arousal each and every time. Had she been teasing him, hoping to make him break?

As much as she wanted to bend to no man, she wanted to surrender to Guntram—here. Now. Wanted to feel his cock stroke deeply and lock inside her, nestling against her womb while his seed poured into her. She'd never experienced that before, the true connection with another of her own kind, her species. She'd denied herself the joy of children in order to maintain her status—but also because she'd been afraid to trust a mate to see to her happiness, to listen to and heed her opinions. Mated females held power in their own right, but only within their pack, and only over each other.

"Guntram, you don't know why I've resisted this. I have reasons for remaining alone."

"And I'm sure they're good ones," he said, a finger trailing along the edges of her sex. "But this is me, Gabriella. You should know by now, I would never hurt you beyond the pain you desire. You've earned respect in your own right among our kind. Do you really think that will disappear once your belly's full and your breasts are nurturing pups?"

A soft sob caught her unaware. The picture that filled her mind was of golden sunlight in a copse, her in wolfskin, cubs suckling her breasts while Guntram kept watch. A sublime image, empty of all her fears.

Even now, tethered to this bench, knowing he would take her whether she gave him the words to grant him that right or not, didn't feel in the least like that other time that haunted her nightmares.

Guntram had indeed earned the right to her body, to her future. He'd earned her trust. But did he love her? She didn't think she could bear to mate herself to him if he felt compelled only by duty.

But she was woman as well as a wolf. And she knew a woman could wield power over the strongest man by her wits and femininity. If he didn't love her now, she would find the key to his heart.

"You know I won't say it," she said, her voice wavering.

"Say what, princess?"

"That I surrender."

"I'd be disappointed in you if you did."

She almost smiled at the wry note in his tone. "Know this, if I were free, I'd give you a fight you'd never forget."

"Are you trying to tempt me to free you?"

"Does it turn you on? Imagining me battling you?"

"I think it arouses you, Princess," he said, thrusting a finger inside her.

"You keep calling me that when you would be my prince."

"I'm not anything more than I've ever been."

"A warrior? It's all I ever wanted from you, steel and muscle."

"You'll still have that, but I promise so much more."

Gabriella slumped against the platform, her arguments drying up. He'd addressed all her fears to her satisfaction. Now, her mind was consumed with thoughts of gaining satisfaction of another sort. "Irkalla will finish with him soon," she said, reminding him there were others outside this cell. "If I can't talk you out of this, you should get on with it."

"I've been cautioned not to ask your pleasure."

"Seems you and Alex have gotten a little cozy," she said, feeling disgruntled at the thought the two men had discussed her proclivities.

"Never."

"Good, because I intend to kill him."

"Not without me at your back."

She smiled full-blown at that. Male wolves tended to push mated females behind them, heading into battle without them. Perhaps accepting him wouldn't be the horrid demotion she'd expected.

"Get on with it," she repeated, summoning her most imperious tone. *Let the game begin.*

Soft laughter gusted over her backside. A rare occurrence with Guntram, and something she knew she would savor and try to entice more of in the future. If they had one together.

Teeth sank gently into her bottom, scraping downward. Lips surrounded her labia and suckled. Her clit was rubbed, plucked, squeezed—and her back arched, her shoulders rising as far as her restraints would allow.

Still, she withheld the moan clawing for release at the back of her throat. She wouldn't give it to him, would fight within her power to resist—just as a reminder that she would never truly submit everything she was to his domination.

"It's all right, you know," he whispered. "To let go with me. I promise I'm strong enough to allow you the freedom to be yourself, always."

Her body vibrated as fingers sank into her vagina, swirling to encourage the honey to flow, and her pussy responded eagerly, wetting his hand and her thighs.

More rustling sounded, higher this time, and she knew

he stood behind her. A zipper rasped. An agonized groan escaped him, and then his hands came down to grip the bench beside her hips and the platform creaked as he climbed on.

"I would have taken my time," he said, his voice tightening, "I would have stroked your flesh until it was red, teased your cunt until you begged—but there isn't time." The blunt end of his cock bumped against her sex, found her center, and rushed inside.

Gabriella's breath left in a strangled groan. Guntram more than filled the aching void inside her, cramming his thick cock inward, stretching her walls as he worked his way inside.

Her gasps grew ragged, and her heartbeats pounded against her chest. Her womb tightened as her sex clasped around him to pull him deeper.

Already she could feel his cock lengthening, the crown swelling as it surged toward her womb. The swollen head stroked over the bundle of nerves finger-length deep inside her vagina, causing sexy jolts of arousal to spark and simmer before gliding past and sinking deeper.

She whimpered, knowing instinctually and intellectually what was coming, but for all the years she'd existed, she'd never experienced a wolf's penetration, never known the "lover's knot."

Her body knew what to do, melting around him, caressing up and down his shaft in rolling waves as muscles spasmed and relaxed rhythmically to encourage his cock to glide deeper.

When Guntram was finally surging against her cervix, her pussy contracted around him, milking him. His knot swelled larger, the pressure, even without movement, enough to keep her on the verge of a powerful orgasm.

"Guntram," she whimpered, as semen began to spurt in warm, intermittent streams inside her.

Still he moved against her, pounding his belly and groin against her body, the moist slaps growing louder, her cries at last clawing their way past her throat to accompany the sounds of his deep, throaty growls.

Finally, he lowered his elbows to the platform, his back covering hers. "It's done," he said, his voice rasping. "With my seed, I plant our future. In return for your submission to me, I offer you my life, my protection, my love."

Gabriella closed her eyes at his formal vow, surprised he used the words. Traditions weren't something he'd ever embraced strongly, proving it by serving a female for all these years and appearing to be content with his role.

But the words soothed her, filling her with hope, with a sense of connection she'd never felt with another creature. Not even Alex. Alex had fought her, subdued her, seduced her, but never really held her heart.

She knew that now, because her thoughts in these past days had clung always to the hope Guntram embodied.

"You don't have to say the words, Princess," he said softly. "I don't expect them to be returned."

"You should want more," she said, fighting tears. "You should demand more of a mate."

"I want only what you will give me."

"I didn't give you *this*."

"This was necessary. Besides, I don't think I could have simply played with your body and let you walk away. Not after knowing this pleasure."

His lips trailed along the back of her neck and Gabriella

sighed. "We haven't much time. Any chance you're emptied yet?"

A laugh pushed her deeper against the bench. "Emptied? Isn't this moment one all females yearn to wallow in?"

His nose nuzzled the top of her shoulder, and Gabriella quivered. Would he bite?

Instead, his lips continued to trail along her skin.

"I'm not a romantic," she said. "Neither are you."

"I would try . . . if it would make you happy."

Gabriella smiled, ducking her head out of his reach so that he wouldn't catch a glimpse of it. "Guntram, don't you know the only thing that will make me truly happy is getting the hell out of here?"

"Almost done," he said, gasping. Indeed, the spurts had slowed. The knot was lessening.

If she were honest with herself and with him, she'd admit disappointment that their connection was ending.

"If we were home, I wouldn't let you leave the bed for the entirety of your heat."

"Who says I'd allow you to keep me pinned to the bed?"

"Think you will be able to resist now that you know what it can be like?"

With her orgasm fading and all her problems rushing back in to choke her, she clamped down her despair. Footsteps drew near. "Better start acting the part, Guntram. We're about to get company."

Guntram pulled out of her and eased off the platform. His zipper scraped.

Laughter preceded the arrival of two men, both human-like in appearance—both naked with their cocks sprung and their arms slung around each other's shoulders.

The dark-haired male eyed Guntram. "When will you be

done with her?" he said, his gaze lowering to her breasts.

"Do you have need of this room?" Guntram asked, his voice taut as his body.

The male's eyebrows rose. "I think we have need of you," he said, his gaze gliding now over Guntram and sliding lower.

Gabriella knew he had to be eyeing Guntram's crotch, and she nearly lost it. Although she couldn't turn to see for herself, she knew Guntram's face was heating.

A low growl emanated from her mate.

The two men stepped back, eyes widening. "We can have you whether you consent or not," the dark-haired one sputtered. "You are here for our pleasure."

"The Master arranged for her pleasure," Guntram said softly.

The other male sucked in a quick breath and turned to whisper to his companion.

Both offered tight smiles and backed away from the cell door.

Guntram snorted behind her.

"How did you know that would work?" Gabriella asked.

"Instinct. Only the most powerful of demons could manage to hold you."

Oddly pleased with his comment, she wriggled on the bench, tugging at the bindings on her wrists. "Can you let me out of these things now?"

"I wouldn't want anyone to think I didn't take my job seriously."

"Wha—?"

Leather cracked in the air above her. "A whip?" she said, incredulous. "You're going to whip me?"

"Don't you think you deserve it?"

Leather slapped one buttock, not as sharply as she expected, but stinging just the same. "I didn't mean for this to happen. It was an accident, my getting pulled into this hellhole."

Another crack landed on the opposite buttock, and she winced.

"First, you had no business volunteering as an emissary to the vampires."

"I'm female, they're matriarchal. It made sense. Even our own clan council thought so."

Again, the leather landed, this time lashing the back of one thigh. "You had no business entering into their coup—it wasn't your battle."

The quiet anger tightening his voice was tightening parts of her anatomy she wished didn't like the punishment quite so much. Arousal stirred again. Guntram had never questioned her before, never rebuked her for a single decision. Now that he'd mated her, was that all about to change?

Another sharp *thwack* stung her ass. "You put yourself in danger, out of your pack's reach, while we scrambled to figure out what the hell had happened."

The leather whip cracked, this time stinging so hard she knew she'd have a welt, but damn, her sex was moistening, ripening, fluid wetting her folds. Again it landed, but this time remained draped over her hip.

His breaths were harsh, his hand, when he smoothed it over her stinging parts, shook.

Gabriella's eyes filled. She'd known he cared for her, but she'd only ever thought about her needs, her desires. That she'd made him suffer hurt a part of her that she thought had turned cold and shriveled.

Her heart ached, imagining his fear and desperation as

he'd entered the enemy's lair and agreed to cross into another realm to find her.

"Let me loose," she whispered.

This time he heeded her request, unbuckling the restraints at her wrists. When she straightened and climbed off the platform, she rubbed her wrists, keeping her head down because she needed a moment to compose herself.

Guntram had taken her for his mate. Not asked. To offer him an apology, to let him see her sorrow—well, he might think she loved him. And that couldn't happen, not if she wanted to keep on an even standing with an alpha male.

Drawing a deep breath, she raised her head and shook back her hair.

Guntram's throat worked as he swallowed, but his chin lifted, his lips thinned.

Gabriella stepped toward him, crowding against him with her naked breasts pressed to his chest, forcing him backward until his back met the wall. "I did exactly as I wanted. Your duty was to follow me."

Guntram's indrawn breath lifted his chest; the thick hair cloaking it abraded her nipples. She rubbed against him, deliberately.

His eyelids drifted down until he watched her through narrowed slits.

"Guntram?" she said, her inflection still hard.

"Yes, mistress," he replied, his posture unbending.

"I want you."

# CHAPTER 14

Freed by her command, Guntram moved fast, snaking his arms around her waist and turning to press her against the rock wall at the back of the cell. With his body shielding her identity, he hoped for a few moments more to lose himself inside her.

Stroking her pale flesh with the whip had had a startling affect on him. His passion had crept higher with each lash, knowing she writhed and wriggled, not to escape the whip, but because her body yearned for the punishment.

Her passion needed pain to creep past her tightly held emotions and release the warm, passionate creature inside her.

Alex had been right. *Damn him.*

Guntram grabbed her wrists and pulled them upward, then clasped them inside one steely grip to stretch them high. Then he reached between them and opened his pants, pulling out his cock.

Before he'd drawn his hand away, one long leg rose to ride the crest of his hip. When his gaze locked with hers, her expression hardened, and the arch of her eyebrows had every red corpuscle in his body surging south to meet her silent challenge.

He growled deep inside his throat. "I don't mind that every time we fuck you'll offer me a battle."

Gabriella blinked. Then her eyes narrowed. "Do you think I care what you want?"

"Princess, you'll care whether I let you come."

Her mouth opened, then snapped shut. "You wouldn't."

"Not on our wedding night. But keep it in mind. Now, be quiet." Rather than let her have the last word, he swooped down and kissed her. Hard. His lips slamming against her tightly closed mouth. Then he opened his mouth and stroked the seam with his tongue while bracing apart his feet and rooting his cock between her legs.

A low, trembling growl rattled at the back of her throat.

He lifted his mouth from hers, hovering just above her pouting lips. "If we wore wolfskin, I'd latch onto your fur with my teeth and bite down until you howled."

Anger and desire warred in her golden brown eyes. She opened her mouth, no doubt to issue a sarcastic jab, but he didn't give her the chance, covering her mouth again and sliding his tongue inside.

Her teeth closed around his tongue, and he waited while

satisfaction and humor glinted in her eyes. But he bent his knees and surged upward, spearing into her, and her teeth freed him as she gasped for air.

"Guntram!"

How he'd longed to hear her say his name, exactly like that, breathlessly, with the slightest hint of a whimper. "It's all right. Everything will be all right. I swear it."

"Fuck me. Fuck me quickly before he comes."

Guntram laid his forehead against her and gritted his teeth. "Don't say his name. Don't remind me. I don't want him between us now."

"Guntram. *Please.*"

He drove into her, ramming her against the wall with the force of his strokes, but she didn't seem to mind. Instead, she lifted her other leg and clasped her ankles behind his back.

He dropped her hands and reached down to cup her bottom, squeezing the softness overspilling his hands. His head dropped to her shoulder as he rutted against her, as he sank again and again in her heat.

"Don't lock with me," she warned. "We haven't time. Someone would discover us."

Nodding against her shoulder, he ground his teeth and willed his cock not to swell inside her, offering instead a human fuck, one made only slightly less pleasurable than the Wolfen version because it was Gabriella's cunt he filled.

How long had he dreamed of this? How much longer would he have to wait to know this pleasure again? But he didn't want to think about leaving her, didn't want to dwell on the demon who'd captured her. Later, he'd exorcise his inner demons—take a few heads as he left—maybe even the Master, who held her bound to him now.

Gabriella was close, her mouth opening as her breaths rasped harshly, her head falling back against the wall.

Guntram watched pleasure flood her features with rosy heat, savored the sight of her plump lips as they rounded. How lovely this view was, up close, skin to skin. If this was all he'd ever have, it would be enough.

At last the strong, deep strokes sparked a fiery orgasm that had them both grinding hard against each other, holding each other tightly, her arms wrapping around his shoulders, his around her lower back. His balls exploded, and he muffled his shout against her skin, as did she hers, pressing kisses against his neck and cheek until he turned and met her lips.

This time their mouths were gentle as they tasted each other's passion, gliding softly as they stared into each other's eyes.

"I've changed my mind," he said gruffly, when he'd mastered his breaths. "Someday, I will want the words."

Gabriella's lips firmed, but her eyes remained moist.

It was enough for now that he'd poked a little hole in the steely armor surrounding her heart. He'd thought he would be content to have her in his bed, to know her loyalty would be his, but now he knew he wouldn't settle for anything less than all of her—body, soul, and heart.

Marduk ground his jaw tight as his hands gripped Irkalla's hips hard, forcing her up and down his cock. Once he'd figured out she intended to draw out their lovemaking in order to keep his attention from Gabriella, he'd decided he'd had enough. He'd give her the requisite orgasm, on his terms and at his pace, and then politely excuse himself.

Not that he was worried about Gabriella. He'd appointed

Dagon to watch over her and give silent warnings to others to go gently or face his wrath. Watching her with Dumuzi had been enraging enough.

But Dumuzi seemed content to humiliate his wife and hadn't let his fist drift anywhere near Gabriella's heart, although the thought of dining on a warm, living heart had to be killing him.

Not that Marduk didn't appreciate the danger Dumuzi posed. Dumuzi might have married the wrong sister, but Irkalla clearly still favored him.

Fingers pulled his beard. "You aren't watching me."

"If I watch I'll be overcome and unable to sustain this erection you ride," he said drily.

Her lips formed a pretty moue. "Your mind is on your new pet. I'd be jealous if I didn't know you're just worried. So many are so interested. But where has she gone?" she said slyly.

Marduk glanced around the room, finding Dagon near the entrance to the corridor with the special cells. "She's fine for now, mistress. May I make you come?" he asked, fire glinting in his eyes because around the others he had to ask.

She sighed. "Yes, but not like this. My thighs ache."

Marduk lifted her off his lap, not liking her expression. She glanced beyond his shoulder and crooked her finger. Marduk stiffened, not giving her the satisfaction of gazing over his shoulder. He'd pretend he didn't care who she invited to join them.

"My queen," Dumuzi's voice came from behind him. "How may I serve you?"

Marduk shot a glance behind him and found Dumuzi standing alone. Another glance found his spouse, kneeling on the floor with her arms crossing her chest, apparently left with instructions not to move. Her chest rose and fell quickly; heat flushed the tops of her breasts. Her fury was palpable.

"Marduk's attention strays from me," Irkalla said. "Perhaps a little competition will help him focus his efforts on my behalf."

"Mistress . . ." Marduk growled a warning, not liking where this was headed.

Dumuzi's sly smile stretched across his face. "I am yours to command, my queen. How may I pleasure you?"

Irkalla's eyes narrowed on Marduk as she reached out to stroke Dumuzi's cock. "Surprise me, but I expect to be overfilled with your lust."

Dumuzi held out his palm. Irkalla took it and let him lead her to a wide, backless lounger, really a narrow bed.

Dumuzi lay down, gripping his staff to hold it perpendicular from his body, and gave her a glance filled with wicked intent. "For your pleasure, ma'am."

"You have always known my heart, haven't you?" she said, her voice girlish.

Dumuzi's face betrayed a momentary sadness before he tugged her downward, helping her to straddle his hips, her knees digging into the cushions while she fit his cock to her entrance and sighed, slipping downward.

Marduk would rather have left them to their lovemaking, which it truly was from the yearning in both their expressions, but he knew he'd already made her angry. He climbed onto the end of the mattress, widening his knees around Dumuzi's outstretched legs. When he reached Irkalla, he wrapped his arms around her waist as she glided on the other man's shaft.

He cupped her breasts, pinched her nipples and twisted, and was rewarded with a sharp gasp. "Shall I slide inside you too?" he whispered, playing the supplicant. "Do you want to ride both our cocks?"

"Marduk!" Her breath caught as she slammed downward. "I would have you both share my woman's channel."

Then this was the punishment she'd planned all along. Marduk barely held back the snarl threatening to curl his lip. Irkalla knew he despised Dumuzi.

His hands tightened on her breasts, then released her. He gripped her shoulders and pushed her to lie against the other demon's chest.

Dumuzi's grin was back in place, and the gleam in his eyes said he knew how this act enraged him.

Marduk cupped Irkalla's ass, his thumbs sliding into the crevice, hoping to stimulate her tiny hole and earn a reprieve. At least he'd have her inner wall between their cocks.

But Irkalla pressed closer to Dumuzi and reached behind her, spreading her folds and stretching the opening. "I want you now."

Marduk had no choice. He guided the tip of his cock into the narrow space she'd made and squeezed inside, gliding into her channel and along Dumuzi's shaft. The pressure was more pleasurable than he wanted to acknowledge.

"Move, Marduk. You will take us both."

Then Irkalla leaned over her first lover and framed his face with her two hands, kissing him as Marduk began to stroke them both, pushing deeper in short thrusts, easing inside as her walls melted and honey eased down her passage.

She lifted her head. "Do you remember my first time?" Irkalla whispered to Dumuzi.

Dumuzi groaned. "The bathing pool, inside your father's palace."

"It was dark. I thought I was alone. I swam nude. I didn't know you were watching until you sat at the edge and called to me."

"I was overcome with lust at the sight of your beauty. I had never seen anyone lovelier."

Her soft snort said she needed more praise. "My sister looks exactly as I do."

"Your sister wears her arrogance in her face. I could always tell you apart."

Her sigh said he'd pleased her. "I hadn't yet experienced arousal, hadn't begun my heat. My sister's came first, and I was jealous. I decided I would have you anyway. I set out to seduce you."

"And I had decided to have you for my own. I'd already approached your father—you were old enough. I didn't understand why he wanted me to wait."

"You didn't know what I was. I understood. But I wished to claim you first because my sister had gleaned that I wanted you and I feared she would take you out of spite."

"Which she did," he growled.

Her finger tapped his lips. "That night, however, you were mine. My first. I had you first."

Dumuzi's gaze darkened. "Love, I remember, how small you were, how tightly your sex clasped my cock. I was overcome. I wasn't as gentle as I'd hoped."

"You hurt me. Stretched me. Like now. I hurt, Dumuzi, but then as now, I relish the bite of a cock stretching me, tearing at my inner walls. Do you feel my heat?"

Dumuzi clasped the corners of her shoulders and squeezed.

"Mistress, move with him. I would feel your inner caress and let it take away my breath rather than let him be the cause of my joy."

Irkalla looked over her shoulder. Her face was softened, dewy. Youthful as she must have been when she and her lover first tasted each other's flesh.

Unaccountably, Marduk's chest tightened, realizing the journey these two had taken, the twisted revenge they'd engineered to punish her sister for enslaving her lover in marriage.

Irkalla had entered the Land of the Dead and seduced Nergal, taking his power for her own. Dumuzi had no way of knowing that Irkalla had paved the way for him to join her when Inanna conspired to have her husband dragged into this realm. He'd been made into a demon, but was allowed to keep his human form since it pleased Irkalla to keep him here.

He must have waited eons, perhaps conspiring with Irkalla, to creep back into Inanna's world and exact their revenge.

Still, for all that Irkalla clearly loved Dumuzi, she blamed him for succumbing to Inanna's lure. Never mind that a human male would never have withstood the lure the wicked bitch had cast with her vampire heat.

Irkalla played with Dumuzi, like now, exposing old emotions that lingered between them both—catching the tattered strands and cauterizing them with her oscillating affections.

Marduk had seen them like this before, but had managed never to get himself pulled into their lovemaking.

His cock burned as he fucked her. Moisture, thick and creamy, coated him and Dumuzi, but the friction between their bodies heated up. His arousal caught the flickering flame and tightened his balls, which bounced against Dumuzi's, adding to the tension building inside him.

He stroked harder, meeting her backward lunges until her back arched against his belly, and then he saw Dagon, entering the dungeon alone. His gaze shot to the corridor where he'd last spotted him, only to see the back of a blond head as the figure hurried down the cells.

Something was afoot, and he knew it centered on his new pet. A shifter of some sort had interfered with her. Fear for her safety drove him to thrust hard and fast, not that the two beneath him seemed to mind.

He forced himself to concentrate on the pressure in his balls, the heat surrounding him, and at last, his seed poured into Irkalla.

Her arm reached behind her, snagging his neck. She turned her head to receive his kiss.

"I will leave you two alone now," he said quietly. "I'm sure Inanna will be very displeased for you to linger with her husband."

Irkalla laughed and turned back to stroke a finger over Dumuzi's reddened lips. "She hates you so much, but her jealousy is stronger. Shall we do more to enrage her?"

Marduk heaved a sigh of relief that at last he was dismissed. He withdrew, rising swiftly, and strode toward the corridor where he'd last seen Gabriella. Each cell was occupied, but none held his woman.

Until the last.

Gabriella was letting down her legs from the flanks of a burly man wearing an executioner's mask. Her mouth was blurred, her hair in disarray, and the room smelled of sex. When they both turned to face him, his gaze caught the widening of her eyes, then slid downward to see the fluids, copious amounts, dripping down her inner thighs.

The man's large cock was similarly wet and still semi-aroused.

He'd known she would be expected to partake in the games. But to remain with one partner, to enjoy the experience as much as she clearly had . . .

Marduk's shoulders stiffened. He narrowed his gaze on the man. "Who are you? I haven't seen you here before."

"I'm newly arrived," came the gruff voice.

Marduk drew in the scents swimming in the air, discarded Gabriella's and centered on the male's. Beneath a floral layer, heated with sweat and male musk, lay something more damning.

"Another wolf?" She'd found one of her own kind to mate with? No wonder they seemed to have such a quick rapport. Even now her hand held the man's forearm, trying to hold him back as though offering him protection.

"I am Wolfen," the man admitted.

"And you just arrived?" Marduk stepped closer, drawing in the scent again. "Yet you don't carry the scent of death."

The wolf didn't respond. Merely curled his fists.

"Marduk, why are you upset?" Gabriella broke in, instantly.

She was protecting this wolf—from him? He held out his hand, palm up. "Come, Gabriella. It's time we leave."

Her wild gaze met the wolf's, whose expression remained stoic. His nod, giving her permission, had anger flushing Marduk's skin. First, he had to get the woman away. Then he would discover whether they were accomplices.

Gabriella laid her trembling hand in his, and he pulled her close, bending to brand her lips with a hard kiss.

Then he lifted his gaze above her head.

The man's face blanched white. His eyes narrowed in deadly intent.

They knew each other. Cared for each other. Before the night was through he'd know how deeply, and Gabriella would know never to betray him again.

When it was done, he'd soothe Gabriella's grief. She'd have another chance to accept her place with him or she'd suffer the same fate as her lover.

As he pulled her behind him, down the corridor and into the chamber, he stopped beside the bull-man and leaned to whisper in his ear. The guard nodded sharply and lifted his fist into the air to alert the other sentries posted around the room.

Marduk kept moving forward, ignoring Gabriella's gasping sobs as she stumbled behind him. "Please," she cried. "Don't harm him."

"He's no longer my concern, love."

When they'd reached the door to the stairway, he halted and bent, dragging her over his shoulder because he wanted to leave quickly before she saw her lover devoured. However well the lesson might have served her, he wished to spare her that.

Behind him there were shouts and screams.

Gabriella wriggled on his shoulder, nearly dislodging herself, but he wrapped both arms tightly around her thighs and continued upward.

Not until he'd left the banquet room and courtyard far behind did he slow his pace.

"What's going to happen to him?"

"You will never see him again."

She kicked her legs. "Dammit, put me down!"

Marduk held firm, ignoring her struggles. “Not until we’re well away. I don’t want you caught in the bloodlust.”

“Bloodlust! Are they going to eat him?”

He didn’t answer. But he wouldn’t be surprised. A fresh living man. Dumuzi would demand his heart. Irkalla would feast on the blood. Everyone had their own preference, and like lions surrounding a kill, they’d tear him apart and wander into their own corner with whatever they’d managed to rip from his frame.

“You have to do something.”

“It’s already too late.”

“You’re a monster! As much as any of them!” Gabriella’s sobs shook her body, and slowly her arms wrapped around his middle as she buried her face into his back. She understood now.

It was a start.

# CHAPTER 15

While the demon hustled Gabriella out of sight, Guntram assessed his chances of making it out alive. He had no doubts the Master would alert the guards of his presence. The cell was the last one at the end of the corridor; the only way out was down that same narrow hallway and through the dungeon, which was filled with creatures that would all want a taste of him.

Not wanting anything obscuring his vision, he ripped off the mask. He considered pulling the garrote from the seam of his trousers, but knew he'd be lucky if he could get near enough to try it before being cleaved in two, so decided to try a little intimidation to bluster his way through. It wasn't much of a plan, he conceded, but all he had at the moment.

Squaring his shoulders he faced the doorway, pulling on his game face, and letting anger fill his muscles with steel as the sound of booted feet hurried toward him.

Two guards, sharing grim smiles, halted outside the doorway. Rather than let them have a chance to think, he rushed through the cell door, knocking the first into the guard behind him. The two fell into a heap, and Guntram stepped over their bodies, arms outstretched, growling loudly as he rushed down the corridor.

He paused to duck beneath a curved sword slicing toward his neck, gripped the man's hand holding the pommel, and dug his heels into the floor, continuing to power forward, turning at the last moment to slam the guard into the metal bars of another cell.

The sword loosened in the man's grip, and Guntram peeled back his fingers, breaking them until he wrested it away.

Then he was facing the next wave of guards. This time with a weapon. Feeling more sure of his chances, he faced five now as they rushed into the narrow corridor. He lowered the sword and stabbed it upward into the next guard's soft belly, driving toward his heart. The guard crumpled, and Guntram rammed his elbow into the one beside him and spun to face the next two.

It was too easy. Were they all so easy to best? So soft and ill trained?

Another slice of his sword severed the head of a goat-faced creature, and the last guard stood in front of him, sword held in a two-fisted grip. His shoulders nearly spanned the space. The nostrils in his horrible bull's face dilated around a gusting snort.

Guntram reigned in his rage, sensing this one wouldn't be so easy to defeat.

The bull-man raised one hand from his grip around his sword, curled his fingers, and then stepped backward.

He expected Guntram to follow. And he did, wanting the extra space inside the wide chamber for this fight.

Once they'd both cleared the corridor, they faced off.

"Xenos, don't bleed him completely," came a feminine voice.

"Have buckets prepared, milady," the bull snarled.

The woman stood on a sofa, her head above the others, watching.

Only sparing a glance, Guntram took in her dark skin and hair, her eyes flashing with excitement.

The room was quickly filling with more guards pouring through the doorway from the stairwell.

Guntram knew he wouldn't leave this room. His glance confirmed the one fact he was grateful for. Gabriella was gone. She wouldn't witness his death.

Again, he felt a welling of fierce satisfaction that he'd found her. That he'd claimed her, if only for an hour.

He'd lived for that moment. It was enough.

Still, he wasn't ready to surrender. He'd die fighting like a wolf.

The bull-man snorted again, and Guntram focused his attention on his opponent. "Is it only you and me? Or should I look for a coward's knife flying toward my back?"

"Take me, if you can. Win another night of life if you succeed."

"Your promise, lady?" Guntram said, raising his gaze to the woman, already having divined that she was Irkalla, the Queen of the Dead.

"My promise, warrior," she said, one corner of her mouth curling in a smirk. "If you are strong enough to defeat my finest, I will want to take a closer look at you."

Guntram took what she said, decided to believe her, and fight the good fight. Another day meant another chance to escape. Gabriella's fate was not yet sealed.

The bull-man began to circle him, flexing his shoulders and swinging his curved sword in slow arcs. With his chest puffed out and his head lifting high, Guntram knew the creature thought this would be an easy contest to win.

Guntram drew in deep breaths to calm his racing heart, then narrowed his focus to his opponent, closing out the sounds of the creatures stirring around him, shouting wagers on the outcome of the battle. He shook his head, loosening the muscles bunched in his neck and shoulders. He raised his sword and curled his fist and pounded at the air, filling his heart with quiet rage. Deep inside, he knew he wouldn't lose this fight. Simon had brought him here for a purpose, and he had to believe this contest wasn't the end.

Tired of watching the other warrior posture for the crowd, Guntram lowered his sword and grasped it with both hands, then ran for the other warrior, slicing toward his neck.

The bull-man met his advance with his own blade, pushed him away, and came back with a wicked chop toward his flanks.

Guntram spun away, agile as only a wolf could be, and lowered his head. "Wolves hunted bison and cattle. Do you really think you can best me?"

"You're a tiny man," the bull-man sneered. "Show me some fur and maybe I'll shiver with fear." He strode forward, raising his arm again and slicing toward Guntram's head.

Guntram met the blow and felt the hard jangle all the way to his toes. "You're powerful, but you're slow." Guntram lifted his upper lip in a snarl and shot out one foot, hooked it behind the other man's knees, and shoved.

The bull grabbed Guntram's shoulder and they both fell to the floor, their swords above their heads.

A meaty fist slammed into Guntram's side, expelling air in a pained whoosh. They rolled, the bull getting on top of him, but Guntram dug a heel into the carpet beneath him and bucked, turning the bull. As soon as he rolled the beast to his back, Guntram rammed his knee between his legs and scrambled away.

The bull roared in agony, his hand closing around his groin. His large round eyes narrowed on Guntram as he came to his hands and knees and rose slowly.

Guntram allowed him the time, wanting to impress the queen with his lack of fear. Besides, he was growing more confident by the second, now that he was gaining the upper hand.

The bull was breathing heavily, his snorts deepening. He was growing angry and was likely embarrassed that he hadn't already defeated his opponent.

Guntram felt a cooling calm wash over him. His focus narrowed again. Every movement, every breath of his opponent was noted while his mind raced ahead to figure out how he would defeat him.

Guntram beat his fist against his chest and growled, letting his wolf's voice rumble from deep inside his chest.

The bull snorted, and a deep roar precipitated another lunging attack at Guntram, but this time Guntram was prepared, stepping aside at the last minute and driving his sword into the back of the beast.

Xenos fell to his knees, his face turning to his queen.

Guntram read the lack of mercy in her cold features, placed a foot against the bull's back and drew back his sword. There could be no mercy shown. He lifted his blade and swung it downward.

Blood sprayed in every direction, showering Guntram and the carpet beneath them. The bull's neck was thick, but Guntram's sharp blade, backed by the power of his rage, drove downward until the head tilted, severing, and dropped to the floor. Blood continued to spurt in pulses from the raw open wound. Guntram wiped his blade on the bull's clothing and then turned to face the crowd, which had grown silent around him.

He didn't spare a single glance for any of them, lifting his gaze instead to the woman still standing on the sofa.

Her eyes were wide, her lips parted in shock.

"You will honor your promise to me?" he asked, his chest billowing with his ragged breaths.

Her lips closed. "You dare to ask me that?"

"I'm standing among demons and sinners. Why should I expect you to keep your word?"

"I'm not a demon. And I don't lie." Her gaze remained locked with his, but she raised her hand. "Take him away. Wolf, you will have to surrender your weapons."

Guntram nodded, throwing down the sword, then bent to slide the knife from the top of his boot. He straightened and let the knife roll off his fingers to the floor.

Before it settled, hands grabbed his arms roughly and pulled them behind his back. A rope was tied around his wrists, and then he was shoved forward through the crowd.

"Make way, make way," came the shout from the guard behind him.

Guntram didn't take his gaze from the woman's until the guard pushed him through the door of the stairway. Out of sight, the guard threaded his fingers through Guntram's hair and slammed his head into the wall. "Give me no problems. I'd hate to have to tell her that you died trying to escape," he whispered beside Guntram's ear.

"I'll cause you no trouble," Guntram said quietly, promising to himself that the first chance he got, he'd kill the bastard.

Marduk dumped Gabriella on the bed and then strode away.

Although she wanted to hide her face in her hands and have a good, long cry, she kept her gaze on him, wiping her tears from her face with the back of a hand.

The Master was furious. He paced the room, his body bristling, fists clenched tightly. He didn't once glance her way.

The door opened, and Xalia slipped into the room, her eyes wide. Her mouth opened to speak.

"Get out, Xalia. And don't hover at the door," Marduk said tightly.

"Yes, Bel," she said, biting her lip and aiming a glare at Gabriella. She left as quietly as she'd come.

The candles they'd lit before they left burned low. The

room was filled with murky shadows despite the bright moonlight that filtered through the curtains. Darkness loomed in the corners and painted Marduk's features with an eerie, ominous cast.

A hiccup caught her by surprise, and she closed her mouth, determined to remain still and quiet so that she didn't draw his attention while he worked through his anger.

Thoughts of what Guntram must be suffering wouldn't leave her mind. She remembered the blood feast in the hall where she'd first arrived. It didn't take much of a leap of imagination to know what must be happening. What had probably already occurred. For all she knew, he was dead, dismembered, his parts hacked away and carried off to be eaten.

A shudder shook her body, and she eased to the mattress, taking her gaze from Marduk at last to press her face into the bedding to muffle her sobs. For most of her life, Guntram had been her constant companion, her rock. Knowing he'd had her back gave her confidence, made her feel invincible.

After she'd been attacked in the forest during her first heat, she'd wandered packless, seducing men for the wealth they showered on her until she'd amassed a small fortune. Only then had she sought her own kind, building her own pack as a lone male wolf might, impressing males into her service with the promise of fortune and adventure.

They hadn't been tied to territory; instead they'd roamed, offering their talents as warriors to whoever paid the most, human or Wolfen, until at last the clans in the region had taken notice. They'd enjoyed a unique position and were prized for their warriors' skills as well as her abilities as a negotiator whenever troubles erupted among the many nations.

When the packs had dwindled in Europe, she'd made the decision to explore opportunities in the New World. Guntram had followed; so had most of the packmates he'd selected. They were loyal to her, but loved him. They'd all looked to him in times of trouble. His stoic presence had seemed immutable.

She'd never fooled herself into believing she alone was responsible for their success and esteemed position. Guntram had made it possible. His support had given her freedom, his presence held back the nightmares.

And what had she given him in return? Respect, yes. Autonomy, certainly. But at the end, she knew it wasn't enough to repay him for all he'd done for her. She'd been selfish, so self-involved she'd ignored what she'd always known—that he hadn't stayed because of duty or loyalty, but because he loved her.

The way he'd covered her in the cell, using all his knowledge of her needs was proof enough—that he'd sacrificed his life for hers cemented her belief.

He'd entered hell to rescue her, even knowing he'd likely fail. Her hand pressed against her belly, and she felt the quickening in her womb. She hadn't wanted a mate, never craved cubs or a family because her own had betrayed her, but she couldn't regret a single moment or the consequence of their mating. She'd cherish this child, keeping it first in her heart as she should have done for its father.

Another sob ripped through her, but she didn't care if the angry demon pacing the floor heard it. Her heart ached over Guntram's loss. That he'd been her last hope to escape hardly seemed to matter anymore. What she wanted most wasn't her freedom after all. She wished with all her heart she'd given

Guntram the words she'd stubbornly refused. Pledged herself and her heart to her one true mate.

Her damnable pride had kept her from giving him that gift. Deep inside, she knew she wouldn't have been lying, even a little bit, if she'd admitted that she loved him.

# CHAPTER 16

Marduk heard her sobs, but wouldn't be swayed by her woman's emotions. She had a harsh lesson to learn, and better she learn it now than cause herself or another harm later. Still, the wrenching cries that shook her strong frame caused his own heart to bleed.

He'd wanted to touch life again, but he'd forgotten there could be such deep sorrow to balance the joys. For the first time, he considered her situation from her point of view.

How she must hate him now. He'd given no thought beyond the need to possess her when he'd divined her presence in the mirror. Hadn't wondered for even a moment what sort of life she'd led, what he'd forced her to relinquish. Did she have family? A husband?

Her body betrayed no signs she'd ever delivered a child, but what did he really know about wolves? What had he robbed her of?

But if that were the case, wouldn't she have pleaded on their behalf? All her begging had been for herself.

But who was the wolf in the dungeon to her? When he'd stalked into the cell and broken them apart he'd sensed something important had happened between the wolf pair. He had no doubt the wolf had meant to help her escape, but was he acting on love or duty?

Gabriella's eyes when she'd gazed at the warrior had been free of challenge, softened by some deeply held emotion. Did she love him?

Marduk couldn't imagine that was the case. Wolves were a loyal breed. If she'd been mated to him, cared for him, she'd never have given herself so easily.

Another jagged sob pulled him from his thoughts and he strode toward the bed. It had been forever since he'd tried to soothe a woman's tears. Zara's tears had been the last to move him. She'd wet his chest with them as she'd clung to his shoulders, unwilling to let him leave her.

He knelt on the mattress next to Gabriella and placed his hand on her shoulder, intending to turn her and offer his embrace.

But Gabriella jerked away from his touch, her wet face lifting, reddening as she drew back her lips and emitted a low, rumbling growl. "Don't touch me."

Marduk let his hand drop and narrowed his eyes. "You're overwrought. But this will pass."

"I won't forget," she said, her voice thick with emotion. "You're responsible for his death. You murdered him. You tried to make me believe you inhabit this place but aren't tainted by sin. That you're better than those consigned here because of their misdeeds. But you're worse. You wield you power to serve your appetite, regardless of anyone else's desires. I want nothing from you. If you demand I stay in your chamber, you will have to rape me to ever have me again."

Marduk froze, cut to the bone by the purpose in her expression. He believed her. Withdrawing from the bed, he turned away from the accusation in her gaze. "I'll send Xalia to attend you.

"Keep your whore away from me."

Marduk blew out a breath, growing annoyed with her stubborn refusal of his help. "Who was he to you?" he asked, although he wasn't sure he wanted an answer.

The corners of her lips slid downward, and her face crumpled. "No one. It doesn't matter anymore," she whispered.

Frustrated because he didn't know how to relieve her anger, he strode from the chamber, slamming the door behind him.

"Bel, what has happened?" Xalia said, falling into step beside him as he quickly descended the steps into the street.

"A wolf followed her here from the other realm. He found her. Now, he's dead and she blames me."

"Did you kill him then?"

"No, but I alerted Irkalla's guard to his presence. I as good as murdered him myself."

"And she doesn't appreciate the depth of your feelings for her?"

Marduk's gaze swung to the demon beside him. Of course, she'd see his murdering a rival as a sign of affection. He halted in his steps, realizing he had expected the same—after she'd gotten over her shock, of course.

Gods, he'd been here too long. Gabriella was right. He'd been here too long not to be tainted by the dark souls around him. And where was he going?

Glancing up the street, he knew his feet led him back to the palace, back to assure himself the wolf was no longer a rival for her affection. He closed his eyes, trying to remember how it once felt to be sure of his own moral superiority.

"Go back to my chamber," he said to Xalia. "Make sure she stays inside. I don't want her doing anything foolish."

"Do you think she would destroy herself to join this wolf in death?" She sounded excited by the prospect, likely found it romantic.

"Xalia, go back. If anything happens to her, I will hold you responsible."

Her breath caught, and she whirled and ran back toward the tower.

The guards at the palace didn't stop him as he reentered and made his way down into the dungeon. Inside, the crowd had thinned. Guards with spears crossed to prevent entrance by the curious stood at the bottom of the steps.

Marduk received a solemn nod and was allowed to pass. Inside the chamber, slaves bustled through the crowd carrying the fallen warriors. The wolf had fought well, judging by the number of the queen's soldiers being carried away.

Dagon drew beside him. "He's still alive. The queen has had him taken to her chamber to interrogate him."

"What happened to you?"

"The wolf and an accomplice waylaid me on my way here.

I awoke with a headache and came here immediately. I'm not sure what their purpose was in assaulting me."

Marduk remained silent about his own suspicions. "I have to get to Irkalla before she does something regrettable."

Dagon's smile was brief and ended in a wince. "Neck hurts."

Marduk pushed past him and hurried to Irkalla's chamber.

Inside, the usual crowd filled every available space.

Irkalla stood in the center of the room, facing the warrior. "Tell me how you came to be here, wolf," she said, her tone imperious.

So, he was still alive. Marduk's thoughts raced. If he could somehow save him from being made into a meal, perhaps Gabriella would be appeased. This could be used to his advantage. He strode toward Irkalla rather than pressing closer to the edge of the circle around the warrior.

Marduk eyed the warrior, knowing what Gabriella found attractive in this other man. His strong, sturdy frame radiated leashed power; his resolute stance betrayed no fear, although he had to know that his days, maybe even minutes, were numbered.

Too, he knew what the man found so attractive about Gabriella—besides the handsome features and glorious mane of hair. Her body was equally sturdy and strong, a good match for the warrior's bulky frame. Her pride and fearlessness engendered an odd protectiveness in a man.

He'd never wanted to see her brought down, have proved to her that her fearlessness was based on nothing. She was a woman, thus vulnerable. For without her fierce pride, she'd be somehow . . . less.

Marduk had vague memories of the prideful woman he'd

loved long ago. The human he'd craved to make his own. In the end, he'd had to abandon her, but selfishly, he'd left her with a curse, thinking that he'd be gone from this place and able to rejoin her in the future. He'd wanted her to live so that he might find her again.

Where she was now didn't matter. He'd never see her again, having never found another worthy of the ring he wore, the seal Solomon had entrusted to him so long ago. Perhaps he was doomed by his immortality to reign as the Master of the Demons forever.

The wolf didn't reply to the question, and Irkalla's cheeks reddened. "You would deny me?" she said, her voice rising in disbelief.

Marduk stepped behind Irkalla. "Imagine that," he murmured, just loud enough for her to hear. "Someone who won't bend to you."

"He'll bend," she whispered harshly. "He'll kneel if I have to cut him off at the knees."

"And miss the chance to sample this one's strength of will? Do you think he can resist a vampire's lure?"

"No one can. Besides, he's a wolf. A base creature. He'll submit for food or lust."

"I know you haven't seen many here, mistress, but wolves are known for their fierce loyalty, their odd desire to stay true to a single mate. Since it appears he's dared enter the Land to save my slave, I wonder if he loves her—and if it's true that he can't be aroused by another."

"What are you saying, darling?" she said, her attention at last leaving the warrior and swinging his way. Her eyes were alight with a glimmer of excitement. "Do you think I should tempt him? What if he resists?"

"No one can resist you for long. And think how demoralizing it would be to him."

"I could snack on him later?"

"Or keep him alive indefinitely as your own personal blood well. He's not unattractive."

Her gaze went back, and she licked her lips. "He's handsome, if one admires someone as scarred and chiseled as he is."

"A warrior who trains often. Who prepares for battle every day."

"He'd be hard. *Inflexible*." Her gaze swept his tall frame and Marduk decided not to press her in case she wondered about his interest.

"You will be kept near my quarters," she said, raising her voice. "My personal cells." She lifted her chin to signal to the guards directly behind him. "You will let them take you."

The warrior narrowed his eyes at the guards who approached and no one doubted, armed or not, that they'd have another fight to the death if they tried to kill him now.

As he was led away, Marduk gave Irkalla a look that he hoped conveyed chagrin. "Do I have to worry that your new pet will replace me in your affections?" he asked, mirroring her earlier comment.

Irkalla lifted her eyebrows. "I'm not so completely self-absorbed that I don't realize when I'm being manipulated. What is your interest in the man?"

"He dared touch my woman. I would like to question him. Alone. Learn something about her that I haven't been able to pry from her lips."

"Why is it important?"

Marduk wrapped his arms around her from behind and bent toward her ear. "I would learn her greatest fears and loves."

Irkalla patted his cheek, her smile widening. "We are much alike. How can it be any other way? You are the other half of me."

"Never let Nergal hear you say that."

"Nergal is lazy. I bleed him until he finds his pleasure. He eats, he sleeps. He's content to let me rule, knowing I would never try to kill him and risk losing what I've held so long."

"He's indulgent. Never think he wouldn't move himself if ever he thought another filled your thoughts to exception."

Irkalla offered him a pained smile. "I love him, you know. He's given me everything my heart yearned for when my sister betrayed me. He gave me the means for my revenge."

"The wolf," he said, bringing her attention back. "You will let me question him? I could try to find the key that will make him bend to you. You would not have to risk having him defy you with an audience."

"I'd have to kill him, and I think I would prefer to keep him near for a while. I've never tasted a wolf's blood. I wonder if their cocks are truly barbed."

A shiver rattled against him, and he squeezed her waist. "Let him wonder for a while whether he's been forgotten. In the morning, I will be back to interrogate him."

He released her and tilted his head, an offhand bow that never failed to annoy her.

"Will you ever learn respect?" she said, wrinkling her nose.

Marduk grinned. "Tell the truth. If I did, you'd grow bored with me. Good night, mistress."

He left her and made his way through the throng, back to the courtyard and out the gate. His steps were lighter, his heart thrilling to possibilities. The wolf was strong, moral.

He had more incentive than ever to keep Gabriella safe. Could the wolf be persuaded to replace Marduk in exchange for her freedom, at last freeing him to return to the realm of the living?

Gabriella cried until her stomach hurt. But at last, her sobs quieted to soft hiccups. As her grief receded, pushed ruthlessly deep inside her, she felt shame at her outburst. She'd acted like a woman—overcome with self-pity. She'd let Marduk see how deeply he'd cut her. She'd given him power over her, exposed her soft heart for him to manipulate again. Guntram would have been disappointed in her.

Feeling more herself, she got up from the bed and wandered to the balcony. The desert stretched as far as she could see. A vast lonesomeness that her heart echoed.

She was stuck here. For eternity. With a man who wanted only her submission, not her love. Something she would have settled for, she'd thought—before she'd been given a glimpse at what her future might have held. Just a glimpse of the terrible yearning that was love had spoiled her for accepting such a shallow existence.

The door to the chamber opened, and she pressed closer to the ledge. Footsteps padded toward her, heavy, measured. *Marduk*.

She considered baring her teeth, shifting to use her natural weapons and take out her anger and sorrow on him by ripping at his flesh, but what would it gain her? She might be consigned to the same fate as Guntram, and while there was a hope she might have conceived, she couldn't betray his memory like that.

Instead, she refused to acknowledge Marduk's presence,

unwilling to give him anything, not even her attention. A pale sort of rebellion, but she didn't have any other feminine weapons to confront him with.

Tears hadn't moved him. Neither had her pleas.

Marduk remained silent for a long moment, only the sounds of his breaths and hers breaking the silence between them. Then his feet resettled, scuffing the ground. "Are you considering jumping?"

"Of course not," she said, lifting her lip in a snarl. "I would only injure myself. And then you'd have exactly what you've wanted all along—me, confined to a bed."

"Is that all you think I want from you?"

"It's all you've demanded of me."

He stepped beside her, his hands landing on the top of the ledge. "I want your happiness," he said softly, turning to gaze at her profile.

"Do you even know what that is? It's not sexual satisfaction; it's not filling your belly with sweet rose petals. Do you have any concept of what happiness really is?"

"Perhaps I just need to be shown the way. I would try to make you happy."

"That's impossible. I'm a prisoner. Kept from the man I might have loved for all my life." She snorted. "I've discovered I'm more wolf than I had thought."

"Because you're still grieving?"

"Because I don't know how I will ever be able to stop," she whispered.

"And if I told you he wasn't dead . . . that there's a chance he could still survive . . ."

Gabriella's heart leapt. She stood frozen for a moment, wondering if he was playing some terrible game with her. Her head swung toward him, hope filling her chest even as dread that he might be lying churned in her belly. "You're not playing with me?" she asked, her throat tight.

"I've just returned from the palace. Your warrior laid waste to half a dozen of Her Majesty's finest men. She's impressed."

Gabriella blinked at the sudden moisture in her eyes, and quickly cast her gaze at the desert rather than let him see. "Wolves can be fearsome adversaries. And Guntram's the best there is."

"That's his name?" he asked, sliding closer. "Guntram?"

She shook back her hair, pride welling in her chest. "It means '*War Raven*.' A name he was given for his prowess long ago."

"You've known him a long time?"

She nodded quickly, sniffing. "For most of my life."

"He came to rescue you, to take you back, didn't he?"

Gabriella nodded slowly, knowing that denying the truth would be a waste of breath and probably piss him off. "Of course he came for me. What will happen with him now?"

"It depends entirely on your warrior. If the queen continues to be interested in him, then he may live. I interceded on his behalf, helped Irkalla see that it might be more to her benefit to let him live a little longer."

Gabriella stared at his face, at the grim jut of his square jaw. "Why would you do that? You don't want him here."

"Not for unselfish reasons, I assure you. I could care less whether your wolf lives or dies."

"You did it for me, then?" she asked, not believing for a moment he did it for any reason but his own gain. He'd expect a reward for his effort. He'd expect her submission.

"Of course."

Whatever his reason, she couldn't help being fiercely glad

that he'd interceded. At last she let her heart hope again, and turned to give him a smile. A smile cost her little, but she had nothing else save her body to give him.

His arms opened slowly, hesitantly, and she stepped forward and nestled against his chest, grateful as she'd never been before. "You will expect to be repaid."

"I will expect you to give me what I'm due," he said, sounding impossibly arrogant. "Regardless of what happens with your wolf. I will tell you that I have no desire to see him killed. But that might still happen if he proves intractable and dangerous. You must tell me how I can convince him to surrender to the queen."

Gabriella pulled away and raised her gaze, seeing now that Guntram only had a temporary reprieve unless she helped Marduk find a way to make her mate cooperative. She crossed her arms and rubbed them, suddenly chilled. "He's loyal to me and would sooner face death than break his trust with me."

"Gabriella, tell me how I can convince him that he must."

She read the earnestness in his gaze and knew he meant to help. "You must convince him that if he doesn't, I will come to harm. He would do anything for me."

"You've earned such loyalty?"

She shook her head. "Never. He gave it freely," she shrugged. "I don't know why."

He raised an eyebrow. "He loves you."

Unbidden, her chin lifted. "Is that so hard to believe?"

"You are headstrong and stubborn. If he didn't love you, how else did he stand aside and let you roam freely and take lovers without it driving him to take action?"

"I don't know," she said, unable to hold back another, softer smile. "Maybe you should ask him. Can I see him?"

Marduk shook his head. "Irkalla would never permit it. I won't, either. You belong to me."

Gabriella felt like screaming, so great was her frustration. Men—wolf or dragon—could be complete asses when their pride was at stake. "I belong to no man. I give myself where I wish."

"And will you give yourself to me?" he asked quietly, his gaze boring into hers.

Gabriella took a deep breath, remembering her fierce refusal of him earlier and turning a deaf ear to the voice screaming inside her that demanded she refuse because she was now bonded with Guntram.

For Guntram's sake, they both had to toss away their pride.

Never breaking with his glance, she promised, "Keep him alive, and I will give you everything you ask."

# CHAPTER 17

Guntram paced his cell. He'd been left alone for hours, cooling his heels. Hours his mind spent jumping from lusty images of Gabriella's surrender to worries about how he would keep his promise to save her. A heavily guarded servant had brought a basin of water for him to wash the blood from his body. He'd drunk from it first, face submerged, until the water had turned pink, and then he'd splashed the rest over his chest and arms to wash away the grime.

His cell was sumptuous for a prison. The floors were a cool black marble, the walls painted a lush bloodred. Even the narrow cot was covered with a plush down mattress and piled with pillows.

Only the bars were unembellished. Strong, too. He'd shaken them, testing their strength, but they held firm. Candles burned in sconces on the wall opposite the bars. His was the only cell and had to be entered through a small closet-like room. Round hooks protruded from the back wall, and he didn't have to guess that this was one of the queen's playrooms.

Why had she brought him here instead of throwing him into a dungeon or a pit? The answer was likely one that wouldn't sit well with him, so he kept his mind focused on planning for every possible scenario he might face when Irkalla or one of her minions remembered his existence.

Light footsteps drew near and he halted his pacing, watching the woman who held his life in her hands approach cautiously.

Irkalla was scantily clothed. Guntram took it as good sign. She wanted something from him. A short, beltless robe was held closed by one small hand gripping the fabric at her breasts. He admitted to himself that she was beautiful—in a deeply disturbing way. Dusky skin, dark hair. A feral excitement glittered in her almond eyes.

She wet her plump lips with her tongue as she drew near.

He wondered whether anyone would come running if he reached through the bars and choked her. The thought was deeply satisfying, but he knew he had to tread carefully. He straightened his shoulders, wishing he had a shirt when her greedy gaze traced the flexing muscle.

"What are you called?" she said in a soft singsong voice.

"I am Guntram."

"Guntram . . ." she said slowly, as though savoring it on her lips. "You do know that you live by my whim?"

He tilted his head—all the acknowledgement he would allow the bitch.

Her head canted. "You aren't afraid?"

"My death would mean escape."

"You don't think you're destined to remain here—after death?"

"I've followed my conscience in all things."

"And you're sure you've always taken the correct side?"

"When a man follows his heart, whichever side he fights on, he cannot be damned."

"Is that something wolves believe?"

"It's what I believe."

Her gaze slid away, a small frown bisecting her perfectly arched brows. "I want to know how you came to be here . . . who helped you."

Guntram firmed his lips and gave her a small, tight smile.

Her lush lips thinned. "There are ways, unpleasant ones, to make a man talk."

"The answer isn't important." Her attire, and the fact that she was alone, decided his strategy. "What is important," he added, deepening his voice, "is that I am here. With you. *Now*."

She blinked, and Guntram nearly growled with satisfaction. However revolting the prospect, if he could tempt this woman into letting down her guard, he would escape.

Her gaze raked his body, color filling her cheeks. Then her attention honed on the crystal strung around his neck. "Come closer."

Guntram cursed silently. He'd forgotten to hide it. He stepped toward the bars, pretending indifference and forcing his expression to soften, his gaze to hungrily devour her body.

Irkalla licked her lips again and reached through the bars, lifting the crystal off his chest.

Guntram held his breath when the crystal no longer touched his skin. But nothing happened, and he wondered if the crystal had any power at all. Or if this place, her palace, was enchanted as well.

A small, cat-like smile wreathed her mouth. "You have given me my answer after all, warrior. I know of another with a gift for working with stones. Simon brought you here."

Stepping back, she let the crystal fall against his chest. "I would spend time with you, but now I have another to find and cage." With a last, covetous sweep down his body, she turned. "I will send clothing suitable for your rank," she said over her shoulder, then disappeared through the anteroom.

Guntram exhaled and wrapped his hands around the bars, wishing he could shake the ceiling down around him. His taut body ached for action. At least, he knew he wouldn't be cooped up here for long, although he did begin to wonder whether he would be the night's entertainment or dessert.

Remembering her warning, he stripped off his pants and removed the thin steel wire from the seam. He hid it beneath the mattress, not knowing for sure whether he would be returned here or not, or whether his new clothing would permit him to hide it again. He didn't like the thought of being weaponless against her guards should he have to fight again.

Then, stretching out on the soft mattress, he closed his eyes and willed himself to relax. He had to conserve his strength, quiet his mind. He held to the memory of Gabriella melting around him at last, to her sweet mating sounds and moist depths.

When he grew restless again, he clasped his fist around himself and eased his body while his mind lingered in the lush dream of a future spent inside her arms.

Marduk drew Gabriella back into the room, relieved she no longer considered him a monster. Again, he drew her close to his body, his hands gliding soothingly up and down her back. "When I leave you, I will find out what has happened with him. Don't worry now. Irkalla's intrigued and keeping him close."

Gabriella raised her face. Her darkening gaze betrayed her worry. "Guntram's so stubborn, so proud. And he doesn't know how to lie or pretend. If he displeases her . . ."

"His strength of will offers her a unique challenge. I'll be sure to stoke her interest."

"Marduk, what will happen to him?"

"Irkalla will never let him go willingly, but I can arrange for him to be returned to where he came from."

"You can send him back to the other realm?"

"A sorcerer lives not far from here. He would help if I ask."

She snuggled closer inside his embrace. "Is there no way you would allow me to leave with him?" she said softly.

"If I must stay, so shall you. I'm selfish enough to want you here. Never think that I would help him from kindness, but to remove a threat to our relationship—and to earn your promise to give yourself freely to me."

"To submit to you, you mean," she said grumpily.

Marduk smiled against her hair. "Has it truly been a trial for you?"

"You know you've given me great pleasure."

He heard what she left unspoken and sighed. "In time, you

will settle. I will treat you well. Give you all you desire . . . and don't say it . . . except for the one thing you want most. It will have to be enough."

"If you save him, I will be . . . satisfied," she whispered.

He hugged her close, then lifted her chin with his fingers. He kissed her, inhaling her distinctive scent, made stronger by her bout of weeping. Her eyes were still rimmed in red, her nose a little swollen. But her lips trembled and parted beneath his, and it was enough.

Reaching down, he cupped her bottom and lifted her.

Gabriella needed no instruction to wind her long legs around his waist. Hastily, he pushed down his clothing and freed himself, sighing when she squirmed to ease her moist channel down his turgid cock.

Locked together, he walked back to the balcony and sat her on the edge. With sunlight catching the red strands in her brown hair, he was reminded again of his sweet Zara. Funny how often of late he'd thought of her.

Gabriella's legs tightened around him. "Don't drop me," she murmured, smiling up at him.

"Never, darling. Hold tight to me." For once, he took her gently, flexing his hips and stroking slowly upward.

Her head fell back, a sigh escaping her soft, pouting lips. "Have I told you how well you do this?"

Marduk felt a grin stretch his lips, feeling suddenly light and carefree. "I'm glad I please you in this at least."

"You please and amaze me. You would any woman."

He heard the underlying exception. She would never love him. Perhaps he could gift her with her heart's desire. Nestling closer between her legs, he bent and kissed her, sliding into her mouth to mate with her slick, sweet tongue while he circled his cock, grinding deeply. Within moments, her snug passage began the sensual caresses that rippled along his shaft.

So simple, this sexual act. So uncomplicated. So lacking the sizzling violence of their previous couplings. Like lovers of long acquaintance.

Breaking the kiss, he slid his lips along her chin and nuzzled her ear, her neck, his hands clasping her buttocks to bring her closer still, until they barely moved.

Her body writhed internally on his cock, massaging his length with succulent clasping. Sweet heat filled his belly, tightened his balls, and then he drew back and slammed forward, a slow deliberate pounding that caused her to moan and undulate as the rapture swept over them both.

When they rested against each other, breathing deeply, their chests pressing together and apart, he leaned back. "I must go."

"Hurry back."

She worried for her warrior. For the gift of the other's life, she would welcome him.

Still connected, he gathered her up and strode back into his chamber, kneeling on the bed and following her down. "Rest. I will send clothing. Tonight, there will be no tribute demanded. All attention will be on the wolf."

Pulling free, he refastened his clothing and strode from the room, silently commanding Xalia to watch the door but not enter. Excitement simmered inside him, making his steps lighter as he hurried to the palace.

When he entered Irkalla's chambers, he slowed his steps. Ninshubur stood in the center of the room, his frail body quivering. "I know nothing, mistress, of another sorcerer inside this city."

"Would you lie to me, old man?" she said, standing close while her gaze watched him twitch.

"Never. Your generosity kept me from the hall."

"If I discover that you have . . ."

Sensing she was almost through with him, Marduk strode closer. "What has happened?"

"The warrior wears a crystal, a shield. Someone powerful is here."

Marduk recalled seeing the false Dagon in the dungeon and silently agreed. "The wolf won't tell you where to find his accomplice?"

"He's stubborn. Bristles his back like a dog when I make my demands." Her sly glance locked with his. "But I think I know how I can make him tell me everything I need to know."

He tensed, knowing whatever she had in mind involved Gabriella.

"You are bringing her tonight?"

He didn't bother trying to pretend he didn't know to whom she referred. "If that is your wish," he said, inclining his head.

"We will see if his pride is as strong as his need to protect her."

Marduk narrowed his eyes. "I would not have her harmed."

"Of course not. I would not overstep," she said, too easily. "I know you would have enjoyment from her for a long time to come. So I will demand nothing . . . fatal."

Marduk held his tongue, although anger crept up his neck in hot waves she wouldn't fail to note. "Let me talk to him."

"Do you think he will tell you, when he refused my command?"

"I don't know, but what harm can come of it? And I can lay suspicion in his mind about what will occur tonight."

Her fierce expression relaxed. A slow smile tipped her lips. "Make him uneasy. Make him sweat."

Marduk bowed. "As you wish." Then he left her, striding through her quarters to her private apartment at the rear and the small cell where she kept those unlucky enough to serve her baser needs.

She hadn't sipped from him yet. This he knew because she expected him to appear at the feast later. Any of the lovers she'd conscripted in the past had suffered long bouts of weakness, having lost blood and vigor to her voracious demands.

The cell was quiet as he approached. The warrior lay naked on the mattress, an arm beneath his head. His dark eyes glittered angrily when Marduk drew abreast of the cell.

"We're alone, warrior," Marduk said quietly, studying his rival.

"Where is she?" he bit out.

Marduk kept his expression carefully neutral. "In my care. Well . . . and sated."

Guntram jackknifed from the bed, slammed his feet on the floor, and stalked toward the bars. "She's mine. My mate. *My wife.*"

Marduk hadn't known, but should have guessed what had transpired inside the dungeon. Females, when mated with a Wolfen male, were bound. "She failed to mention that fact when I fucked her last."

A growl erupted and Guntram reached through the bars. But Marduk stepped back, unhurried, gauging the rage in the other man and wondering just how far his need to protect and own the passions of his mate would lead him. "She will be at the feast tonight, but you won't be allowed near her unless Irkalla allows it."

"Why are you telling me this?"

"I would bargain with you."

"What can I offer? I'm caged like a beast. No wealth to offer. You own everything I want."

Marduk stepped closer, unafraid that he was entering the other man's reach. "I have been trapped here for nearly three thousand years," he said softly. "Forced from my own wife's arms, but I can't leave unless another takes my place."

"Your place?"

"I am the Master of the Demons, a title and responsibility bequeathed me by Solomon himself upon his death. As he ascended into the heavens, I was cast into hell."

Guntram's brows lowered as comprehension dawned. "You would have me become the Master? Why would anyone follow me? I'm not a demon and have no special powers beyond my skills as a warrior."

"You seem a just man. Strong. Resolute. *Incorruptible.* The power resides in my seal," he said, curling his fist and raising it to show him the ring. "With it, I command the lesser demons, those outside Irkalla's immediate circle. I am second in rank in Kur-gal. Whatever you want, whomever you want, can be yours."

"And Gabriella?" Guntram asked, his voice straining.

"Her disposition is entirely your choice. You may keep her by your side or let me take her with me when I go."

The warrior didn't immediately reject the latter offer. *Interesting.*

Guntram took a step back, his fearsome scowl fading. “Must I decide now?”

“Tell me your decision later. I’ll find a way to meet with you again. In the meantime, my mistress expects me to come back with a certain piece of information.”

“What makes you think I will tell you when I refused her?”

“She said precisely the same thing.” Marduk shrugged. “I had to ask in order to be able to answer her honestly that you refused again when I return.” He turned on his heels, and then glanced back. “She is sweet—your Gabriella. Prickly on the outside, but soft at the center.”

“You have not raped her?” Guntram said hoarsely.

“She’s given herself to me, sweetly, from the start.”

Guntram’s proud shoulders slumped. “Thank you.”

Marduk stared, disconcerted by the selfless nature of the man in front of him. Guntram preferred knowing his wife had sought her pleasure with another man rather than knowing she had suffered. “Last night . . . it was the first time you were together?”

Guntram nodded, his expression growing guarded again. “Why do you ask?”

“I don’t think she knew she loved you.” Why he felt the need to share that, he couldn’t have said. Perhaps he wasn’t as corrupted as he’d come to believe. He felt empathy for the man. Understood his lack of anger, because he hoped Zara had been treated well by whoever lay with her.

Marduk gave Guntram a nod. “Tonight, do your best to please the mistress. Stay alive another day.”

“I won’t sleep with her.”

“Even if Gabriella would want it?”

“I’m not like you.”

"Or her, it would seem."

"I'm pledged to her."

"So you'd prefer to die to prove you love her?"

"It's our way," Guntram gritted out.

"Again, apparently not hers."

"I don't care what she must do. What she wants to do. But I would have her know I honor her."

"Don't be an ass. Prove your love by surviving. Prove it by being there to ensure her future."

"I won't be made a spectacle of."

"There is that possibility—whether you're forced to pleasure your mistress or feed her. Irkalla doesn't care about you, only about her pleasure. If you give her disrespect in front of an audience, she will crucify you. Remember that Gabriella will be watching, and she will carry that memory all of her life."

The wolf's fingers tightened around the bars, but he nodded, resignation in his burning glance.

Satisfied he'd made his point, Marduk left. He had ruffled feathers to smooth, and Gabriella to prime for the evening's events. But at the end, he felt a shining hope that at last he'd be free.

# CHAPTER 18

Once more, Gabriella entered the Queen of the Dead's hall, dressed only in her short skirt and baubles, and shoring up her courage to play her part in tonight's performance. Marduk, dressed in his familiar black costume, had remained silent since they'd left his quarters.

He hadn't told her how he would manage it, but before they'd set out, he'd promised to get her close to Guntram so that she could add her pleas for him to cooperate until they could find a way to free him.

She'd leave out the part about not accompanying him back to the other realm. She'd agreed to exchange her freedom for his life, although Marduk hadn't asked her to repeat that vow when he'd returned. He assured her that Guntram was well and at least considering behaving.

The hall was filled with the curious, all benches crammed to overflowing and more creatures standing in the back. They knew another living wolf had trespassed and hoped to witness the carnage of his murder.

Again, Gabriella knelt on a bench beside Marduk on the dais. From her lower vantage, she had an excellent view of Irkalla, who sat with a cat-like smile curving her lips, her dark eyes glittering with ill-concealed excitement. Beside her, Nergal, the one most feared due to his dominion, sat rocking back and forth, a vapid, listless expression on his face. Gabriella wondered if Irkalla had drained him to ensure he left early.

The seats beside her, reserved for Dumuzi and Inanna, were still vacant, and Gabriella hoped with all her heart that neither showed up, because they would take an especially perverse interest in seeing how Guntram fared in Irkalla's custody.

Her hopes were quickly dashed when Dumuzi strode through the doors, his powerful body held erect, his gaze on the dais, and his hand wrapped around the end of Inanna's tether.

Marduk plucked meat from some sort of fowl and held it in front of her. "You must eat," he said aloud. His gaze reminded her to hide her fear.

She opened her mouth, washing her expression free of tension. Tonight, she'd be a happy sex slave, waiting on her master's every whim. The meat was tender and well spiced, but tasted like cardboard against her dry tongue. She swallowed hard, hoping she wouldn't choke, but gave Marduk a nod to let him know she was all right.

The Master of the Demons had proven he did have the capacity for compassion. Something she hadn't expected. Something she could hold on to as their relationship stretched into an endless shared future. Her life wouldn't be so bad here. Perhaps, in time, she'd even come to love him.

Dumuzi slid into the seat beside her and raked her with his gaze. It was all she could do not to snarl.

"Forgive our tardiness, mistress," Dumuzi said, leaning forward to meet Irkalla's irritated glance. "My wife required . . . instruction."

A glance Inanna's way confirmed the tale. Color blossomed on her latte cheeks. Her lips were crimped into a tight, narrow line.

Irkalla laughed. "You are forgiven. We both know how headstrong my sister can be. *How willfull.*"

Gabriella wondered at the venom that could keep a millennia-old grudge alive. She shivered and pressed closer to Marduk's thigh.

"Your slave has learned some affection for you, Bel," Irkalla drawled.

Marduk petted Gabriella's hair, tugging secretly to remind her not to bare her teeth. "I am kind when served well."

"An interesting concept. One I don't embrace, though. All here live to serve my needs . . . our needs," she amended, patting her husband's hand, who seemed unaware of his wife's words and action. "I offer no softness unless I'm pleased beyond simple gratification."

"You offer softness to me," Marduk murmured. "Should I be flattered?"

She gave him a flirtatious sweep of her thick dark lashes. "You need no flattery, sir."

Dumuzi moved restlessly beside Gabriella. "What of this new wolf? You didn't bleed him dry yet, did you? Does that mean you are going to offer him as the main entrée at tonight's feast?"

"He will be brought to us shortly, but only for all to assess my new pet's attributes and admire him. I have wicked plans for the beast."

Gabriella's belly tightened upon hearing the sultry note entering Irkalla's voice. She wondered if Guntram knew he would be expected to service her tonight, and whether he had enough interest in his own survival to please the bitch. He certainly had the skills and stamina. She still burned from the memory of his taking.

Dumuzi leaned across Gabriella, deliberately pressing his thigh against her. "Will you offer him up for entertainment or savor him privately with perhaps a few close courtiers?" he asked, sounding hopeful.

"Do you desire a private audience?" Irkalla asked slyly.

"I desire less noise. Less distraction for my conquests."

Irkalla's chest rose and fell quicker, her interest evident in her deepening color. Did Guntram or Dumuzi inspire her lust, or was it the thought of having all three males at her disposal that left her breathless?

Then Gabriella caught Marduk's frown as he eyed Dumuzi. It was subtle, and quickly replaced by a bored expression.

"Husband, you tire," Irkalla said, turning to Nergal and placing her hand against his cheek. "Would you like to be escorted to your bed?"

Nergal's head turned toward Irkalla, and his beautiful round eyes rested on his wife. "I am tired, but you will know this. You please me, wife," he said, his words slurring slightly. "Have your fun. But don't forget that I wait."

Irkalla blinked and smiled radiantly as Nergal pushed away from the table and stood.

Gabriella shook her head, wondering about their relationship and how so powerful a demon could be led by his balls and be glad of it.

When he'd left the room, Irkalla's head turned to sweep their table with a glance. "Shall we bring out our guest?" With just a wave of her hand, the doors at the rear of the hall opened. All heads swiveled to watch.

Gabriella forced her body to remain still, her breaths even, as Guntram strode into the hall.

He was nude but for a short linen slave's kilt. His body gleamed with sweat, or was it oil? All the musculature of his chest, abdomen and thighs stood in relief as torchlight gleamed on the rigid curves. With his short hair, stiff posture and proud, furious expression, he looked like a Roman warrior of old.

Her breath caught, her chest tightening around her aching heart. His gaze met hers, and then quickly flitted to the queen's. Of course he couldn't betray too much interest. Irkalla would use his feelings for her against him. Against her.

Still, the fleeting glance had struck her. Tonight might be the last time she saw him. Touched him. And he'd never know for certain that she carried his child. Not unless he noted that her heat, which had burned so hotly the previous night, had retreated, its purpose fulfilled.

The room grew silent as he strode deeper, unescorted into

the hall, the slap of his bare feet on the cool tile the only sound as he approached the dais.

Unable to resist, Gabriella lifted her nose to scent the air, welcoming his unique smell.

His nostrils flared and she knew he shared her elation, her primal impulse to bathe in his rich, masculine aroma.

When he stood in front of the dais, she held her breath, caught by how beautiful he was. His body radiated power and pride.

Irkalla lifted her chin, waiting. Marduk cleared his throat.

Guntram's lips tightened, but he knelt on one knee and lowered his head.

He remained silent so long, Gabriella worried he'd refuse to offer obeisance. She leaned forward, hoping to give him a signal, but Marduk laid his hand on her shoulder.

Guntram glanced toward that hand, then lifted his gaze to Marduk's before turning to Irkalla. "Mistress, I'm here at your command."

"What do you offer?"

"As I am naked, I have only myself to render tribute."

Irkalla leaned back, her skin flushing and her eyes glittering. "Will you obey me in all matters?"

"I am yours to command."

"Nicely done," Marduk said softly, bending toward Irkalla. "His pride speaks well of his respect for your authority."

"It does. He pleases me in many ways. I think I would learn the measure of his skills. A private audience then?" she said, tipping her chin toward Marduk.

The room erupted in muttered complaints.

Marduk's mouth eased into a sensual smile. "Will I have to worry about your affection?"

"Never, for you know I am voracious." She turned to the guard at the end of the platform. "Take him below."

Gabriella heaved a sigh as Guntram was led away. The less time he spent here, the less opportunity for her blunt warrior to condemn himself.

Marduk's hand pressed into her shoulder, a silent warning that she heeded without knowing why he cautioned her. But since he'd managed to maneuver the queen to serve their interest, she would trust in him a little while longer.

Marduk's mind raced with the opportunity unfolding before him now. So many questions had been answered in the last few minutes that he fought hard to keep his excitement from showing in his face.

Ruthlessly, he forced his breaths and heartbeats to remain even.

Irkalla lifted her hand, and Marduk stood to help her up, turning his back on Gabriella, but she got the hint and backed off the platform. She'd follow his lead without question this night.

Marduk led Irkalla down the steps, then fell in behind her, standing to the side and gesturing to Gabriella to follow his mistress, then allowing Inanna and Dumuzi to precede him, as well. Dumuzi dropped the leash.

When they entered the dark stairwell, Marduk snaked out his forearm and wrapped it around Dumuzi's throat, drawing him back.

"Keep your voice down or I'll break your neck," he whispered.

Dumuzi's hands tightened on his forearm, but didn't try to break the hold. "How did you know?" he replied quietly.

"The demon you impersonate loves a larger audience to witness his wife's humiliations. Who are you?"

The mage, who wore Dumuzi's face, replied wryly, "I think you know."

Marduk jerked his arm against his neck. "Tell me why I shouldn't bring the guards down on you."

"Because I'm the only one who will open the portal for you."

Marduk loosened his grip, letting the mage take a step downward. The mage filled his lungs with air. His face, Dumuzi's hateful visage, was imbued with a gleeful mirth. "Be ready."

Marduk nodded. "We'd best not call attention."

They hurried down the steps, falling in behind the others and entering the chamber, which was lit by dozens of torches and candles but empty, save for two guards.

Irkalla glanced around her at the empty sofas. "What do you think, Marduk?"

"I think one of the cells would serve us best. The larger one at the rear, perhaps?"

Inanna didn't move to follow, eying Dumuzi as Irkalla led the procession to the cell. Her gaze narrowed and a frown bisected her perfectly arched brows. "Husband . . ."

The man wearing her husband's face turned, his mouth curving downward with displeasure.

"Something doesn't smell right," she said softly.

Marduk halted, his heart thudding hard against his chest. If she revealed them now, all would be lost.

The mage bent toward her, wrapping her leash around his fist and pulling her close. "Inanna," he said into her face. "I think you know who I am."

Inanna's eyes widened as she returned his stare. "Where is he?"

"Do you care if he suffers?"

Her nose wrinkled in disgust. "Of course not."

"Would you not like to exact a little revenge for how badly he has treated you?"

"Why shouldn't I demand you take me with you when you return to *Ardeal*?" she asked, her voice shaking.

The mage's expression hardened. "Because you know I will not, even if it means I must sacrifice my mission. Your husband lies asleep and bound in your bed. If you hurry, you can keep him there indefinitely."

Inanna's lips parted, her indecision clear in her glittering eyes.

The mage leaned closer. "Won't you enjoy your sister's fury when she realizes she's been betrayed? You will be there to soothe her, to remind her of your familial bonds. She will grow to trust you again."

Inanna backed up a pace, then whirled and ran for the steps.

As she disappeared, Marduk said, "Do you trust she won't simply alert the guards above?"

The mage lifted one brow. "She hopes we will kill her sister. Her need for revenge against the two of them will be too much for her to resist. Let's not keep Irkalla waiting."

Irkalla stood inside the entrance of the cell, a frown creasing her forehead. "Where is my sister?"

"It's too crowded in here," Marduk said easily. "I sent her away. She was disappointed at not being here to enjoy the wolf's submission."

Irkalla didn't look pleased at the bit of news, but her gaze strayed to Guntram, whose gleaming physique rippled as he tensed his fists. "It is crowded. Do we need the girl here?"

"If you prefer, she can wait outside the cell and watch. You like watching, don't you, Gabriella?" Marduk said, careful to keep his tone crafty.

Gabriella's eyes widened, then her gaze went to Guntram, a desperate plea in her gaze.

Irkalla's lips stretched. "I think she does. Outside, girl."

Marduk tamped down his disgust and jerked his chin toward the door.

Gabriella walked stiffly outside, then leaned against the far wall, her face hidden in the shadows.

Guntram's chest rose, his fists curling tighter. Marduk hoped he wouldn't spoil the moment he sensed was coming by moving too soon. Guards still lingered in the hallway. They needed to press closer.

Irkalla approached the warrior and slipped a finger beneath the top edge of the garment that covered Guntram's hips. "Take it off."

Guntram kept his gaze above her shoulder, pinned to Gabriella, and slipped the knot at his hip.

Irkalla released the breath she'd been holding and reached down to clasp his flaccid cock. "I admire a man who doesn't lack self-discipline. But I also find great satisfaction in testing his limits." She caressed his cock, lifting it and touching the smooth cap with a finger. "I've heard things about a wolf's cock. How it expands when aroused to lodge inside a female. I would know what that feels like. But first I'd like to see it."

A muscle flexed at the side of Guntram's square jaw. The grinding of teeth was audible.

"Must I bring your female inside and tie her to the bench for you to watch another rape her, or will you give me what I command? You did give me your vow."

Guntram closed his eyes, and his expression betrayed a hint of anguish as he seemed to sink into a memory. But his cock slowly filled inside Irkalla's grasp.

"Not so terrible, was that? You've surrendered only a little of your pride." Irkalla knelt in front of him and opened her mouth, taking him inside and suckling, drawing back her head to milk him and tug him into a full erection.

When she was satisfied she sat back on her heels. "I would have it all. Don't withhold."

Guntram reached down, pushing her hand away, and then manipulated his cock, gripping it tighter than she had and squeezing until blood filled the tip and it swelled.

The thick, rounded knot appeared to fascinate her, and she bent again to take the cap in her mouth and suckle. "It's hard," she said when she came off. "And so broad." She met his narrowed gaze, then glanced over her shoulder at Gabriella. "But you would know that. Could you feel the difference deep inside you?"

Gabriella wouldn't meet Guntram's gaze. Marduk wondered if she didn't dare because the emotions she'd felt when he'd been locked deep inside her would have shown on her face. "I felt the difference," she said softly.

"Why should you deny yourself the experience, my queen?" Marduk murmured.

"Why, indeed?" she replied, laughing. "But will you be jealous? I might find his cock more memorable than yours."

"I wish only your pleasure, mistress."

"Of course you do." Her tone held no irony. The bitch believed that everyone was concerned for her pleasure.

"You should let him take you like the dog he is."

"On all fours?"

"Bent, your sex presented for him to sniff and nuzzle before he ruts." Marduk gave Guntram a look, reminding him of the need to cooperate, but Guntram's lips flattened into a furious, thin line.

"Your new pet doesn't know how precious the gift of your attentions can be. The rewards cannot be measured," Marduk said slowly.

Guntram grunted, but his expression eased into a passive façade.

"The bench, darling," Marduk urged. "You needn't grovel on the floor."

"What say you, Dumuzi?" Irkalla said, as though just remembering that he was there. "You've been so quiet all evening. Does the thought of me rutting with a dog disturb you?"

Dumuzi's head inclined. "When the shine dulls from your latest acquisition, you will remember who serves you best."

"I can always count on you, can't I?"

Dumuzi's face reddened. How did the mage do it? Assume the emotions of the one he impersonated? Dumuzi would have been quietly furious at the reminder of the one time he hadn't been so dependable, when Inanna had seduced him, taking him for her mate as his lust ruled him.

"When I am not at the mercy of a sorcerer's tricks, you know well that you can count on me."

"Yes I can. So why don't you help me onto the bench, and watch over me in case this wolf decides he must pin me with his jaws?"

The guards outside the cell shifted restlessly on their feet. "Ma'am, should we not be inside with you to protect you?" a thick-necked guard said.

"I have protectors here. The warrior prides himself on honor, and he wants to live another day to free his woman. Incentive enough to cause me no harm. He won't dare savage me."

With her hand inside the mage's, she stepped onto the platform and bent over the padded bench. "Shall I restrain your hands?" the mage whispered.

Irkalla laughed. "Why not?"

Marduk knew the thrill of eminent danger fueled her arousal as much as the thought of experimenting with the unusual cock. Both hands were bound in leather cuffs. "Leave off the ankle restraints. I will want to move."

Then Marduk ambled toward the cell door, ostensibly for a better view, and turned his back on the guards just outside the open door. Dumuzi took up a position on the opposite side of the door.

Guntram gave them both a surreptitious glance, then lifted his gaze to Gabriella.

Marduk held his breath. He needed to arouse the queen and distract the guards with their lusty play, leaving them less vigilant.

Marduk cleared his throat, pulling Gabriella's attention to him. He gave her a small nod. Her wide gaze went back to Guntram, a silent plea in her golden brown depths to accompany the small, tight smile she wore.

Guntram's jaw tightened, but he stepped behind the queen and bent. First his hands landed on her buttocks, smoothing over them then gripping them firmly to hold them apart. Then his head dipped and the wet sounds of a tongue lapping in profuse moisture followed. For long, tense moments the watchers held their breaths.

Irkalla's head lifted, her back arching, her bottom lifting

higher. Her face was radiant, skin flushing a deep rose, her lush lips forming an excited circle.

The guards beside him breathed deeply, their gazes likewise glued to the queen's rapturous expression.

Just a few minutes more and they would make their move.

"Come inside me," Irkalla crooned. Her hips lifted, her knees settling deeper onto the cushioned squabs.

Guntram rose, his face red, his lips moist. He fisted his hand around his cock and squeezed, increasing his girth before kneeling on the step behind Irkalla and bending over her.

He breathed deeply as though girding himself to accept a great burden.

The moment he entered her, everyone knew because Irkalla's eyes slid shut and her mouth opened around a soft gasp.

The first slam of his hips rattled the wooden platform. The second forced air from Irkalla in a soft, feminine grunt. By the third, Guntram's desperate gaze met Gabriella's and Marduk knew they had to move now before the warrior ruined their chance by exposing his anguish to everyone there.

# CHAPTER 19

The queen's heat clasped Guntram's engorged cock and his stomach tightened with revulsion. The only woman he'd ever wanted to slip inside was only paces away, watching as he pleasured another.

Feeling as vile, as amoral as the vampires he despised, he lashed his hips at the bitch beneath him, slamming hard to punish her and her kind for the fact that he was here, punishing her for the fact that he and Gabriella suffered for the *convenience* of others.

Gabriella's eyes were glassy, filling quickly, but Guntram hadn't the strength to reassure her, to tell her silently that he'd get past this. Instead, he bared his teeth and hammered harder.

While blood rushed to his sex and to his head, he did note subtle stirrings from the other two men. *At last.*

Perhaps they'd make their move, and he could withdraw before he gave Irkalla her pleasure, before he spewed his precious wolf's seed into her whore's cunt.

He let go of her ass and bent closer, his hand sliding to the thin wire he'd hidden in his fist, then stuffed beneath the cushions of the bench when he first entered the room.

His excitement over the battle to come increased his sexual fervor and Irkalla groaned, no doubt thinking his escalating ardor was all about her. But Guntram had had enough. If the men were still waiting for the right moment, he'd give it to them.

He leaned over her back, still rutting into ripe heat, and slid his hands forward, carrying the wire beneath Irkalla's outstretched neck. Then he straightened, pulling his hands up, tightening the garrote—just enough to slice shallowly into her tender skin.

Irkalla let out a muffled shriek and bucked against him.

"Easy, now," he whispered, looking up.

The guards, their eyebrows lowered, stepped toward the entrance, but Marduk was already moving, shoving them both against the corridor wall and looping an arm around the one closest to him—tightening, then twisting, breaking the guard's neck and letting him fall silently to the ground.

Likewise, Dumuzi caught the other, halting his shout with a knife slicing across his throat. As blood spurted, he pushed him to the ground.

Gabriella's expression grew taut, fear and excitement shivering through her.

Guntram pulled out of Irkalla, looped the garrote twice

around the queen's neck, then tied it below the bench. "The wire's very sharp," he rasped. "If you move, if you try to shout, you'll risk severing your own head."

Then he was off the platform, pausing to tie the slave's skirt he'd been given to wear around his hips and lifting a sword from the ground beside one of the fallen guards. He straightened, his muscles flexing as adrenaline spiked his blood, and followed the others down the corridor toward the empty chamber.

"How are we going to get out of here?" he asked quietly.

Marduk's smile was tight, determined. "You'll follow the dragon."

Then they were racing up the steps, Marduk in the lead, Guntram at the rear. When they entered the hall, all gazes swung their way.

Gazes locked, expressions shifting from suspicion to shock at the sight of the wolf carrying a sword and the blood spatter that coated the other three.

Guards at the back of the hall shouted and began to run through the crowd, shoving away anyone in their way.

Marduk leapt atop a table, spread out his arms and transformed, crushing the table beneath him. His tail swung in every direction, lashing out, clearing a path for them, then he lifted his head and a fiery explosion blasted a hole through the ceiling.

"Get on his back," Simon shouted, once again wearing his own face.

They all climbed on, one behind the other between his wings, and Marduk rose on his hind legs, his forearms pulling at the edges of the hole in the ceiling to widen it. With one powerful downward flap, they were shooting through the hole and into the darkened sky.

Below them, shouts erupted, arrows whistling silently behind them—but they were already too high.

"There's a cave beneath the ridge," Simon shouted. "We have to get to it. I have what I need to open the portal there."

"*Hold on*," came a voice inside Guntram's head, Marduk's voice.

Guntram wrapped his arm around Gabriella's waist and clasped a spiny ridge, then bent forward as Marduk soared downward.

"*They won't be far behind us. Already the guard is spilling out of the gates.*"

"Why are they following? Why aren't you repelling them, Marduk?" Simon said.

"*Have to conserve*," he replied. "*Save something in case we need it later.*"

Shrill shrieks came from off to one side, and Guntram swung toward the sound. Winged, black-skinned demons were bearing down on them.

Marduk skimmed downward between hills of sand and then turned upward, his wingtips hitting the tops of the dunes and spraying sand into the air behind them.

But the dark, winged demons were undeterred, continuing to gain on them, their strange, shrill cries filling the air.

"*They will try to unseat you.*"

The creatures behind them were faster, more agile, and Guntram knew he'd spoken the truth. "I'd rather make a stand on the ground with a sword in my hand," Guntram shouted.

"*Hold tight!*" Marduk executed a sharp turn, heading back toward the ridge. "*Where is that damned cave?*"

"Midway up, just to the left," Simon said

"*I see it. You might have mentioned how small it is.*" Marduk flew straight for the opening, then lifted his wings and angled them forward to brake. Turning, he hovered near the entrance. "*You have to jump.*"

"Fuck me!" Guntram muttered, staring down at the steep drop, but he stood first and waited for the next downward flap of wings to clear the cave's entrance and leapt for it, landing at the lip of the entrance. Then he turned, grabbed a jagged edge of rock and reached out to help Gabriella, who also sailed safely across, landing hard on her bare knees.

He helped her up, then turned to await Simon, but Gabriella's soft gasp behind him had him turning back. She sat huddled on the ground, her face leeched of color.

"Touch her," Simon shouted from Marduk's back.

Guntram reached down and clasped her shoulder. Her eyes cleared, focusing on him, and he realized there really was power in the crystal strung around his neck. "Keep your hand on me, Gabriella." Then he turned back to wait for Simon.

When Simon made the leap, he hugged the side of the cave. "Give Marduk room."

"He'll never make it," Guntram said. "He's too damn big."

But Marduk seemed to have no such qualms, flying upward, then curving down again, swooping toward the entrance. When he thrust his head and forearms inside the opening, he transformed.

With Gabriella's hand planted against his back, Guntram rushed forward to catch Marduk by the arms before he slid off the shelf. He pulled him into the cave.

"Guntram," Simon said softly, "we're going to need that sword."

Guntram had noted the *V*-formation flying straight toward them. "I know, those damned harpies are coming."

"Don't piss them off. But they aren't who I'm worried about."

Guntram heard the steely edge of Simon's voice and turned slowly. Flat, reflective disks, a matched pair, shone from the back of the cave. Then a low, ominous rumble reverberated, shaking stones from the ceiling.

"Simon?" Guntram whispered harshly.

"This is an *anzu* den."

"And you didn't think to mention it before?"

"It didn't matter when we arrived because I knew we wouldn't meet a bird when we arrived."

As the creature neared, its paws, then its fierce lion's head, entering the moonlight spilling into the cave's entrance, Guntram lifted his sword, swearing. "If I keep it occupied, you might be able to slip past it."

"It'll kill you," Gabriella said, coming around his side. "I'll transform to help."

Guntram stepped forward, shoving her behind him as he eyed the creature slinking ever closer. "You'll do no such thing. I didn't come this far to lose you like this."

Simon turned to Marduk, who nodded. "You'd better get against the walls again," he murmured.

Marduk stepped past Guntram to stand in the center of the tunnel. He held the creature's gaze and stretched out his arms, hands extended palms up. He closed his eyes, and a light blinked beneath one upraised hand, then flickered and glowed strongly, subduing the shadows pressing around them.

Marduk opened his eyes then and stared at the creature

creeping closer, then drew back the hand wearing the ring with the seal and slammed it forward. A sound like a sonic boom exploded all around them, and the *anzu* fell flat, whimpering, against the cave floor.

Marduk gasped and dropped his hands. The light surrounding his hand faded.

"You didn't kill it," Guntram muttered.

"It's not inherently evil. Just hungry. Something to remember," he said, aiming a sharp glance at Guntram.

Guntram nodded his understanding, then turned as shrill cries from outside the cave entrance grew in volume. "This cave's getting crowded."

"Best plan I could manage," Simon said.

"Glad you think you have it all figured out. What are they, anyway?" he asked, eyeing the dark creatures who lightly touched down before them one by one.

"*Lillum*. Vicious demons. If they get close enough they'll rip your throat out."

Guntram thought they looked like creatures from a nightmare. Completely black, their shiny skin reflected the moonlight. Long black hair hung in tight ringlets down their backs. Their breasts were small, their nipples cone-shaped like a young girl's. Their expressions were also girlish in a frightening way. Girlish even when black incisors slipped over the edges of their lips.

One stepped forward, as graceful on land as in the air, her naked body swaying. "Master," she said, her gaze locking with Marduk's. "Why have you betrayed us?"

"Aya, darling," he said softly. "It's time for me to leave."

"Don't you love us anymore?"

"I will miss you."

Her head canted as though listening to something buzzing beside her. "Our queen has asked that we sever your hand and retrieve the ring. Already Dumuzi leads her army. She will give him power over us." Her eyes grew wide. "Who will protect us?"

"My hand will stay where it is. And if you let us pass, I promise a replacement who will please you every bit as much as me."

"But will he love us?"

"You will have to show him the way. You enjoyed training me, did you not?"

Aya grinned. "Do you think to sway us? Even Nergal has left his bed. Even now, more *anzu* are winging their way here."

Guntram peered toward the sky. More lion-headed birds soared toward them, their wings flattened as they arrowed downward.

"Stay clear of my fire, Aya. For the sake of our love, I wouldn't want you singed."

She laughed, then spread her wings and leapt off the ledge, spiraling upward, the others of her flock following.

"I don't like this," Guntram said. "We're trapped. Simon, go get that damn bag."

"We must do something first," Simon said quietly.

Guntram looked to Marduk, who nodded, then lifted his hands. He tugged the ring past his knuckle, his chest lifting as though surrendering a great burden, and handed it to Guntram.

Guntram looked at the ring lying in his palm, then lifted his gaze to Gabriella. She was shaking her head, her eyes filling. "No. No!" she said, turning to Marduk. "You promised that if I stayed you'd let him go."

Guntram glared at Marduk. "He promised that if I took his place, he'd help you get back."

Marduk shrugged. "I made two agreements, each better than the last. You may come with me Gabriella. Guntram has given you into my care."

Guntram fisted his hand around the ring, unable to meet Gabriella's eyes. "You'd better get going. Now."

Gabriella grabbed his forearm. "I can't. I'd rather stay here with you."

His heart slowed, pounding purposefully as he looked into her face one last time. He cupped her chin in his palm. "Don't make this sacrifice count for nothing. Go. You may even now be carrying my children. I don't want them born in this place."

Simon cleared his throat and stepped into their tense circle. "Sorry to disappoint you both, knowing how much you want to prove you love each other, but the ring is meant for me." He cupped his hand over Guntram's closed fist. "I hoped I'd make it this far. And if I did, I made arrangements. I will remain as Master of the Demons. You will both take your places in your clan."

"Simon . . ." Guntram couldn't believe it. "Why?"

"My job is done. Alex has been prepared, his place in the Nation affirmed. Gabriella needed a strong mate at her side. Don't let your bitterness over this unfortunate chain of events cloud the fact that you and Alex will need each other in the future. Don't burn bridges." His lips quirked. "Don't make my sacrifice worth nothing," he said, stealing Guntram's words.

Guntram's jaw clamped tight, and he drew a deep breath. He unclasped his fist.

Simon plucked the ring. "Now, let's go. We haven't much time. I'll not activate the ring until you're gone."

Taking Gabriella's hand, Guntram forged ahead into the darkness, waiting for the telltale sounds of the arachnids' arrival. "Be sure to keep moving your feet."

When light began to glimmer all around them and the faint chirping sounds grew in volume, Gabriella squeezed his hand.

"Keep moving, they won't harm you if they can't swarm you."

They reached the boulder where Simon had stashed the crystal orb.

The mage quickly unwrapped it and tossed away the canvas bag. "As soon as I've opened the portal, I'll give this into your care, Guntram. It belongs to Alex now. He'll know what to do with it."

"Why shouldn't I just smash it? Isn't it too risky to let it exist?"

Simon glanced up. "Haven't I proven you can trust me?"

Guntram ground his jaws but nodded. "I'll do it."

Then Simon was standing still, spiders running up his leg, but the light was already beginning to flicker inside the clear stone. When the rays burst and curved and the shimmering circle shone, Guntram shoved Gabriella through, then waited for Marduk, who didn't look back to enter it.

Glancing back, Guntram gazed at Simon's lonely figure. "Thank you," he said, his throat tightening.

Simon's smile was strained, but his expression was serene. "She'll have twins, you know."

Guntram smiled as moisture blurred his friend's figure, and he thrust out his hand. "Until we meet again."

Simon nodded. "Better go." Then he handed him the crystal and the claw base.

Guntram hugged them close to his chest and stepped through the portal.

When the light blinked out behind Guntram, Simon swiped the spiders off his hair and shoulders and trudged toward the entrance of the cave. A large male *anzu* was stalking into the entrance.

Simon slipped the ring onto his finger. "*Must I invoke its power to subdue you?*"

He sent the message telepathically. One of the gifts of the Master—the gift to communicate with all the creatures in this realm.

The *anzu* hesitated, its head shifting left and right and sniffing at the air. Then its gaze zeroed on the beast still whimpering on the floor. The *anzu*-bird gave another low, ominous growl, but backed up a pace. Finally, it lowered its head to the floor and knelt on its forelegs.

Simon understood even though no answering thought entered his own mind. He strode forward, unafraid, and slid a leg over the back of the beast, gripping its thick mane.

The beast pivoted quickly, rushing toward the cave entrance. It leapt outward, its wings extended, catching the air beneath its golden feathers and taking to the skies.

Soaring upward, Simon felt his heavy heart lighten just a smidge. Madeleine was lost to him forever. Turned human at last. Alex, whom he'd loved like a son, had his own destiny to fulfill. He, Simon the former Knight Templar, had his own new destiny to chart. One handed down from God to Solomon. Here, he'd guard against intrusions into the other realm while Alex kept watch over his expanding family. Although separated, they'd both serve the greater good until the dark day when hell unleashed its demon hordes in the final battle.

With a phalanx of *anzu* and *lillum* waiting to escort him, Simon Jameson entered Kur-gal as the Master of the Demons.

# CHAPTER 20

Guntram felt the tip of a blade prick his throat as soon as he stepped through the portal. Light burst behind him, then blinked out, leaving splotches of color dancing before his eyes. He blinked his eyes as they adjusted and drew in a familiar scent.

"I'll take that," Alex said softly, holding out his hand.

"The sword or the rock?"

"Don't be an ass, now. We have Gabriella and that demon you brought among us."

Guntram held the orb away from his chest.

Alex grabbed it with his free hand and gave it immediately to one of his men. "The sword?"

Guntram dropped it beside him.

Alex slid something from his pocket and held it in front of Guntram's face. A linked silver chain. "Just until you're out of my territory. A precaution, you understand."

Guntram scanned the room for Gabriella and found her standing beside Marduk, two spots of furious color on her cheeks. Both wore similar collars. "Alex . . ." she said, her tone low and deadly.

"Sorry, love. You'll remember whose foolish action started your little adventure. I just want to make sure that you arrive back in Wolfen territory without incident." When he turned back to Guntram, he lifted a brow. "Will you do it, or shall I have my men hold you down?"

Guntram grabbed the chain and dragged it over his head, allowing Alex to fix a small lock at the side. "Is this really necessary?"

"I have work to do. This allows me one less worry."

When he was done, Alex stepped back and faced Gabriella. "You'll have the trade agreements your clan wanted and more. Free movement inside my territory to escort your shipments to the docks. Will this satisfy you?"

Gabriella's lips firmed, then her glance strayed to Guntram.

Guntram cleared his throat. "It satisfies me."

Alex's eyebrows rose, and his glance slipped between them. "Congratulations are in order."

Guntram didn't ease his expression, waiting to see if the bastard would add something about being glad he'd taken his advice. The last thing he wanted to explain to Gabriella was that he'd listened to anything Alex said about wooing her.

But Alex stayed silent, his only acknowledgement a subtle curving of his mouth. "Your men are being loaded on a transport. I have a limousine to take the two of you wherever you wish to be dropped across the border, so long as you promise my men safe passage back."

Guntram gave him a stiff nod. "What about him?" he said, lifting his chin toward Marduk.

Alex lifted the orb. "I'm sending him back."

Guntram grunted, liking the idea—a lot. But Gabriella shook her head.

Guntram heaved a sigh. "You can't. Simon agreed to take his place to allow him to leave."

"Simon made whatever agreement he had to make to assure both you and Gabriella were returned safely. That was his sacrifice."

"Marduk isn't evil," Gabriella said heatedly.

Alex gave her an exasperated look. "He's a demon."

"He can be useful," she replied, her chin lifting another notch.

"I can't risk it."

Guntram eyed the choker around Marduk's neck. "Do you think that chain can restrain him?"

"No, but if he transforms, he'll sever his own head."

Marduk shrugged. "He's correct. I am at his mercy."

Gabriella stepped in front of Marduk. "I can't let you harm him."

"Gabi," Alex said. "You know what he is. What he's capable of . . . Did you let him seduce you? Are you in his thrall now?"

"She did what she had to do to survive," Guntram said before either Gabriella or Marduk could respond. "And he acted honorably toward her, toward both of us. Simon said we have need of strong alliances. What better, stronger ally than him? He's walked in their world. He knows their every manifestation."

Alex raked a hand through his hair. "I won't have him in my territory."

"I'm not so eager to have him in mine," Guntram muttered, "but he can find his own way, his own place on this earth."

Alex eyed Marduk, who held himself still beneath the inspection. "Do I have your word you won't intrude on our affairs?"

Marduk stared back for a long, charged moment. "You have my word. I want only to visit my old home and try to find what I lost long ago."

Alex nodded slowly. "All right then. You'll accompany them to their territory. After that, I'll leave your travel arrangements to Guntram." Alex returned to Guntram. "Your transport awaits."

With the security force forming a gauntlet of grim-faced vampires, Guntram led the way out of the conference room, across the tiled foyer and onto the veranda. A long black limousine awaited them at the bottom of the steps.

As they began to descend, another car pulled in behind the limo, a small low-slung sedan, and three females climbed out: the blonde Born he'd wrestled in the woods outside the gates when his wolves had been captured, a slender dark-haired woman, and Alex's redheaded phoenix.

Marduk sucked in a deep breath, halting on the step beside him.

Guntram shot him a glance, then, noting his frozen expression, followed his gaze to the redhead.

"Zara," Marduk whispered.

Gabriella nudged him. "Of all the billions of women on this planet . . ." she said, worry pinching her brows together. "You can't," she whispered fiercely. "You gave your word. She belongs to Alex."

Marduk tightened, and Guntram knew he was about to lunge. He grabbed his upper arm. "I don't know what this is about, but don't even flinch. They'll take us all down. Get in the car."

Marduk shook his hand off his arm and continued down the steps, sliding into the backseat, his gaze still following the woman as she climbed the steps and entered Alex's arms.

Guntram eyed Gabriella, who gave him a tight-lipped shake of her head.

When the door closed, Gabriella lifted her chin toward their driver, reminding him they weren't alone. "Later. I'll fill you in later." Then she reached for Marduk's hand, which was wrapped around his knee, the knuckles white.

"Sometimes, we have to let go," she said softly. "It's been so many lifetimes since she knew you. She has a new life. And no memories of you."

Marduk's jaw clenched, and he turned his gaze to stare at the trees lining the long drive out of the estate. "I held to that one hope . . ."

"I know. But she is happy."

He nodded, not looking back.

Guntram caught her gaze. Her eyes softened immediately, and he remembered what Simon had said. *Twins.*

As they pulled away, he leaned forward and pressed his lips to hers, a quiet promise to trust and honor her. Her hand might rest inside Marduk's at the moment, but he had no doubts he held her heart.

"Maybe we should take him to the forests with us before we load him on a plane," Guntram said, not believing he was making the offer. "Think he might like to breathe pine trees and green grass after sucking down sand for three thousand years?"

Gabriella raised Marduk's hand and kissed his knuckles. "Would you stay with us for a while?"

Marduk's gaze left the scenery and scaled the interior of the car. He blinked. "I think I should take some time to acclimate. I thought I'd kept abreast of the changes . . ."

"I understand," she said smiling gently. "And there's all the time in the world."

Alex fed the kestrel a bite of steak, which he'd sprinkled with the powder Simon had left him. He'd administer a dose of humanity every day for a week. When she transformed, he'd give Madeleine the news that she was alone.

The bird plucked at the meat, turning its head to tug it away, then jerked back its tiny head to gulp it down.

Chessa rushed into the salon, carrying a large box. "What do you think of the stroller? Do you think Bianca will like it?"

Mention of his daughter, who'd been born only days ago, dispersed the melancholy that pulled him down when he thought of Simon and Madeleine.

"Bianca loves only two things at the moment, neither of which Nicolas possesses. Can't you hear her squalling?"

Chessa tipped her head to listen for the thin cries emanating from the nursery upstairs. "That's where Nic is, huh?" she said grinning. "Is he ready to pull out his hair?"

"Go rescue him. He refused to let her cry on the nanny's shoulder. I don't think he trusts anyone but you with her care."

Chessa squeezed her breasts. "Ugh! I'm leaking. Just wanted to drop this box with you. It needs assembly," she said, then rushed out the door again.

Mikaela strolled in after her, her lips curving. "I can't believe she's flying around the place already."

"It's her vampire metabolism. We're quick healers." Alex set the bird back on her perch and patted his leg.

Miki settled there, laying her head on his chest, and sighed. "Is all the excitement finally over?"

"The wolves were safely delivered. Our men are on their way back. I think, for now things will quiet down." Another furious little cry sounded from the second floor. "There might be one very small exception."

"She looks like Chessa," she said softly. "Do you think our child would have looked like me?"

Alex sighed and hugged her closer. Although Mikaela had been reborn without memory, he'd given her his own. She felt the same pain he'd suffered knowing their baby had died inside her body when Dumuzi had taken her heart.

"She would have had dark auburn hair," he said softly, nuzzling her red locks, "a heart-shaped face, and mossy green eyes. And she'd have been just as lovely as her mother."

"I'd like to try again."

"Isn't that what we've been doing every night?"

"Like you said, the house is quiet, no wolves or demons underfoot . . ."

"Are you feeling neglected?" he asked, blood rushing to fill his cock with heat.

"Just a little empty," she said, tilting back her head and giving him a saucy look.

Alex sprang from his seat, and carrying her close to his chest, walked up the curved staircase. He headed to the wing opposite the nursery and Chessa and Nic's rooms, toward his own bedroom that he shared with his new wife.

Once inside, he kicked the door shut and walked straight for the bed, not stopping until he settled her in the center and crawled over her body.

Poised above her, he smoothed her hair back and leaned down to kiss her.

Miki sighed against his lips and melted. "It doesn't get any better than this."

Alex made quick work of removing only essential items of clothing. When he was stroking deep inside her, passion rising, he remembered the look that had crossed the demon's face when he'd first spied Miki.

A flush of happiness, followed by dawning horror had crossed his features, and Alex had known instantly that Miki would never be safe.

Riding her sweet curves now, he branded her with his heat, plunging deeply, trying to give her the one thing that would bind them together forever.

Guntram stuck his nose into the pine needles, searching for her scent. The pack had shed their clothing at the edge of the forest and transformed—wolves loping into the woods, while Marduk took the sky, skimming along the tops of the trees to follow.

Gabriella hadn't been content keeping astride the pack,

she'd streaked ahead, her tail wagging happily, daring him to keep up.

He'd lost her in thick underbrush, but at last picked up the trail. With his head bent toward the forest floor, he hurried forward, letting his brothers peel off to continue their run while he sought another sort of release from the tensions of the past few days.

They'd stopped briefly in Atlanta to report all that had happened. When they'd told the tale of entering the Land of the Dead and returning, he'd noted the incredulous expressions. Not until he'd introduced Marduk and given him the nod to prove their claim had they believed. Marduk's transformation in the center of the cozy study had them all scrambling for the door.

The wolves hadn't been happy to know a demon existed and remained among them at Guntram's invitation, but what could they do? They had everything they'd wanted and more. Guntram had steered the conversation afterward, offering his plans to create a headquarters in Memphis, just up the river from the vampires in New Orleans, to oversee their operations.

Gabriella had sat at his side, her lips firmly sealed, although he invited her input. She'd told him later she didn't want anyone doubting their claim of having mated. Glances had slid between the two of them, seated side by side, and not one of the males had demanded she be removed from the room. He'd set their expectations from the start that they'd forged a partnership rather than a more traditional union.

Gabriella had been suitably appreciative of his efforts . . . later.

Guntram found Gabriella in a clearing. Pine needles cushioned the pads of his paws as he drew near the woman, lying with her arms beneath her head as she stared up into a starry sky.

Shaking his fur, he drew on his humanskin to join her.

Her lips were curved in a smile that was at once lusty and sweet. Her head turned to catch the fading sounds of the *whomp-whomp* of Marduk's wings. "He's leaving us."

"I know. I arranged the tickets. He's heading to the Middle East to visit old haunts," he said, kneeling beside her. Holding her gaze locked with his, he asked, "Will you miss him?"

"I think I will."

"What precisely will you miss?"

Her eyebrows rose. "Not what you're obviously thinking. I haven't had sex with him since we left Kur-gal."

"Will you be satisfied with just one lover?"

"For the rest of my life?"

Guntram swallowed hard, prepared to accept either answer she gave him. He loved Gabriella, loved her lusty nature and her stubborn belief in her own invincibility. Placing bonds on her unfettered passions might kill the very qualities that attracted and held him bound to her.

Gabriella's eyes shimmered with moisture and she reached up to slide her hand over his chest, pressing her palm above his heart. *"With my vow, I grant you dominion over me and our children; I place my heart in your keeping. I pledge my troth to you and promise to honor our commitment."*

Guntram held still, drinking in the words. His skin felt hot and cold at the same time, as a lush warm breeze sifted through the trees and bathed them both with fresh scents of the woodlands and their own rising passion.

"Thank you," he said simply, because he hadn't the words to express his happiness. "You won't regret it."

"I won't let you disappoint me, you know." She lifted her arms and opened them.

Guntram slid over her, welcoming the clasp of her strong, sturdy thighs around his hips. His cock nudged between her folds and he laid his forehead on her shoulder as he stroked inward.

Fingertips raked his scalp, and he groaned, lifting his head to press a kiss to her lips.

Their tongues stroked together, silky slides that tasted and aroused. As his mouth lapped, sliding over hers in drugging, gobbling circles, he gathered his knees under him and drove harder toward her core.

At last, she broke the kiss, gasping as her body began to undulate, curving her hips to meet his steady strokes. "My Raven," she whispered, gliding her lips along the side of his neck. "I love you."

Guntram stroked once, then withdrew, coming to his knees. "Turn around," he said, his voice rasping.

Excitement sparked in her eyes, and she quickly complied with his command, rolling to her belly and coming up on her knees. She eagerly scooted her ass backward until she rubbed against him.

Guntram smiled, knowing if she looked back now, she might begin to worry a bit. Feral pride filled him. She'd given him her heart. Pledged her fidelity to him alone. She'd gifted him with her love. Everything he'd ever wanted was his for the taking.

Given freely.

There was enough of the proud male wolf inside him to want to howl his triumph to the moon.

He laid his palms on her buttocks and stepped backward on his knees. Then, bending over her, he tongued a spot, wetting it, and then nipped it. He repeated the action over and over until she was jerking and trembling, her breaths coming in soft gasps.

When he pressed his nose to her skin and nuzzled, her back sank in the middle, lifting her bottom, and raising her sex—offering herself for his exploration.

Guntram rubbed his nose and chin in the dampness, stroked her labia with his tongue and drew the thin inner lips between his teeth.

He nibbled and stroked, moving downward. His tongue glided over her clit, then retreated.

Gabriella widened her stance, giving him greater access. He swooped downward, spread her folds with his thumbs and stroked his tongue inside her, lapping at her cream and groaning because his own body was wound tight, close to exploding.

"Guntram, *please*," she moaned. "Come inside me."

And only because he'd teased himself beyond resisting her plea, he straightened, grasping the notch of one hip and funneling his cock through his fingers to slide into her silky, wet sex.

On his knees behind her, he flexed and pushed inside her, cramming past soft tissue that was already beginning the sexy caresses heralding her orgasm. He scooted closer, bending over her, sweeping her long hair over one shoulder to bare it.

"Yes, yes," she cried as his teeth clamped down on the tender curve of her shoulder and held her immobile. He ground inside her, letting himself go. His balls tightened, and blood surged toward his crown, filling it, expanding it until he filled the narrow space behind her womb and locked with her.

He reached beneath her and palmed a breast, squeezing it and then tugging at the spiked tip. His other hand slid between her legs and drew wet circles on her clit.

She bucked beneath him, her inner walls convulsing as he ground harder, relishing the connection that tied their bodies together as they both exploded and his seed poured in scalding spurts inside her.

Still locked, they both began the slow descent. He pulled them down to the ground, never retreating from her womb, and held her against him, unlatching his jaws to press kisses to her shoulder and neck. "I love you, Gabriella," he whispered in her ear.

Her hands covered his, clutching her belly and her breast, and they lay like that until his balls had emptied and the rigidity of the knot slowly waned.

Gabriella turned her head and they kissed. Just a brush of lips. Her hand cupped his cheek. "I don't think I've ever been happier. Why did you wait so long?"

Guntram smiled. "You weren't ready. I wasn't sure."

"I don't regret a moment of our journey."

"Do you think it's ended?"

Gabriella's smile was wide, her eyes teary. She pushed his hands to her flat belly. "Our children were conceived there."

"We'll birth hellions then?"

"I'm counting on it. Fierce, independent wolves—with a warrior and a princess for parents, how can they be anything less?"

"Alex and his brood had better be ready."

Letting his sex slip from her body, he turned her to face him. With her soft brown gaze locked with his, lying side by side in a fragrant bed of pine needles with the distant stars sparkling overhead, he kissed her, renewing his vow as he intended to do every night of their lives.

# Delilah Devlin

Until recently, award-winning romance author **DELILAH DEVLIN** lived in south Texas at the intersection of two dry creeks, surrounded by sexy cowboys in Wranglers. These days, she's missing those wide-open skies and starry nights but loving her dark forest in central Arkansas, with its eccentric characters and isolation—the better to feed her hungry muse! For Delilah, the greatest sin is driving between the lines because it's comfortable and safe. Her personal journey has taken her through one war and many countries, cultures, jobs, and relationships to bring her to the place where she is now—writing sexy adventures that hold more than a kernel of autobiography and often share a common thread of self-discovery and transformation. To learn more about Delilah, visit www.delilahdevlin.com.

# BOOKS BY DELILAH DEVLIN

## INTO THE DARKNESS

978-0-06-116123-0 (paperback)

"From its intriguing and twisted storyline, in-depth and well-written characters, to the torrid sex scenes, *Into the Darkness* is a must read for those paranormal lovers who love to live on the edge."
—*Romance Reviews Today*

## SEDUCED BY DARKNESS

978-0-06-116124-7 (paperback)

"Devlin's intricate vampire society is filled with compelling personalities. The chemistry between the characters is explosive. . . . [It] will raise your temperature, and the ending will leave you begging for more. "
—*Romantic Times*

## DARKNESS BURNING

978-0-06-149820-6 (paperback)

"A dynamic heroine with a mysterious past and hidden strengths pits herself against a truly magnetic hero capable of drawing the reader—and the heroine—into a world of pleasure and sexual excess."
—Kate Douglas, author of *Wolf Tales*